MERCI SUÁREZ PLAYS IT COOL

MERCI SUÁREZ PLAYS IT COOL

MEG MEDINA

CANDLEWICK PRESS

Copyright © 2022 by Meg Medina Books, Inc.

First edition 2022

Library of Congress Catalog Card Number 2021953123
ISBN 978-1-5362-1946-3

22 23 24 25 26 27 LBM 10 9 8 7 6 5 4 3 2 1

Printed in Melrose Park, IL, USA

This book was typeset in Berkeley Oldstyle.

Candlewick Press
99 Dover Street
Somerville, Massachusetts 02144

www.candlewick.com

TO THE READERS WHO HAVE FOLLOWED
MERCI FROM THE START

CHAPTER 1

"SHUT THAT SCREEN DOOR, Merci! You're letting in mosquitoes!"

Mami's sharp voice makes me jump as Tuerto dashes between my legs. He doesn't even stop for a chin scratch in his race to escape the heat.

It's early, but Mami's already in her scrubs for work, though she's still padding in bedroom slippers and a sloppy ponytail. Her eyebrows aren't drawn in yet, either.

"Sorry. I was just letting him in before he got too loud," I say, swatting at the half dozen bloodsuckers that are now darting around the kitchen.

The sun was barely up when I heard the meows. They echoed through our backyards, sounding like one of those spirits that Abuela warns about—a tátara-something-or-other buried back in Cuba who gets testy if they think they've been forgotten by their descendants.

Anyway, when I flipped on the light, I found Tuerto glaring at me from outside, his front claws clinging high and wide against the screen like he was the victim of a stickup.

"Did that cat shred the mesh again?" Mami asks, exasperated. "Your father just fixed it last week."

"No." I move my body to hide the new tear near the seam. She's not above making me pay for the repair. But can I help it if our cat is a genius? He's learned to yowl and shake the door to let us know he wants to come in. I've taken videos of him doing that trick because, one, my friend Wilson and I like trading funny cat videos when we're bored, and two, while it may be lousy door manners, we've seen pets on *Those Awesome Animals* on TV win the $5,000 prize for less. Maybe we'll get lucky.

"And anyway, you can't blame Tuerto for wanting to come in from the heat, can you? He's wearing a fur coat, you know, and it's his nature to survive." I motion at the thermometer we keep hanging on the patio. The needle is pointing at the red numbers. "It's already ninety degrees!"

It's the best defense I can think of, though I hope she doesn't point out other less flattering parts of Tuerto's nature, namely that he's a heartless murderer. He kills everything: birds, mice, voles, lizards—even baby possums—and leaves them as grisly presents. I think back to the first time Tuerto left us a dead sparrow in Lolo's garden. I was so angry at Tuerto for killing that pretty bird. "We feed Tuerto!" I cried. "He doesn't need to kill things." But Lolo just cradled the little body in his palm and helped me bury it so its spirit could live in the flowers. "There's no stopping Mother Nature in the end, preciosa," he told me, though we tied a silver warning bell to Tuerto's collar after that.

Mami sighs and yanks the chain for the ceiling fan, trying to circulate the air-conditioning that never quite keeps up with Florida in July.

"I suppose you're right about the heat," she mutters. Then she reaches under the chipped saltshaker on the kitchen table and hands over today's List of Doom.

I try not to look bitter as I review my list of chores. I should be with Papi and Simón this morning, way out past the cane fields in the Glades. If they finish that job early, they're planning to fish on Lake Okeechobee for a little while.

Mami, however, had other ideas for my time and ruined the fun. She says chores build character.

Which is porquería.

"You have to clean your room today," she tells me, as if I can't read her list myself. "It's a mess. Tuerto is nesting in sweaty underwear."

"It's mostly Roli's," I say. "Go see for yourself—if you dare." It requires the moves of a ninja just to get past our door with Roli's boxes from college all over the room. He hasn't unpacked from when he came home in May.

Naturally, she ignores this. "Let him sleep," she says.

Roli worked the graveyard shift at Walgreens again last night, so he's out cold, snoring cómo si nada on the other side of the curtain that divides our room.

Mami loads the percolator with El Pico and lights the flame. "You have your summer reading, too. Don't forget. There's only a couple of weeks left before school starts."

From the corner of my eye, I see the incriminating stack of library books sitting on the shelf near the back door exactly where I left them three weeks ago. I read the business book (my free choice) in two days, but I haven't even started the other two, mostly on principle. Why should I do homework for a teacher I haven't even met? But the not-so-secret faculty motto at Seaward Pines Academy is apparently *Work 'em till their eyes bleed.*

"It's kind of hard to read if I have all these other chores, too," I say. "Besides, is summer reading even legal to assign during an official vacation period?"

"Legal?"

I grab my phone from the charging station and type the word *vacation* into the dictionary. "It says right here: 'Vacation: An extended period of leisure and recreation.'" I give her a knowing look. "We'd never get away with this kind of infringement on an employee's personal time in the business world." I should know since I am currently writing the Sol Painting, Inc., employee handbook for Papi. "In fact, I'm pretty sure my rights are being violated. I may have a case here."

"Only if you mean a case of poor planning," Mami says. "We've been over this, Merci. Reading *is* recreational."

I give her a look. "Not with *those* books."

"How would you know if you haven't started them?" She peers out the kitchen window toward Abuela's house, where the lights are on. There's a small flash of worry in her face.

"What?" I say, walking over. The summer has been tough on my grandparents, especially Lolo. The heat seems to have melted his mind like butter in a pan—and *that* has everyone around here on edge. His new medicines were supposed to help with that, but if anything, he seems worse.

"Nada," she tells me, although I'm not sure whether to believe her. "It just looks like they're up already. Check in with Abuela before you get started. She might need you to watch Lolo while she showers this morning."

I try not to make a face at her. I hate when she calls it "watching Lolo." It's not like he's a baby, or worse, like the twins, who are every babysitter's nightmare. Lolo has always liked to walk the neighborhood, though every once in a while now, he forgets where he is, which makes Abuela jumpy. What is that like? I wonder. To suddenly not know your own block or recognize our houses or, on some days, even know your own name?

Anyway, I try not to think about that too much. And I don't mind taking walks with Lolo, either, even if we're moving slower these days. He's quiet, but I can still tell Lolo anything I want and be 100 percent sure that he won't tell anybody else.

Mami shakes a box of bran flakes into a chipped bowl. "You want some of this?"

It looks like a stack of bark shavings. "No, thank you," I say, holding up my hand. "That stuff tastes like Styrofoam."

She shrugs and pours milk over her cereal. "It also keeps the digestive tract moving," she says. "I noticed you took a long time in the bathroom yesterday."

I give her an icy stare and head to the refrigerator. It's bad enough that my screen time is closely monitored, that I'm required to store my phone in the kitchen overnight, that I have to do chores during my vacation. Now my bowel habits are being surveilled, too? Prison inmates probably have more privacy.

The cool blast from the freezer soothes me when I yank it open. I pull out the last two packets of blueberry toaster waffles I hid at the very back. At least Roli hasn't devoured these yet. Maybe he read the sticky note that I taped on the box, the one with the skull and crossbones I drew: *Hands off the stash, Bro.* These waffles are Lolo's favorite, and mine, too, even though Mami and Abuela claim they're not "real food."

"Where are you going?" Mami says as I head past her and down the hall with my breakfast.

"To attend to my digestive tract," I say, trying not to sound too snarky. "And then to check on Abuela."

CHAPTER 2

IT'S BEEN WEEKS SINCE I've seen anybody from Seaward Pines. Once summer started, we all went our own ways. Wilson spends all of July with his dad and cousins in New Orleans. Hannah is away at a prisoner-type summer camp in Georgia, where they don't allow phones except for calling home once a week. Lena and her dad left on an RV trip to the Badlands in South Dakota to photograph bison. So, it's been lonely. I'd even be happy to hear from Edna Santos, who can pluck my last nerve at times, but she's been away, too, sunbathing on some island near Boston called Nantucket.

And where have I been? Right here at Las Casitas, of course, same as every single summer since I've been alive.

I haven't even had a chance to hang out with Roli much since he's working all the time. If he's not at the pharmacy, he's helping Papi.

I pull open Abuela's screen door and step into her kitchen, which is just as hot and steamy as ours. She's at the stove, scrambling eggs and frying ham steaks, and the smell is heavenly. The house is already loud, too, with cartoons blaring from the TV and the crash of dominoes coming from the next room, where Axel and Tomás, still in their pajamas, are hanging out with Lolo. They hate to wait for Tía to wake up and make them breakfast, so sometimes they ditch their place and come next door to Abuela and Lolo's instead.

"You're early!" Abuela says, glancing at the clock on the wall. It's 7:45 a.m. "Lolo and the boys haven't eaten yet."

"I know, but I was up already, and I thought Lolo and I could take a walk before it gets even hotter out there."

She flips the sliced meat around in the frying pan with her long fork and gives me a stern look when she sees me put the frozen waffles I brought over in the toaster.

"You'll spoil his appetite," she says.

I press down the lever and watch the coils turn bright orange. "But he'll need more energy to take a walk with me, Abuela," I say. "It's just a pre-breakfast treat."

She *tsks* her tongue and slides the eggs and ham onto

dishes that she carries to the table. "Go get them while I rinse out these pans, then."

I wait for the waffles to pop up and take them with me to the living room. Their scent of berries is irresistible.

"Breakfast is ready," I say, making my way to Lolo's chair. The twins have set up long, curving courses of dominoes that start at his feet and reach all the way around the coffee table. Abuela made this an electronics-free zone, except for TV, so they have to get old school and creative when they come here. Lolo and I used to play the same way when I was little, too. We called it Caracól because of the snail shape we set in motion when we made them collapse.

But nobody answers me. The twins are too busy, of course. And Lolo, I see now, is asleep in his chair despite the blaring TV. He's been falling into lots of naps this summer. On the porch rocker. In his chair. I click off the remote and walk closer to wake him up with a whiff of blueberry.

"Lolo?" I say, louder. "I brought you something."

I move the waffle under his nose, but he doesn't stir. His hands have gone slack around the tin in his lap, and his chin hangs down to his chest. I shake him gently.

"Lolo, wake up."

That's when he keels to one side.

10

A chill rises along my back, and I drop the waffles. The air in the room seems to change around us instantly. The twins look up from their construction and stare. Tomás slides his two middle fingers into his mouth, a habit Tía has been trying to break, now that they're almost seven. Axel wraps his arms around his knees, watching.

I take a tiny step back, knocking over their fichas. The *click-click-clack* of the chain reaction sounds loud in my ears as I wait for Lolo to wake up. *Please*, I think. *Please wake up*.

But something is very wrong.

"Abuela!" I manage to call out. "Come quick!"

The seconds drag through mud as I listen to the slap of her chancletas getting closer. She comes to the doorway drying her hands on a dishrag, frowning the way she does when she has to break up another squabble between me and the twins.

"¿Qué hay? The breakfast is getting cold!" She looks around at the dominoes. "And who's going to pick all this up?"

I stand next to Lolo, my tongue thick in my mouth. Though a million words are running through my mind, none cuts loose. All I can do is point at Lolo in his chair.

In a flash, Abuela's face changes. She moves toward us faster than I've seen her go in a long while. "¡Viejo!" she

11

says as she reaches his chair. "¿Qué te pasa?" She swats her dishrag at him, tries to shake Lolo awake, like he's having a bad dream. His eyes flutter open, but he doesn't seem to see her. Instead, a long string of saliva drips from the corner of his mouth. "Leopoldo!" She says it louder, firmer, like he's just needing some discipline.

He still doesn't answer. His skin looks gray, like recycled paper.

"Quickly, Merci." Her breath is raspy and heavy, the same huffing sound she makes after she finishes bathing him, getting him dressed, tying his shoes. "Find your mother," she tells me, "or Inés—anyone!"

Tomás's and Axel's eyes are wide and scared. I can't leave them here to see this, so I drag them off to the kitchen.

"What's wrong with Lolo?" Tomás asks.

"Why won't he wake up?" Axel says.

"I don't know, but I'm getting help," I tell them. "Sit down and don't move."

Then I'm out the back door, racing along toward my aunt's house.

I poke my head in her side door and call out. "Tía! Come quick! We need you!" I shout again, even louder. "Tía!"

The shower is running. I don't wait.

I do an about-face and tear toward my house at the other end of the path, just as Mami's car lumbers down the driveway toward the street. I run toward her, waving my arms.

"STOP!" I shout at the top of my voice when I reach the car. I bang my fists down hard on her trunk, and the sound makes her slam on the brakes.

Mami glares at me in the rearview mirror and rolls down her window.

"What—"

"It's an emergency," I say, trying to catch my breath in gulps. "Lolo."

She turns off the car and leaves it right where it is as she grabs her medical bag from the back seat. Then we run back along the path. By now, Tía Inés is out in the yard, too, tying a robe around her waist, her hair dripping as she hurries toward us.

"I heard yelling," she says, clutching the lapels to cover herself.

"Your father," Mami tells her without stopping.

The twins are still at the kitchen table when we get there. They make a beeline for Tía as soon as they see her, trying to wrap themselves around her waist.

"Lolo won't talk," Axel tells her.

"His eyes look weird," Tomás adds.

"Shh," she tells them, stopping at the threshold with me as Mami charges in.

Mami lowers Lolo to the floor. Then she grabs a stethoscope from her bag and listens to his heart. She takes his pulse, then starts on his blood pressure.

"How long has he been like this?" she asks as she waits for the reading.

Abuela looks to me.

How long? I shake my head.

"Call 911, just in case," Mami tells Tía quietly. She slides a cushion from the sofa under Lolo's legs and turns to me. "I need a cold washcloth."

I grab Abuela's dishrag from the floor and run to the bathroom to soak it under the stream of water, cursing the fact that it never gets too cold. When I come back, I press it against Lolo's forehead myself, exactly the way Mami shows me. He still looks blank and pale, but he's blinking now, alive. I slip my hand into his and give it three small squeezes, the signal he used to give me whenever I felt shy about trying something new. *It's OK. You can do this, preciosa.*

Meanwhile, Tía is on the phone giving information to 911. It feels like a long time, but eventually sirens grow louder from somewhere in the distance.

And then everything happens choppy and fast.

The sound of tires on our gravel as the ambulance

maneuvers around Mami's abandoned car. Rescue workers in gear that makes them look too big for the room, like the wrong-size dolls in a playhouse. I drop Lolo's hand as Tía pulls me back toward the kitchen.

Roli barrels in the back door, barefoot and shirtless, his hair a mess. "What's going on?" he says. "Why are the EMTs here?"

Two workers crouch on the ground, where they're strapping Lolo onto a flat gurney. A few seconds later, they lift the steel legs that unfold like that scissor lift Papi sometimes uses when he has to paint a high spot. And then Lolo gets wheeled away.

The ambulance pulls out of our driveway, sirens wailing, as I stare after it from the open door. A man walking his dog has stopped to gawk. Across the street, a few of the condo residents are out on their balconies looking into our yard, too.

"Roli, throw some clothes on while I get the car." Mami says. She turns to Abuela. "Gather the medical records from his last checkup at the doctor—and get the current medicine list, too. They were in that yellow envelope, acuérdate." She talks over my head as she reaches the door. "Inés, meet me at JFK when you're dressed. And call Enrique, please. Tell him what's happened."

"*I'll* call Papi," I say, interrupting.

Mami glances at me and then at Tía, who's still holding her robe closed, the twins clinging to her waist. She nods at me. "Tell him JFK Medical Center. Will you remember?"

"Yes," I say.

"JFK," she repeats, like I'm a baby. "He should meet us there."

"I heard you, Mami," I snap.

"Come on, boys," Tía says. "We need to get dressed. Hurry."

Everyone scatters.

I stare at the dirty footprints from the rescue workers' boots on Abuela's normally spotless tile floor. Blueberry waffles have been ground to pieces everywhere.

Outside, Mami starts her car, beeps for my brother to hurry. I can hear Abuela in her bedroom, opening the sticky drawer where she keeps her important papers.

My brain feels flooded, like I'm moving underwater as I walk to the kitchen and sit down at the table. The yolks from Lolo's uneaten breakfast are orange and congealed now. The smell of cold eggs makes me light-headed.

I manage to tap Papi's contact with shaky fingers.

He answers on the fifth ring.

"¿Y esto? A call instead of a text?" Papi says. "I'll bet you butt-dialed me by mistake!"

16

I stare out at the mess of dominoes on the living room floor. My throat has closed into a fist.

"¿Me oyes? Do we have a bad connection?" His voice gets serious. "Merci? Is there something wrong?"

"You have to come home," I blurt out.

And that's all I can manage before I finally start to cry.

CHAPTER 3

WEIRD FACT: I'VE NEVER really been alone at Las Casitas. There's always an adult around here, even if I can't see them. Abuela's sewing machine makes that rapid-fire sound that lets you know she's stitching something in her back room. Tía pulls the squeaky laundry line as she pins our clothes on, tugging the next length with her fast rhythm. Mami's voice carries too loud when she's talking on the phone to her patients, especially the ones who are hard of hearing. Papi's van squeaks when it lumbers up the driveway at the end of the day.

I used to hear Lolo, too, mostly his humming as he weeded the garden or his laughter when I told him a funny story from school. I heard those silly arguments he used to have with Abuela about getting too much sun, too. But lately, it's the rattling of his walker that tells me he's near; even with those tennis balls at the bottom of the legs to help it slide, you can still hear it clicking as he slowly makes his way around. I don't like his new sound as much. It tells me it's the new Lolo, the unsteady one, the one who can't remember, Lolo with Alzheimer's—not the Lolo I miss.

But now, I wish I could hear any of those sounds, especially Lolo's walker. The quiet feels all wrong. It's been five hours and twenty-six minutes since everyone left me here with Axel and Tomás, and as each hour ticks by, Las Casitas feels lonelier, like there aren't enough of us to fill the space the right way. There's only the engine sounds of the twins playing an old race-car video game on Roli's tablet, even though they're not supposed to touch his things. I gave them permission, though. How else could I keep them from asking their million questions? *Why did he look like that? Why can't he talk? Why is he at the hospital? When is he coming back?* And the worst one, *Is Lolo going to die?* Which made me say, "God, Axel, shut up already."

I know everything living dies one day. I'm not stupid. But I can't bring myself to think that might mean Lolo, too. Just thinking about him dying scares me, not to mention how mad it makes me at God, if that's who's making the arrangements. Why does somebody good like Lolo have to die when there are plenty of horrible people in the world who could go instead? People who make wars or burn villages down or plant bombs.

It's totally unfair.

I'm just settling into the book I've been trying to read when my phone finally buzzes. The sound makes me jump so hard that I drop it. I've called Mami five times today, and each time it has gone to voice mail, so I've hung up. Who leaves messages anymore? Roli and Tía have been ghosting me, too, ignoring my texts. Is it because Lolo has died? I've typed the question and deleted it half a dozen times.

But it's not anybody from my family. Instead, it's Wilson Bellevue from school, who is still in New Orleans.

Check it. Albalacerdus on the loose!

He's sent along a picture of himself with two younger boys—his cousins, I guess—standing near an enormous white alligator. Wilson is mugging for the camera, making a fake-scared face.

I can't help smiling. Albalacerdus is a new character that will be introduced to the Iguanador Nation universe this fall, according to *Fleet*, the newsletter we both get as members of the Iguanador Nation Fan Club. Albalacerdus stands twelve feet tall and is a hybrid human and albino reptile, who eats live pigs and other livestock to survive. (This does not earn him friends.) For now, no one knows for sure whether he's going to be an ally to Captain Jake Rodrigo—despite his wacko digestive needs—or just another villain mucking up the galaxies. Wilson and I like to trade theories and make bets. I smell a bad guy.

I stare at Wilson's goofy expression and get that weird tingle in my stomach. I miss him, although I'd never say so, of course. I mean, who else would admit to being in the fan club except him? We both know it's kind of corny, but we still like it. Plus, he's fun to hang out with, even long distance the way we do. Twice this summer, we plugged into our favorite movies in the series and texted comments to each other while we watched at the same time. Nobody can spot clues for what might be a plot spin-off like Wilson.

I take a deep breath, my thumbs paused over my keypad. Should I tell him about Lolo? I want to, but maybe that's just an awkward downer, especially since it looks like he's having so much fun. What kind of pal throws a wet blanket on your good time? Maybe I'll tell him later.

> Cool. Glad you didn't get eaten, especially acting like such a ham.

> Ha ha. Still alive. And coming back to Florida next week. What's up there?

My stomach zings again, and not just because it's going to be nice to have him back around. What do I say? *Lolo got rushed to the emergency room this morning.* And then, what I don't want to tell him. *I'm scared.*

But just then, I hear a car coming up the driveway. I hurry up and attach a thumbs-up icon to his message.

Gotta run! More later.

I pocket my phone and rush to the bedroom window. Roli is behind the wheel of Mami's car. No one else is with him.

"Quick, shut that game off and go to the kitchen," I tell the twins, who barely react.

"NOW!"

They get off the bed and toss the tablet back inside one of Roli's boxes. Then we dash through the house. Luckily, it still takes Roli a while to park a car properly, even if it's just pulling straight into the driveway. I wait patiently as he tries not to sideswipe the carport posts again like he did the last time he drove Mami's car. You can still see her car's paint on them. When he finally stops the engine, I call out, "What's going on? Is Lolo OK?"

Roli climbs out, looking just as disheveled as he did when he drove off with Mami all those hours ago.

"Well?" I ask again as I trail him into the kitchen. The

twins look up innocently from the table, pretending to read Papi's newspaper. Geez. Not suspicious at all.

Roli narrows his eyes for a second, but then he turns to the sink. "From the evidence, they've concluded that he experienced a syncope," he says.

"What do you mean he peed?" Tomás asks, appalled.

"I said *syncope*," Roli says.

I shake my head. A year away at college has crammed even bigger words in that science brain of his. It's exasperating.

"Speak plain, will you?" I say.

Roli turns on the faucet and washes his hands to his elbows, even scrubbing his nails with the vegetable brush like a surgeon. The twins watch, transfixed, as his arm hair turns bubbly.

"In a word," he says, "Lolo fainted."

In my mind, I can still see Lolo limp in his chair, the saliva in long drips from his mouth. I shudder to clear it away. Not even Abuela has ever mentioned sitting in a recliner as a fainting hazard—and she frets about every possible combination of health dangers, including death by sudden fright and electrocution by toothbrush.

"That can't be right," I say. "He was just sitting in a chair."

"Being seated has nothing to do with it. Syncope is very common in older adults, especially in cases of poly-pharmacy." He dries his hands and starts down the hall to our room.

I follow close behind. "Poly-*what*?" I ask.

He pulls off his sweaty shirt and tosses it near our nightstand, along with the rest of his smelly laundry. "Don't they teach prefixes anymore? Poly means many . . . as in polymeric, polyandrous, polyethylene—"

"ROLI!"

He sighs. "The mix of *many* medicines he's taking," he says. "Sometimes drugs interact differently in older people, and they cause trouble instead of helping."

"Then why bother taking them?" I think of Lolo's pill-box that Tía fills with medicines every week, each com-partment marked for the day of the week and the time of day he's supposed to take it. There's a blue-and-yellow tablet in the morning. A pink one with an *M* on it in the afternoon. Two white ones at bedtime. And of course, all his vitamins. I knew all those pills he takes were creepy. If it's not fruity and chewable, it's suspect in my book.

Roli grabs the curtain that divides our room. "Benefits versus risks. It's always a balance in medical treatments. Now, do you mind? I have to get to work by four."

"Again?" I say. Roli's been working nonstop this

summer at the twenty-four-hour Walgreens, where he rings up customers and announces the bonus points coupons over the loudspeaker in English and español. The job he really wanted was as a research assistant on campus this summer, but he didn't get it. Believe it or not, the professor passed on his talents. The position went to a graduate student with an even bigger brain than Roli's, apparently, which is hard to imagine. Honestly, I think Roli is in shock. He's not built for failures like I am; they're more or less a feature of my daily life. Still, I feel sorry for him. He needs the money for school—*bad*. He found out that his college scholarship was going to be a lot smaller this year, and Mami and Papi don't have much spare cash to help. Now he's going to have to take a semester off and take classes at the community college so he doesn't fall too far behind. Plenty of people get degrees that way, but Roli had other ideas for himself.

We all tried to cheer him up.

Abuela said, "Qué bueno, you'll be able to eat real food again and won't look so skinny anymore!"

Papi said, "I can really use your help with some jobs in the summer and fall."

Mami reminded him that a semester goes fast and that working in a drugstore would give him some real-life experience with people and medicine.

Roli didn't argue, but you could tell he was, and is, pretty bummed. He wanted more than telling people what aisle they could find the aspirin in.

He doesn't answer me from behind the curtain, so I decide to retreat to my side of our room. I'm almost to my bed when I accidentally step on a charger he's left lying around. The metal prongs get jammed between my toes, slicing off some skin.

The pain is immediate and so is my scream. "Ow-ow-ow-ow-ow!"

"What's the matter?" Roli peeks around the curtain to see what's wrong.

My little toe is already ballooning as blood pools around the cuticle. Now it's me who's going to faint. I hate blood, mine or anybody else's. "I've been amputated!"

I hop the rest of the way to my bed to assess the full damage.

"Is my toe hanging off? Can you see bone?"

"Wash that scrape out and get ice for your toe," he says after a quick look. "And watch my stuff, please. It's delicate." Then he disappears behind the curtain again to finish changing.

"*That's* your medical advice? What kind of doctor are you going to be?"

"Probably a very old one by the time I'm through," he mutters.

I lie back on my bed, trying to bend my crushed toe. Sharing a room with Roli again is a challenge. For starters, he's blind to the blue painter's tape that I ran down the middle of our room to mark our sides. Still, I have to admit that I'm a little glad he's staying home, even though it's not what he wants.

Anyway, I'm not crossing the land mines again to get ice. Instead, I reach for the jumbo-size Iguanador Nation tumbler I keep on my nightstand for when I get thirsty at night. There's still plenty of water in it, so I put it on the floor. Then I point my toes like a ballerina and slide my foot in carefully. I close my eyes as soon as I notice the water getting pink.

When the sting starts to subside, I call out to him. "Is it the all-night shift?" I ask. When he works overnight, it means no snoring to bug me, but also no Roli to keep me company. I like when I have somebody to talk to if I can't sleep. I can ask him stuff about Lolo and he tells me the truth.

He sighs. "That's tomorrow."

I don't ask any more. He's prickly these days since all his friends are getting ready to go back to campus. They have parents who can pay for their dorms and food and all the things they need, I guess.

He throws open the curtain and adjusts the plastic name tag on his work shirt.

"Did the twins eat?" Axel and Tomás are still in the kitchen, but we can hear them from here, opening and closing cupboards.

"They had chips and stuff," I mumble, checking my toe. I guess I just forgot the sustenance part. I don't mention that they never ate their breakfast either.

"Weakening those two through starvation, are we?" he says. "Feed them something, Merci."

"But I'm injured." I pull my dripping foot from the cup as proof.

"Uh-huh." He glances at the box nearest his bed and frowns. "And don't let them play with my stuff unless I'm here. I thought we agreed." He grabs his tablet and moves it to a different box.

Then he walks to the door.

"When is everybody coming home?" I ask.

"When the doctor signs discharge papers to spring him."

"So, he's going to be all right?"

He turns to me before he leaves. The shirt is too boxy on him somehow. His name tag is crooked, too. "You know he's not all right, Merci," he says quietly.

I think about our recent nighttime talks about body systems, about how the heart, brain, and lungs are all connected. About how things break down until . . .

"For now?" I insist. "It's not all broken right now, right?"

He sighs and gives me one of those long looks.

"Roli?"

"Right." He motions to the kitchen with his chin. "Now, get those two some food before they decide to cook something for themselves and torch the place."

Sadly, my only culinary expertise is for something called a Dog Cruncher, which Hannah and I invented last year in the cafeteria by accident, when she discovered that Justin Aldrich had crushed her bag of chips to powder when she wasn't looking. Anyway, it's a hot dog split down the middle and stuffed with half a bag of crushed potato chips and the contents of one ketchup packet. It's scrumptious. So good, in fact, that Wilson and I even tried to sell a few at the school store last year. We would have made a killing, too, except Chef—who's running a cafeteria monopoly—reported us to Miss McDaniels. She shut down DC Xpress in a flash, though not before she enjoyed one herself.

Anyway, I haven't shared that particular treat at home. Mami only buys fake soy cylinders called Not Dogs, and let's face it, the magic of a Dog Cruncher would be lost if we used those. So, I'm standing on one foot at the stove, figuring out how to make one last grilled cheese sandwich without burning the bread black, when the rest of our family finally comes home. The twins hear the cars first and shoot out the door, leaving their burnt sandwiches on the table.

Papi pulls up in the van, Lolo riding shotgun in the front seat, the way he used to when he still went along on jobs. Tía, Abuela, and Mami are following in Tía's car.

The twins sprint across the yard.

"Lolo!" they yell when they see him, awake and smiling.

"Take it easy, you two," Papi tells them as they clamor around the passenger side. "Give him some room to get out." He sets up Lolo's walker and opens the door for him. "Vamos, viejo," he says quietly. "Llegamos."

The twins crowd around anyway, ignoring most of what Papi said. Maybe relief is washing through them, the way it is for me.

"Roli said you synch-oh-peed," Axel tells Lolo.

Tomás nods in agreement and slides his hand into Lolo's. "We can finish Caracól."

"Sí, claro," Lolo tells them quietly.

I guess now isn't the time to explain that I put all the dominoes away this morning, even the ones that had scattered under the sofa and behind the planters.

"Tomorrow, muchachos," Papi says. "Lolo has to rest today. Doctor's orders. There's been a lot of excitement."

By now, Abuela and Tía have gotten out of their car, too. You'd think it was Abuela who fainted for how pale and frazzled she looks. She's holding another big envelope and using it as a fan. This one has a big JFK Medical Center logo in the middle.

"Come on, boys. Your tío's right," Tía says, walking over. "It's been a long day. We'll play tomorrow." She looks over her shoulder at me. "Thanks for watching them, Merci."

Then she reaches for Lolo and helps him to his feet.

Maybe it's my sore toe. Maybe it's the walker that's hard to work around. But I'm nervous as I step forward and slide my arms around his soft middle. I take a deep breath against his chest as I hug him. There's a faint smell of rubbing alcohol in his shirt that shouldn't be there. It's the scent of a doctor's office, of shots and scary needles. I listen there for his heartbeat and his breathing.

"You OK now, Lolo?" I whisper. *You scared me. I thought bad things.*

He takes my face in his hands and smiles at me. I know that look. It says that I'm the only girl, the nieta, the special one, la preciosa.

"Sí, claro," he repeats, and then he chuckles a little, although I don't know at what.

I hug him again and then watch him amble down the path between Tía and Abuela, the twins already racing ahead. Papi slips his arm over my shoulder as we turn to go, but it's not a comfort somehow. I want to shake him off along with this uneasy feeling that won't settle even though Lolo is home, right here in front of my eyes. *He is all right, just like Roli said,* I tell myself. He just fainted, that's all. A syncope.

"You OK?" Papi asks quietly.

"Fine," I lie. Nothing about today feels fine, though.

I slip away from Papi and go inside.

CHAPTER 4

WE DON'T OWN a swimming pool, like some kids at school. But that doesn't mean I don't ever go swimming. That's because Papi's friend Gustavo, who manages the condos across the street, lets us use theirs whenever we want. It's a trade-off for all the times Papi has painted vacant units over there for cheap. It's just a bean-shaped pool, and there's no diving allowed since it's only six feet at the deepest part, but it's better than roasting, especially on a day like today.

Hannah, Lena, and Edna are coming over at lunchtime, so I'm trying to hurry through my chores today. They're all finally home, so we're going to spend the whole day together catching up.

Mami went on overdrive with today's to-do list, but for once I'm trying to get to everything so the place looks as good as possible. Hannah and Lena have visited plenty of times, so I'm not worried about them. But this is the first time Edna is coming over to hang out, and it makes me nervous. Edna has always been the kind of girl who notices everything you don't want her to, and there's plenty of that around here. Toys in the yard. Ladders with broken rungs, old paint buckets. Lolo and Abuela's garden in dusty ruins. I've never been to Edna's house, but I can pretty much imagine it. She has her own room with matching everything, I'll bet, not to mention Diamond, her miniature terrier that wears nail polish.

Anyway, so far, I've wiped down the kitchen counters with bleach, brought in Abuela and Lolo's mail, emptied the trash, and set out the recycling bin for pickup. But I still have a load of things left to do, like hose off these chairs and read a few more chapters from that infernal reading list before school starts next week. I swear, it's like being Cinderella, except without the fairy godmother to do me any favors.

I guess I can't really complain, though. Roli has an even worse job than I do—for once. Mami asked him to help Abuela bathe Lolo before he leaves for work. He told me last night after he got home. We were talking in the dark, the way we sometimes do.

"The summer just keeps getting better," he grumbled.

"God," I said, staring up at our ceiling. "That means you're going to have to see his privates. All wrinkled and stuff."

"Thank you, Merci," he said. "Just what I want to dream about."

I'm wrestling the hose across the yard when Roli finally appears at our patio table wearing the gym shorts and T-shirt he slept in. Mami is long gone to see her new rehab patient, Papi's out on a job, and Tía and the twins are at the dance studio, so it's just the two of us. He pulls out a chair and hunches over his fried-egg sandwich as he scrolls through his phone. It takes him a few seconds to notice that I'm pointing the hose at him like a gun.

He stops chewing. "Don't even think about it," he says.

I hold my aim steady, two-handed. "Then move," I say, not bothering with manners. "I have to wash the spider-webs off the chairs before my friends get here, which is any minute."

He scoops up his plate and stands just inside the door to watch me work.

But when I squeeze the grip, I get blasted in the face

with a spray instead. Sputtering, I drop the hose, water dripping off my glasses.

Roli lets out a snort.

My hair has puffed to enormous proportions in this humidity, and now I'm drenched. My temper boils over like rice out of a pot.

"It's not funny!"

"Oh, it absolutely is," he says, still laughing. He puts down his sandwich and walks over to inspect the nozzle. "Gimme that. I suspect sabotage."

"What do you mean?" I'm still dripping.

"Didn't you tell the twins they couldn't stay home to swim today? What did you expect?"

I think back to the morning guiltily. It's true. They asked and I said no because if the twins were there, they'd be hanging all over my friends, butting in and listening in on our conversations. Shouldn't I be able to have my friends all to myself?

He fastens the grip back on the metal threads and does a test squirt to make sure it's on right. "There you go."

Just then a shiny SUV comes up the driveway slowly. BTS's newest song is playing from inside. They're Hannah's current obsession.

"Oh no. They're here." I look like a swamp creature. The patio still needs to be hosed off. Dirty spiderwebs dangle from the screen door and the chairs. "I'm not done with Mami's dumb list."

Roli heaves a sigh. "Go," he says. "I got this."

"You're going to do chores for me?" I ask, suspicious. "What's the catch?"

"They're waiting," he says.

"I owe you." I turn to go and then hesitate. "I don't suppose you'd like to read two novels and do a book report for each of them, too?"

He squirts a jet of water at my feet. "Get out of here before I change my mind," he says.

He doesn't have to tell me again. I run down the driveway to where Hannah, Lena, and Edna are climbing out of the back seat. Hannah is lugging a gigantic cooler with the lunch stuff she offered to bring. Lena has both their backpacks, one slung on each shoulder. Edna steps out and looks around, more or less like she's landed on the moon. When Lena and Hannah see me, though, they drop everything, and the three of us run at each other, screaming for joy. Edna watches for a second before she saunters over, grinning.

Then there's a weird moment when we all just stare at one another. How can we all look so different in just a few weeks? Edna is suntanned to a deeper brown and has her hair gathered in a slick ponytail. Lena is rocking red cat-eye sunglasses, and there's new hair color in her spikes to match. She's wearing turquoise earrings, too. Hannah has gotten taller than us—by a lot.

"Snap!" I say. "Did they put you on a stretching rack at that camp?"

Hannah grins and waits patiently as Lena, Edna, and I run our fingers across the tops of our heads to see how tall we are in comparison to her. None of us reaches past the middle of Hannah's forehead now.

"You're a good height for modeling," Edna says.

Mrs. Kim turns off the music and steps out of the car. She's in a linen blouse and perfectly pressed walking shorts.

"Hello, Merci," she says. "How was your summer?"

I tug self-consciously on the wet shorts that are riding a little too high and pulling across these new hips I've gotten. "Fine, thanks," I say, even though I know Mrs. Kim isn't really listening. She's too busy glancing around and politely snooping.

"Your parents are well?"

"Mami and Papi are at work already," I tell her, offering up the intel I know she's after.

"Oh." She darts a glance at Hannah, who I'm guessing didn't mention that my parents wouldn't be home today.

"My grandparents are here, though," I say.

"Lolo!" Lena says. She really likes him. "Is he feeling better?"

I shift on my feet. "Yes, he's fine."

Mrs. Kim glances at their house. "That's right. Hannah mentioned he'd been under the weather," she says. "Such a lovely man."

The thing is, everybody loves Lolo. Papi calls it "the Suárez man charm," which Mami calls "the corny joke-telling gene." I don't know how much of it is left, though. Lolo has been quieter since he got back from the hospital. And though it's been a week since his fainting spell, he still looks a little pale. I don't want Mrs. Kim to see that. She might decide there are no competent adults here to watch us. So, to head her off, I point toward the backyard in desperation. "And my older brother is home until he goes to work later. You remember Roli? The genius?"

It's a stretch, but having Roli around is usually the golden ticket for parents. Mrs. Kim is a tough case, though. She turns toward the patio and waves at Roli, who's hosing off the table and chairs like a pro. I can see from her frown that she's not entirely happy. Hannah's mom is super cautious, especially about what she calls "teenage males," which she puts in the same category as werewolves and other dangerous creatures. I guess that includes Roli since he's not twenty yet. But what could *he* possibly do? Bore us to death with scientific notations? Besides, he's going to be busy bathing Lolo—not that I can tell her that.

"It's fine, Mom," Hannah says. "We all know how to swim. And I have my phone."

"I'm CPR certified," Edna adds. She's looking around, seeming kind of bored. "Since I was, like, ten."

Mrs. Kim seems unsure. "Well, why don't I at least drive you girls to the pool and get you settled in?" she says.

"Mom," Hannah whines. "I told you, it's right across the street. We can walk."

"That's true," I say.

"But it's so hot today," she says, pleasantly. "If I drive, you won't have to carry all these heavy coolers and bags in the heat."

We all know Mrs. Kim doesn't care one bit about us lugging stuff. How many times has she made us haul boxes for one of her PTA events? We're practically her pack mules. No, she wants to walk us over so she can scope out where we're going to hang out. She is no joke when it comes to keeping tabs on Hannah. I'm never sure what she's scared of since Hannah *never* gets in trouble on purpose. Still, Mrs. Kim always has to know the exact details about where we're going, how long we'll be there, what we're going to do and all that. Even my parents think Mrs. Kim is overprotective—and that's saying something for people who consider sleepovers at a friend's house a risky activity.

Hannah gives us a shame-faced look, but then Edna pipes up.

"I'll take the ride. I mean, it *is* pretty steamy." She puts her sunglasses on top of her head to reveal what I hope is waterproof mascara.

Lena shrugs. "Besides, we'll be able to compare schedules faster." She reaches into one of the backpacks and pulls out her school envelope to tempt us. I look at Hannah and we break into a smile. Our schedules came this week, but we all promised not to open them until we were together so we could see what classes we share. Eighth grade, here we come!

"Then it's settled," Mrs. Kim says, turning to me again. "I'll wait in the car. She takes in my drenched shirt and frizzy hair. "Come find me when you get cleaned up."

Hannah looks like she wants the earth to swallow her up as her mom walks away.

"Will I ever breathe free?" she grumbles under her breath. Her shoulders slump her down almost to her old size.

"Probably not," Edna says. Then she looks at me. "Pedal to the metal, Merci. I'm melting."

"Wait here," I tell them, and hurry inside to get my things.

A little while later, we're at the Palm Villa condominium pool. I punch in the code and let us all through the pool gate, looking around in case any other residents are here. Gustavo always says we should say we're visiting a relative if anybody asks.

Luckily, the coast is clear today.

I pick a spot at the best table under one of the palm trees and try not to think about what Edna is thinking as she looks around. Edna's family lives up in Jupiter, and I know she has her own pool, her own room, her own everything. Hannah's been there. She says when you visit Edna, you have to stop at a gate where a guy named Edmund takes down your license plate and calls the house to see if she's expecting you—which Hannah's mom loves for the safety aspect alone. I also hear that if you get bored at Edna's pool, you can go to another pool, the one that the community shares. That one has an exercise studio, a hot tub, a ballroom (for parties), and even a tiki bar where you can get fruit, waters, or sodas—*for free*.

I'm still waiting for my invitation, but whatever.

Here, things are different, of course. Nobody is teaching Zumba to moms. Instead, the big game is shuffleboard, even though the courts are buckled and faded. The fiberglass furniture is chipped and unsteady, which is why, on gusty days, the umbrellas are the source of Abuela's dire warnings. She's sure they'll come loose and go off like giant discs to decapitate somebody.

Edna walks over to the clubhouse and cups her hands against the sliding glass doors to peer inside. Not much to see, I want to say. Just the exercise bikes that are older than we are and a few folding tables stacked against the wall. I hold my breath until she walks back to us. I've got to wonder why she agreed to come today when her pool options are so much nicer.

"Stay in the shade," Mrs. Kim tells Hannah as she presses the remote ignition to get her car started. Then she opens the squeaky gate to let herself out. "Reapply your sunscreen in an hour and keep that hat on in the water, too, Hannah Kim," she calls out. "You've cooked your skin quite enough at camp, and you don't need heat stroke, either."

Hannah doesn't look up from under the brim of her baseball cap. Her SPF 90 sunblock is already thick as caulking on her neck. I can smell it from here.

"Bye, Mom," she says.

We all watch Mrs. Kim through the shrubs as she finally gets in her car and pulls away.

Hannah lets out a heavy sigh.

"What's next for you?" Edna says as the car disappears around the corner. "Installing a locator chip under your skin?"

"I wouldn't be surprised," Hannah says.

Edna reaches into her bag and pulls out a pack of gum that she holds out to each of us. "Are there rules about gum on the pool deck here?" She looks around at the globs of bird poop and everything else on the pavement. "I guess not."

"Forget all that mom stuff!" Lena says, folding a stick of gum inside her mouth. "We've got more important things to do. Like figuring out our schedules!" She pulls us over to where she's arranged four chaises, side by side. Edna frowns at the unsteady one with tiny mold stains on the straps. They're my guests, so I take that one.

Then we all dig in our bags for our identical Seaward Pines Academy envelopes.

"On the count of three," Lena says, and then, on cue, we rip them open.

It's a big computer printout. I run my finger down the grid. "I'm in homeroom 810," I announce.

Hannah shakes her head. "Crud. I'm in 812 with Mr. Kowal. How about you, Lena?"

"I'm in 812, too," says Lena, happily.

"Ditto," Edna says.

"What?" I blurt out. "I'm by myself?"

"Don't worry, Merci," Lena says. "It's next door, and it's just homeroom. How about first period?"

"I've got English first with Tibbetts," Hannah says.

Lena fist bumps her. "Yes!" she says. "Ms. Tibbetts lets you choose the books you read."

But I find that my first period slot doesn't match theirs either. "I've got Mrs. Watson for science first hour."

"How about civics, then, with Ms. Donner, for second period?" Edna says.

We go on like that through our whole schedule, class by class, twice, but in the end, the horror sets in. They're in several classes together, but I'm in exactly *none* of the same ones.

I'm stunned.

"I hate my schedule," I say, trying not to let the panic show in my voice. "All we have together are lunch and PE. How am I supposed to live with that?"

"What's the big deal?" Edna says. "Have your mom write a note to Miss McDaniels to change you into one of our classes. My mom does that all the time."

"Not mine." I lie back on my chaise and stare hard into the bright sky, trying to disguise the fact that my eyes are watering. Mami isn't like Mrs. Santos, who donates money and volunteers for everything, and then cashes in on the favors she does for our school. Mami will just say something dumb, like how middle school is the time to expand my horizons and make new friends and all the rest of those lies. It's like she doesn't understand the basic facts of life: It is never a good thing when you are separated from your herd in the wild.

So, I stay quiet and let the sun shrink the skin on my cheeks while Lena, Edna, and Hannah keep comparing notes on the classes they have together and what they know about this teacher or that. Their happiness is a hot-air balloon rising while I'm here shriveling in the sun. I'm trying not to be mad at them for it, but it's not fair that they'll be together without me. Couldn't they at least be a little more upset?

Finally, Edna looks over at me. "Are you going to sulk? This is supposed to be fun, you know."

"Edna," Lena says.

Edna heaves a sigh and reaches for her phone. Soon, her thumbs are flying over the screen.

"What are you doing?" Hannah asks.

"Hello? Basic reconnaissance." She scrolls and swipes like a pro to reveal different people's socials. After a couple of minutes, she looks up at me. "Avery Sanders and Mackenzie Lewis are in your homeroom, according to Insta. Didn't you play soccer with them?"

"Yes."

"Well, there you go."

I scoot closer to look over her shoulder at a picture of Avery and Mackenzie together at soccer camp this summer. People are leaving zillions of comments about how cute they look and all that. One of the posts has little applause icons and mentions my same homeroom. Avery was our center forward last year, and Mackenzie and I subbed in as the attackers flanking her. We played off each other pretty well. The thing is, though, that they don't really get too chummy with me, unless we're on the soccer field.

"It's not the same as you guys," I say.

"Obviously," Edna says. "But it's something. And even if they ignore you, at least you know you're not in a loser homeroom where they've thrown all the outcasts." She looks at me sheepishly and then mumbles, "Not that you're an outcast."

I don't even bristle. I mean, I've never been especially

popular, but it's Edna who really knows what it's like to be tossed to the curb. It wasn't that long ago that her old friends shut her out of the A-list. Avery and Mackenzie aren't mean girls, but they're still the opposite of outcasts. They're those girls who are good at everything and nice enough, to boot. They make it feel like a big deal if they say hi to you in the hall.

Edna tosses her phone in the bag. "So now that we fixed that, let's swim," she says. "It's way too hot."

I look at the water half-heartedly and shrug. Hannah nudges me with her toe.

"Edna's right, Merci. Cheer up. Even if your mom doesn't fix your classes, we'll have lunch together every single day."

"And don't forget, we have the eighth-grade sleepaway trip this year," Lena adds. "We'll definitely be roommates for that." She wiggles her eyebrows and breaks into a huge grin, until I do the same. The trip is a Seaward Pines middle-school tradition, and it's always fun. Three days in Saint Augustine during October, with none of our parents to bug us.

Lena puts her schedule away and pulls off her T-shirt and her glasses. "So what we should do now is . . . have a cannonball contest!" She runs for the deep end of the pool and jumps high, pointing her toes like a gymnast as she curls up her knees. Her splash makes a perfect arc of water that drenches the pool deck, almost to where we're sitting.

"Wait for me!" Hannah says. She tosses off her hat and goes chasing after Lena, the glitter on her suit making her look like a beautiful mermaid. There's another perfect splash, and then they're bobbing at the surface, laughing together in the pool.

"Come on, guys! Get in!" Hannah yells.

Edna is next, but she doesn't run. She more or less slinks to the pool edge and looks at the surface one last time, probably checking to make sure it's clean enough before jumping in.

I back up to get a running start toward the water, ignoring the pain in my toe that's still healing. I grit my teeth and let the pavement singe the bottoms of my feet as I race toward the deep end. I leap as high as I can, trying to make my own glorious splash. But I lean back a hair too far and then—*smack!*—I've only done a back slap.

The world goes quiet as I let myself go all the way to the bottom like a bag of sand. Above me, I can see the three of them treading water. They'll be together a lot this year, and I'll be stuck mostly alone. I wait as long as I can below, sullen and watching them through the ripples, until finally, I have no choice but to push back to the surface to breathe.

CHAPTER 5

ROLI AND I ARE dressed in our Sol Painting T-shirts and caps the next morning, waiting for Papi to finish his shower so we can leave for the job. Normally, I'd be psyched. I mean, Roli and I haven't done a paint job together in a long while, and today's a good one. We're heading over to Loxahatchee. Gustavo's wife, Zenaida, works as a house-keeper there and got us the job. She says there are horses and everything.

Even so, I'm barely awake as I pick at my waffles. I don't know what made sleep harder: my sunburned shoulders or worrying about who I'm going to talk to in any of my classes. I spent all night rubbing aloe cuttings on my skin and checking people's stories to see if anyone else was mentioning their schedules. It's exhausting to do all this spying. I wish you could just ask outright without looking desperate. But no, you can't, and after all that work, so far, all I know for sure is that I have a couple of classes with Avery and Mackenzie.

I'm trying to decide if we're going to get friendlier. Being on the same team with them means I have a temporary pass inside their social club, which is kind of cool, since Avery is always thinking of fun things to do, like putting looped clips of her favorite moments from the National Women's Soccer League games on her feed or organizing us to decorate our lockers before games. But after we hang up our cleats, things change. Avery and Mackenzie have a closed group of friends that the rest of us can watch but not join. People notice what that group wears and where they hang out and what shows they talk about at lunch. They have boyfriends and girlfriends. They go to parties and sometimes invite each other on family vacations.

Anyway, it's not that Avery or Mackenzie has ever been snotty, like girls in some of the other biodomes around here. They're nice to me, especially during the season, when I've heard Avery say things like "Sure-foot Suárez" in front of her other friends at the locker, when she's describing one of my good moves. It's just that after the season is over, so is our closeness. Coach Cameron was always lecturing our team about thinking of ourselves as a soccer team "family," but it never really took hold. Maybe Avery doesn't think of family the way I think of it. Whatever the reason, after the season, we were all on our own and back to our own groups.

Roli leans into the refrigerator, planning his breakfast raid.

"Leave me the string cheese," I warn. He'll suck up everything in sight if I'm not careful.

"Oh," he says. When he straightens, I see he's got my last mozzarella stick hanging from his lips like a cigar. "Sorry."

He comes back to the table also carrying the tub of arroz con leche that Abuela sent over yesterday. It's Roli's favorite dessert, and I'll bet she made it to thank him for having to see Lolo desnudo. Whatever the reason, there's enough rice pudding for an army. Still, he grabs his spoon and starts digging through the cinnamon top all by himself.

"Save me some of that. I like it too, you know," I say. "And Abuela said to share."

He ignores me. "Aren't you done with those yet?" he asks, motioning to the books I'm stuffing in my backpack for the ride.

I scrunch my nose at him, wincing a little from the sunburn. Tiny blisters have formed at the tip of my nose, but they don't sting as much as his comment. He knows I'm a slower reader than he is. And slower at math, and slower at science . . . and you name it. "I still say summer work shouldn't even be allowed," I mutter.

He takes a heaping spoonful and doesn't answer. I can see that he aims to finish the whole bowl unless I stop him, so I put my things down and go in search of a spoon from the drawer. My back is turned for just a few seconds, but when I come back, I find him scrolling through my phone without permission.

"Hey!" I say. His signature sneaky move this summer has been snapping dumb pictures of himself—like a close-up of his eyeballs—and making them my home screen when I'm not looking. "I don't need your mug on my screen again."

He swivels in his chair and squirms out of reach. "Hang on, will you? This will only take a second."

I hear my text message ping as he's working. "Roli, I mean it. Give it back or I'll scream." My cheeks are flaming now—and not from the sun. What if it's something private, like Wilson texting me? I don't want Roli to know.

"What is with you?" he asks, getting to his feet. "Just wait."

He towers over me now, of course. With his back turned, it's easy for him to block me from grabbing my phone while he works at something on the screen. Finally, he hands it back. "Here you go."

"What did you do?" I ask.

"Provided the answer to your suffering," he says.

I look to see what he means. The covers of the books on my reading list fill my screen. When I scroll, I realize he's downloaded the files from the library's audiobook collection.

A tiny bubble of hope flutters inside me. Why didn't I think of this before? I hold my breath, staring at the phone and fighting the urge to kiss his stubbly face.

"It will take you exactly twenty-one hours, give or take for bathroom breaks. You can start listening while you're painting today."

"Is this allowed?" I whisper in case Papi is still lurking. He'd be one to think audiobooks are cheating since there is less suffering involved. And who knows if my new teacher will think like that, too?

"Too late to worry about that. You start school on Monday. You want a zero on the first day?" He scrapes the sides of the bowl and savors the last morsel without me. Then he heads for the door just as Simón is pulling into the driveway.

"I'm going to help Simón start packing the van," he says from the doorway. Then he grins and adds in a sing-song voice, "By the way, *Wilson* says he's home."

Simón, who's riding shotgun with Papi, slides down his sunglasses and whistles as we pull up to the job. He's Papi's best guy—and now Tía Inés's, too, if you know what I mean. I don't really like to think about adults' love lives, but as gross ideas go, those two aren't bad. And the twins really like Simón. He plays with them. He laughs at their dumb jokes.

"Look at the size of this place!" he says. "These people must have a huge family to fill all the rooms."

Papi stares through the windshield. "I think it's just the lady and her husband."

I squeeze in between their seats to see for myself. The house is enormous. "If we were painting all of it, we'd be making a boatload of money, Papi!"

"¡Cabal!" says Simón.

"If only," Papi says, shrugging. "La señora just wants us to paint two rooms."

"Better than nothing, hermano," Simón adds, shrugging.

We pull around to the back of the house on a long driveway that opens to a yard big enough to be a park. It's been cleared except for tall pines here and there. Beyond the trees, two horses graze in a white-fenced paddock. It looks like a painting, especially this early when the grass is dewy and the sun still feels gentle.

Zenaida is at the back door, waving us in.

"¡Buen día!" she calls out.

It's weird to see Gustavo's wife here, instead of back home at the condo. It's like she's a different person. She's dressed in navy blue pants and a collared shirt, like she's going to a doctor appointment or something. At home, she's always in flip-flops and colorful sundresses, wandering around the condo walkways to check in on residents, which is her favorite pastime. Abuela says that if it weren't for Zenaida, the ancianos over there wouldn't have anybody to talk to all day long.

"Los pobres. If they didn't have you, their tongues would dry up in their mouths," Abuela told her the other day when Zenaida dropped off a roscón from the bakery, the kind she knows Abuela likes.

Anyway, I'll bet Zenaida's job as housekeeper here keeps her plenty busy, too—and not just making conversation or snacking on guava-filled treats. What's the chore list on a place like this? It must take hours and hours to clean it.

"This way," she tells Papi and Simón as she opens the door for us. Then she sees Roli and me. "I see you brought your best assistants, too!" She smiles wide and kisses us on the cheeks, glancing at our shoes to make sure they're clean. We know the drill, though, so we all slip on our paper booties and follow her inside.

Almost as soon as I step into the kitchen behind her, I feel like Alice in Wonderland after she shrinks. The room is wide open with lots of stainless steel and dark wood cabinets. Strangely, not a single thing is on any of the counters. At our house everything is out in the open. Bags of crackers. A fruit basket. The old coffee can Mami keeps near the stove for draining the used cooking oil.

"¿Quieren agua?" Zenaida asks. The refrigerator door has a small see-through compartment filled with bottled waters. "It's going to be another hot one."

Papi says no since we bring our own drinks in a cooler. Then she asks how Lolo is feeling, and they make small talk in Spanish. I try not to eavesdrop since I know what's coming. It's like our whole neighborhood sort of knows that Lolo isn't himself these days. I hate it. The worried looks, the sighs, the times when people say things like "qué lástima."

Roli and Simón go out to the van to bring in the paints we picked up at the store this morning. I unfold the tarp and drape the kitchen table and upholstered chairs in plastic, taking extra care to cover everything. If we drip anything on this stuff by mistake, we'll never be able to pay for it.

I'm taping down the ends when I hear sneakers squeaking against the tile, and then a tall lady appears. She's about Mami's age, with short hair and very tan legs, like the runners on our school track team. She's in a pressed golf shirt and matching earrings. Even from here, I can smell some sort of perfume.

"I thought I heard voices," she says. "Good morning."

Roli and Simón nod a hello. Zenaida stops talking with Papi midsentence and switches all at once to English.

"Good morning, Mrs. Ransome. I was just letting in the painters." She smiles at her boss and gives us a curt nod before heading out. Just like that, it's as if she doesn't know us anymore, like she's never stood at Abuela's window, chatting in the shade.

Mrs. Ransome turns back to us and smiles brightly. "You're right on time, Mr. Sol. I like that," she tells Papi.

"It's Suárez," Papi says. "Enrique Suárez. Sol is the company name."

"Like the sun," I say, motioning to the logo on our shirts.

She peers over at me.

"These are my children, Rolando and Mercedes," Papi says, using our full names, like all the extra letters in them make us more important. "And my assistant Simón. All excellent workers."

I won't lie: it feels good that Papi says I do good work, but I can see that Mrs. Ransome doesn't look too convinced, so I try to stand a little taller. *Go ahead,* I think. *Ask me the difference between satin finish and flat. See if I can estimate how much paint you'll need to cover the wall square footage of this room.* I'll bet she doesn't think that I put Roli to shame with a roller, to say nothing of my freehand edging skills on trim.

"Well, let me show you the space. It's this room, of course," she says, motioning around the kitchen, "but also the den. Follow me, please."

"A den?" I whisper to Roli. "Like bears?"

"Shh," he says.

We follow her down the sunny hall and into another room that opens with double doors. It's even more immense than the kitchen, with tall ceilings and wood beams overhead that make the place look like both a church and a farmhouse at the same time. One wall is made entirely of tinted windows that overlook the paddock, too. The horses, I notice, are still grazing.

"I'll need you to take extra care around those beams," she says, pointing at the ceiling. "They're cedar."

Simón pockets his hands and glances up the height of

the room. Then he takes a step toward the bookcases and squints to admire a framed diploma beside it.

"Mira, Roli," he whispers, elbowing him. "Isn't that where you study?"

Papi turns to look. Then he grins proudly. "My son is studying to be a doctor," he tells Mrs. Ransome. He taps his head to show he means that Roli's got brains. "Smart, like his mother."

Roli's ears become tomatoes as he pretends to study the wall surface, running his hands along the paint. I feel for him instantly. Public parental adulation. Ouch.

Mrs. Ransome turns to my brother, surprised. "Really? A doctor?"

Geez. *Yes, really.* All anyone would have to do is talk to Roli for five minutes to know it. Who else would use words like *amyloid plaque* and *subthalamic nucleus* in casual conversation? If you ask any of his old teachers, they'll tell you that Roli was pretty much college-ready the day he finished kindergarten. I think back to his valedictorian speech at his graduation last year. When he got to the podium, all the honor-society bling around his neck made him look like a nerdy rapper at the mic. He talked about having purpose and helping others and a bunch of other stuff that made Mami and Papi get weepy in their seats.

Afterward, our headmaster, Dr. Newman, pumped Roli's hand like my brother had already cured cancer. "I know you'll do big things in this world, Rolando," he said.

Maybe Mrs. Ransome can't imagine Roli as a doctor since he's in his uniform right now. A doctor's coat and coveralls are both white uniforms, but they are not the same at all. People look at you differently, even if you're the same person wearing both. I wonder, though, what *do* future doctors look like, if not like Roli?

He turns to her. "I'm in the biology program right now," he says quietly. "I'd like to specialize in neurology one day." He doesn't mention Lolo or why he wants to learn how to fix people's brains.

Mrs. Ransome's eyebrows shoot up even higher. "My goodness, that's impressive! When do you graduate?"

I steal a glance at Roli, who slides his hands inside his pockets, just like Simón. It's a simple question, but it's got a gnarly answer that depends on so many things—but mostly, as usual, on money.

"I'm not sure." Then he turns to Papi. "Where do you want us to start?" he asks.

Papi nods and gives Roli's shoulder a squeeze. "Right," he says. "Let's prep the kitchen, mijo."

Out in the hallway, Zenaida has been listening. She

catches my eye and smiles as we walk by, but she keeps dusting without a word. We're supposed to be "the painters" here, I guess, and not friends and neighbors. I get it.

So, I put in my earbuds, make my face blank, and call up my first book as we start.

CHAPTER 6

ON THE RIDE HOME, I send Wilson a picture of Mrs. Ransome's horses and add "Welcome back" in multicolored letters. I took the shots at lunchtime, when we all ate at a picnic table near the paddock. I caught them in dappled sunlight, which makes them look magical with the filter I used.

Zenaida brought some snacks so I could feed the horses treats, but at first neither one came over.

"Horses can be shy," Simón told me. "Give them time." He knows because his grandfather had a farm in El Salvador when he was a kid, so he grew up around them.

So, I waited until Jack, the brown one, finally came over to the fence to see what I had in my hand. He lowered his silky muzzle, sniffing around, and lifted the carrot away from my palm with his big yellow teeth. He let me pat him a few times on his neck, too. Then he trotted back to his friend in the field. I guess horses can be a lot like people, a little nervous and unsure if they don't know you. Weird, since they're so big. It's like they have no idea of their own power.

As soon as I send the picture, Wilson tags it with a thumbs-up.

See you Monday.

School starts next week.

I pause over the keypad. Should I ask about his schedule? I haven't seen him post anything about it, but it would be great if Wilson were in at least one of my classes. That way, I'd at least have *somebody* to talk to. Then again, that could be trouble. It might be weird to sit next to each other. People would start rumors, which is the worst. What would we do then?

So, I just text back some confetti and a party hat.

See you Monday. Eighth grade!

I stare out the window, thinking about school and trying to look on the bright side. I've been making a mental list of things I've been looking forward to, now that we're the oldest grade in the middle school. Eighth-graders are usually the starters on the middle school soccer team, so I won't have to sub in anymore. I've got a pretty good shot to be a teacher's assistant for my community service job, which is cushier than anything else I've had to do. How hard can it be to deliver notes and run copies for somebody? Best of all, the eighth-grade annual sleepover trip is in a few weeks. Lena, Hannah, Edna, and I will definitely be roommates for that, just like we said.

"Who was that?" Papi asks.

I turn back from the window. "What?"

"Who texted you?"

Roli turns to look at me from where he's sitting on an overturned paint bucket in the back. He raises his eyebrows but keeps his mouth shut, thank goodness.

Papi doesn't seem to notice. "If it's Mami, tell her we'll be home in thirty minutes." He stretches his neck and winces as it makes a cracking sound. Those cathedral ceilings gave him more trouble than he expected. Mami will have to twist him this way and that to fix his pinched nerve later.

"OK," I say.

I text Mami that we're coming home. My phone pings a few seconds later with her reply. The words make the back of my neck feel prickly, so I read the message out to Papi.

"'Glad you're on the way. It's been eventful around

here.' What does that mean?" I ask. My mind goes to Lolo as a cold feeling springs up inside me. "You don't think he fainted again, do you?"

"Cálmate," Papi says, watching me in the mirror. "Mami would have called right away if there was a problem."

Simón turns and gives me a reassuring look. "That's true. Bad news doesn't wait."

"Then what does she mean?" I ask. A squeezing sensation starts in my chest.

"Please, Merci." Papi twists his neck again. "Don't jump to conclusions. We're going to find out soon enough."

When we get home, Papi makes me get out at the end of our driveway so I can pick up the mail for everyone. Mostly, it's junk mail and bills, but as I hurry along, sorting everything into stacks the way I'm supposed to, one letter catches my eye. It's addressed to Axel and Tomás. I slow down and study it. They've got pen pals? There's a return address in grown-up handwriting, I notice, but no name. I know better than to open it or even to hold it up to the light. Tampering with the US mail is a felony, number one. Plus, that would qualify as snooping in Mami's book, which I'm not supposed to do. She'd be worse than the feds if she saw me peeking inside.

Simón is already out of the van and standing on Abuela's porch, where Lolo and Tía are side by side on the porch glider. The sight of Lolo makes me feel better. He's OK, at least.

Simón is already on the porch saying hello. He should be helping us unpack the supplies that need cleaning, but it's no use mentioning that to him when Tía is around.

"Señor," he says politely to Lolo in greeting. Then Simón kisses Tía's cheek and says, "I thought you were going to be at the studio today, Inés."

"I went," she says, "but I had to come home early." She wipes sweat from her neck and lets her eyes flit to Lolo. "We had a little incident, so I had to cancel the afternoon classes. Aurelia is still over there in case anyone shows up."

Papi stops unloading the back of the van and walks over as soon as he hears that. He puckers his lips and motions with his chin to ask what's up.

"Nada," Tía says. "Someone just went missing for a little while."

"Again?" Papi says.

"Again." Tía pats Lolo's hand.

Papi's shoulders droop. He shakes his head and studies a pebble he grinds into the ground with his boot.

Lolo has been slipping away when Abuela isn't looking—and he's quicker than he looks for a guy with a walker. It's like he's been taking lessons from Tuerto, who can vanish in an instant. "The disappearing acts," as Papi calls them, are scary because we have canals where Lolo might wander too close and a busy street that leads to the condos, where Lolo likes to visit. Every time he does it, Papi gets mad at Lolo, even though it's not anybody's fault—not even Lolo's, when you think about it. When you have Alzheimer's, you forget things, like rules. How can you follow a rule if you can't remember it?

"Where's Abuela?" I ask, looking around.

Mami comes through Abuela and Lolo's front door just as I ask.

"Lying down," she says quietly. "Today took a lot out of her." She walks over to kiss Papi on the cheek and then gives him a knowing look.

"How far this time?" he asks.

"We searched for forty-five minutes before Gustavo called," Mami says in a low voice. "He spotted Lolo near the bus stop."

We all stand there, stunned. The bus stop is several blocks away, and it's at a busy intersection.

Papi tosses down his rags in frustration. The tiny vein in his temple looks thick and wormy.

"Viejo, you can't walk away from the yard anymore. Remember? It's too dangerous. There are too many cars.

And people can't leave work to come look for you!"

"Enrique, please," Mami says.

"What, Ana?" he snaps. "It's making us crazier than a bunch of cabras!"

I watch Lolo carefully as Papi scolds him. I feel bad for him. It's no fun when everyone's mad at you, even if it's because they love you. The weird thing is, though, that he doesn't seem to care that he's worried us again. Instead, he looks out over the yard.

"He's not hurt, hermano. That's the main thing." Simón shrugs and moves away to tend to the truck. He's like family around here, but he's careful not to get too mixed up in the big stuff. Lolo is the biggest stuff for us right now. It's what can make Tía cry if she's tired. It's what Mami and Papi whisper about if they think I can't hear.

"Simón is right. It's over now," Tía says. "But maybe one of you will have better luck convincing him to go inside. We've been out here a couple of hours, and I'm roasting." She looks at the mail I'm holding. "Any of that for me?"

"Sorry. I almost forgot." I hand her the letters and slide in next to Lolo. His shirt feels damp against my skin.

"It's hot out here, Lolo," I whisper to him. "Why don't we get a cool drink? We've still got Jupiñas in our fridge. And I can show you the cool pictures I took today. The lady had horses."

I take Lolo's elbow so I can help him to his feet. He loves pineapple soda almost as much as he likes frosty batidos de mamey from the bakery. But this time, he just draws back his hand and stays put, even though beads of sweat are all along his forehead.

"The bus is late again," he says, frowning at me. "Very late."

For a moment, nobody says anything. What is Lolo talking about? Papi's jaw is clenched so tight you can see it moving.

"There's no bus, viejo," he says firmly. "You're here in the yard, roasting to death."

Mami reaches for Papi's shoulder. He swallows hard, staring at Lolo hopefully, but then, clicking his tongue, he moves off to finish unloading and maybe to calm down. Tía just stares into her hands.

It's Roli who steps forward. His glasses are speckled with the pale blue paint we used in Mrs. Ransome's kitchen. Sweat marks have made large, dark circles at his pits. He looks beat, but I know he's trying to hurry so he can get to his night shift at Walgreens in a little while.

"I think you missed it," he tells Lolo. "You'll have to get the one that comes by tomorrow." He sticks his hands deep into the Styrofoam cooler he's brought from the van and pulls a bottle of water from the melted ice. "Why don't you drink something for now? No sense getting dehydrated while you wait." He unscrews the bottle and holds it out to him.

Lolo shifts his gaze to Roli and squints, as if trying to see something tiny and far away. Sometimes he calls Roli Enrique. Sometimes other names. But he finally accepts the bottle and pulls long, thirsty drafts, his Adam's apple bobbing as water dribbles to his chin. When he finishes, he gives Tía the empty bottle without even looking at her.

"Tomorrow," he says. And then, as if it's all been decided, Lolo lets me help him stand.

What happens tomorrow? I wonder as we walk inside together, the heavy thump and drag of the walker marking the way. And the day after? And the one after that? When is the day that Lolo will not be OK anymore?

CHAPTER 7

IT'S ONLY FIVE BLOCKS to Sharp Shears, but the car ride has been much worse than a hot walk would have been, even dragging the twins along. I should have known this ride would be murder. When we got in, the seat burned the backs of my thighs. And even now, with all the windows down, we're all wilting.

"I'm dying, just so you know." I put my face right on the air-conditioning vent in Tía's car, but it's blowing warm air again. What can you expect? It's a secondhand one that Papi scored at the junkyard until she can get the money for a new one.

"I'm canceled," Axel says, leaning his head against the door.

"Me, too. Let's go baaack," Tomás whines. "I'll wear a man bun."

I can't help but laugh.

"We're almost there," Tía says as the light changes.

I close my eyes and feel a long streak of sweat make its way down my back.

It's Haircut Day for the twins, a thankless job I'm always roped into since it's at least a two-person effort. Basically, it works like this: Tía keeps the first victim still in the salon chair so they don't lose an ear while I make sure the other twin doesn't steal all the candies from the bowl by the cashier. The "salary" is usually a slice of pizza afterward. But today, Tía sweetened the pot by announcing that we're going shopping for new school shoes, too. And not at Frugal Foot Hut this time, but at the mall. Normally, that kind of outing isn't something to throw a party about, especially if you're required to wear school loafers like I am, but at least I don't have to go with Mami, who makes me try on every pair and parades me up and down the aisle until she's satisfied with the fit.

We cross over Lake Worth Road and pull into the only shady spot in the parking lot. Tía cuts off the engine and swivels in her seat. "No squirting people with the sink hoses, amorcitos," she says.

Tomás and Axel bolt out of the car without even answering.

Sharp Shears isn't a fancy salon like Pierre Citrus downtown, where a lot of girls from school get their hair done. It's right here in our neighborhood, and Tía's friend Consuelo owns it. Her claim to fame is reliable neighborhood gossip and a team of stylists who cut fast and cheap. As far as Tía's concerned, that's a winning combo.

By the time we get to the door, we look like we've survived a trek through the rain forest. My face is so slick that my glasses have slipped to the tip of my nose. I'm pretty sure my deodorant has already failed, too. Consuelo looks up from her appointment book and waves us in.

"¡Ay, qué calor! Come inside quick."

She comes out from behind the counter and kisses Tía Inés on the cheek. Then she offers the twins lollipops from her stash. It's a preemptive bribe. Smart move.

"Look how tall they are now!" Consuelo says as they wander off. "How old are they?"

"They'll be seven in a couple of months," Tía says. "Can you believe it?"

"¡Dos caballeros! And look at you, too, Merci," she adds. "You've become a woman, ¡que Dios te bendiga!"

"She wears the same shoe size I do!" Tía says.

Geez. I stare down at my feet, wondering if my

dogs are freakishly big. Maybe. Especially now, with a smashed-up baby toe that looks like a blue sausage. I can't bother with that worry for long, though. I'm parched, so I head straight for the water cooler to quench my thirst.

I glance around while I gulp down a few cones of water. Most of the stylists are lounging by the bonnet dryers in the back of the shop, looking bored and watching shows on their phones. There's only one customer in here, an older guy, who's getting his eyebrows and ear hair trimmed. I recognize him right away. It's Señor Humberto, one of Lolo's old friends from the bakery where Tía used to work. Señor Humberto and Lolo used to hang out most afternoons during Tía's shift, trading jokes and eating free snacks. The twins have already spotted him and are mesmerized by all the weirdness of hair in odd places. I make a mental note to hide the scissors when we get home in case they get ideas to work on each other.

"¿Qué me dices, muchachita? I haven't seen you in a long while!"

He pulls down his top lip so the lady can snip near his ample nostrils.

"Hola, Señor Humberto," I say.

"That guy has long nose hairs," Axel says a little too loudly. I give him a squeeze on the shoulder to shut him up.

The stylist repositions Señor Humberto's head and moves on to trimming inside one of his ears. "And Suárez?" he asks. "How is he these days?" All the old-timers just call each other by their last names.

I stare at his reflection in the mirror. How should I answer? Is Lolo fine? He woke up today and had breakfast, same as always. But what do you say about a grandfather who now waits for imaginary buses? No answer seems right, so I finally offer a shrug. "Pretty good," I say.

Señor Humberto glances back at me through his reflection and stays quiet as the stylist finishes. When his trim is done, he inspects the final results and hands her a two-dollar tip. He stops near me on his way out.

"We miss him at El Caribe," he says. "A fine old friend, that Suárez. I'll have to stop by soon to tell him some new jokes." Then he pats Axel and Tomás on their heads and goes to pay at the front desk.

He probably won't come. At first, Lolo's friends came all the time to sit on the porch and have a coffee. But I've noticed fewer visitors these days. Tía says people feel uncomfortable when he can't remember them. They don't know what to say when he gets confused. It hurts them to be forgotten.

"Manuela! Imani!" Consuelo says a couple of minutes

later. "We have young customers here, and you're next in the queue."

I brace myself for a chase. This is normally when these two make a break for it. But to my complete shock, Axel and Tomás follow the hairdressers to the sink station without any drama.

I give Tía Inés a wary look. "What's the matter with them?" I ask. "Did they get heat stroke from the drive over?"

Tsk. Tía sucks her teeth at me. "Crushing on the ladies is my guess. They're getting older, you know. It was bound to happen."

I look over. Manuela and Imani *are* pretty, although they're also about Roli's age from what I can tell, so way out of the twins' playground league. They're wearing false eyelashes and bright lipstick, like they're going to a party instead of getting ready to wrestle almost-seven-year-old twins. But Tía might be right, since the twins are blushing and giving each other weird looks. It's hard to imagine them thinking about girls except as victims of their pranks, but here it is. Romeos in the making.

"Or maybe God has finally answered my prayers and they're learning how to behave," Tía continues. "Miracles happen."

I cross my arms and turn to her. "Be serious. Have you already forgotten the supermarket fiasco?"

She sighs. It wasn't even a week ago that the twins ripped opened packages of knee-high stockings in the cosmetics aisle without paying. They pulled a few over their faces to squash down their noses and mouths so they could look like the undead and scare people in the produce aisle. We were escorted from the store by the manager.

"Don't jinx it, please," she says. "We still have to go shoe shopping after this, remember?"

"Shoe shopping!" Consuelo shakes her head, overhearing us. "I have to do the same on my next day off. More money out the window! Te lo juro, my little one needs new shoes every three months. I can barely keep up."

Tía nods sympathetically. "Normally, I can't either, but this year I've had some help."

"Lucky you! The new man in your life?" Consuelo says, arching her brow.

Tía blushes a little and glances at me.

"Of course not," she says primly, but she doesn't explain any further. It's one thing to hear gossip, according to Tía. It's another to *be* the story. Mami and Papi are always the ones to lend Tía money when she needs it, which is usually before school starts, for supplies, and at

Christmas, for presents. Who'd send her money for the twins' school shoes? I'm about to ask when a walk-in customer steps in the salon. Tía knows the lady, so they all start talking and then discussing the price of a Dominican blowout. I take a seat and plug in my earbuds to find where I left off on the last of my audiobooks.

A few minutes later, I'm just falling back into the story when I feel someone touching my hair lightly. I open my eyes and press pause.

"And how about you, Merci?" Consuelo says, examining my dry curls. "No haircut today? You could use a trim on those dry ends so they don't frizz."

I shrug. "Mami cuts it for me every year. She can do it tonight."

Consuelo looks like I've thrown a bucket of guts at her. "¡Ay no, chica! You should turn to the professionals! We're even running a back-to-school special." She taps a manicured nail against the ad that's propped on her counter. "Shampoo, cut, and blow for thirty dollars. You won't find a better bargain."

I try not to let my mouth hang open. Thirty smackers on hair? Puh-leez. Still, I try to be polite, the way Mami is always reminding me.

"Thanks, but I don't have that much money today," I say. "I'm supposed to get school shoes."

Consuelo breaks into a grin. "Well . . . maybe someone generous can help with that." She gives Tía a pointed look and bats her eyelashes.

Tía puts down the perfume sample she's been rubbing on her wrist and looks over at me. "Why not?" She gives Consuelo a conspirator's smile, and they both turn to me like I'm something to eat.

My brain starts firing emergency warning signals. The coconut smell in the shop suddenly seems too strong as my eyes trail over all those brushes, scissors, and razors lining the counters, all those combs floating in blue liquid like specimens in a science lab. For a flash, I consider running out of here like the twins used to do. But how far would I get in this heat?

"That's OK," I say carefully. "I'm fine with Mami's trims."

"But you're going into the eighth grade," Tía says. "What better time to get a new look?" She flips back to a page in the magazine she's been perusing and holds it out to me. "How about something like this?"

She points to a picture of a curly-haired model with chin-length hair that's been cut at an angle. That girl has no glasses or pimples like I do, though. Plus, she's wearing lip gloss, and her lashes curl up to touch her eyebrows.

They're probably fake, like the ones Manuela and Imani are wearing. I am not that girl.

But Consuelo nods in approval as if it makes perfect sense. "¡Mira qué monada! And it's super easy to take care of with the right products. I promise."

Tía leans in. "Imagine walking into school looking like someone brand-new," she says. "Merci 2.0!"

I sit there blinking at the thought of being upgraded.

Should I want to be someone new? For sure, almost everyone looks different on the first day of school, even though we're dressed in our uniforms. Braces come off. Voices get deeper. People get piercings in odd places. We're taller or fatter or skinnier than before. Just look at Hannah, who got all stretched out, and Lena with those awesome red spikes in her hair and the bold frames on her new glasses. What would happen if I shook things up, too, for once? It might not be so bad to look like an almost–high schooler, like Avery and them, especially now that I'll have to walk into homeroom without my friends.

Consuelo takes my hand in hers before I can change my mind. I trail her to the wash station, past the twins, wrapped in smocks, who make faces when they spot me going by in the mirror. They're getting buzz cuts with little parts shaved in. I can already see it makes them look older, like real second-graders, all big-toothed and brave.

Consuelo whips out a smock like a bull fighter's cape and fastens it at my neck. "Trust me. This is going to be a new you."

I lean my head back into the sink and stare at the ceiling.

But what about the old me? I wonder. *Where will she go?*

CHAPTER 8

LATER THAT AFTERNOON, we end up at the Gardens Mall. I walk along catching glimpses of myself in the mirrored display cases. A couple of times, I don't even realize it's me.

The twins are swinging their shoe bags and hopping from one gold tile to another, trying not to touch any others. It's pretty crowded today with back-to-school shoppers. Lots of kids from school come here, although I haven't spotted anyone I know. A few girls have even had their birthday parties here. Edna says you can have a private runway fashion show of your own and then they bring racks of clothes from a few of the stores so you can shop.

I never shop here unless it's to sample stuff at Lush with Hannah, Edna, and Lena, who usually have to drag me. I just don't like shopping. And, besides, Mami says most of the stores are too expensive, which is true. Even at Finish Line, where we bought Tomás and Axel their new kicks, the sneakers were crazy pricey. My eyes bugged when I saw the triple-digit number that lit up at the register.

But Tía kept her cool and pulled out two crisp hundred-dollar bills from an envelope when she paid. I recognized it right away as the one that was addressed to the twins in the mail yesterday. One end had been sliced open carefully.

"Who sent Tomás and Axel that kind of dough?" I asked. "I might need them as a friend."

But Tía didn't answer. She just smiled at the clerk who was ringing us up. "Next stop, Sears, for your loafers," she said. "And then lunch."

Anyway, I made a beeline for the uniform rack, and in no time, we bought two new uniform blouses and my plastic torture loafers. Now, at last, we're on our way to eat.

"Grab us a table," Tía says. "I'll get in line for the pizza."

"Pepperoni," I say, and then head after the twins, who are already scoping out a table near the potted orange trees beneath the skylights.

There are only three chairs here, so I look around for a

spare one. I walk to the table nearest ours and ask the lady.

"Are you using this seat?"

She looks up from her salad and smiles. "No. Help yourself."

"Thanks," I say, and start to drag it away.

"Merci?"

I look back, and that's when I get a look at the person sitting across from lady I just talked to.

It's Avery Sanders.

My feelings twist up in a knot of surprise. This must be her mom, which I can tell right away. Same eyes. Same shape face. I even remember her on the sidelines from some of our soccer games.

I feel my face flame and my tongue grow thick. "Oh, hey, Avery."

"I didn't recognize you for a second with your new haircut. It looks good." She looks at her mom. "Merci goes to Seaward." She doesn't mention that we play soccer together. And Mrs. Sanders doesn't look like she's ever seen me before in her life when she breaks into a big smile. "Lovely to meet you," she says.

Head explosion, followed by huge awkwardness. "Thanks." I look over at the chair that's still at the table between them. It's piled high with bags from Forever 21, Lulu, and Anthropologie. "Shopping?" *Of course she's shopping. What a stupid thing to say. Why else would she have all those bags?*

Avery nods. "Some stuff for school."

I stand there praying that she doesn't see my Sears bag. "So, how was soccer camp?" I ask. At the end of last season, Coach gave us all flyers for camp at IMG Academy in Manatee County. It's a sleepaway camp, supposedly for "the most serious players." Papi laughed when he saw the fees and said that people had finally gone crazy.

"Pretty good except for the food," she said. "I've got some beast moves for the team this year, though. I'll show you after school one day if we hang out." She shrugs. "Or maybe when we start clinics."

My heart is racing a little. *Hang out?* "Yeah, that'll be great."

"Merci!" Tomás's voice is a pin in a dream balloon, too loud in this echoey space. When I turn to see what he wants, I can see that he's pointing at Tía. She's waving at me, signaling for help carrying the drinks. "I'd better go help my aunt. We're here with my cousins."

She nods and looks over at the table. "Oh, they're cute," Avery says. Then she waves at them and smiles.

Just like that, Tomás and Axel are hypnotized. It must be the brightness of her orthodontically perfect smile.

"Well, I'll see you Monday," I say, not daring to mention

that I've been shadowing her Insta. "Bye, Mrs. Sanders."

I drag the chair the rest of the way and then go to Tía.

"Who was that?" she asks as she piles straws and napkins on my tray.

"Nobody. Just a girl from school."

But somehow, I can't get the smile off my face.

CHAPTER 9

MAMI INCHES ALONG the car loop on our way to the drop-off point at school. My new uniform shirt feels stiff against my bare neck, and my toes are already screaming at me from inside these loafers that I might have bought a little too small. I'm not going to complain, though. At least my hair looks good, just like Consuelo promised, even if my neck does feel naked.

Ahead of us, a shiny SUV stops to let out passengers. A white girl with puny legs climbs out. She's lugging a backpack with a big patch that reads ORLANDO CITY SOCCER CLUB. Can she kick anything with those stick limbs of hers?

"Was I that small in sixth grade?"

No answer. Mami is tapping another message into her phone, exactly like she shouldn't be while she's driving. She's been so distracted this morning. I had to tell her twice that the traffic light had turned green on the way here.

"Mami."

"What?" She turns to me as if just I've just appeared in the seat beside her.

"I said, was I ever that small?"

"Small as what?" she asks.

I sigh. "Never mind. What are you writing that's so important, anyway?"

"Trying to find someone who might be willing to work with Lolo for a few hours a day. He's getting to be a handful for Abuela. Things are . . . advancing."

I stare out the window. Usually advancing is a good thing, like on a job. But not with Alzheimer's. Lolo didn't recognize me yesterday at Sunday dinner, for instance. Tía tried to make me feel better by telling me that my haircut threw him off. "It's me," I told him again and again, but he didn't look like he believed me, even as I sat in the same seat I always do, right next to him. He kept giving me wary looks, all the way through dessert, like he didn't trust I was telling the truth.

"Work with him doing what?" I ask.

"Daily living tasks," she says. "As an aide."

89

I've been around her physical therapy universe enough to know she means showering and eating and other super-basic things like that. Abuela is the one who does everything for Lolo, though, and she's a pain if you don't do things exactly the way she says. Roli says she even got on him for putting the wrong deodorant on Lolo. Who in the world can remember how she likes to part his hair or match specific socks with his footwear?

Mami puts down the phone and moves up in the line.

I look across the quad at the middle school building as we wait for our turn at the drop-off space. Here's the strange thing. I'm psyched about eighth grade, but I'm still going to miss being in sixth and seventh grades. I know every inch of those halls, like which water fountain had the best stream and which exits led to a shortcut to the cafeteria through a space in the bushes. Everything is going to feel new and strange again in the eighth-grade wing. I'll have to figure out all-new terrain.

Just as we pull into the drop-off spot, I see Hannah, Lena, and Edna waiting for me, just the way we planned. Wilson is there, too. The sight of them calms me down somehow. I check myself in the mirror and give my new haircut another fluff. The new Merci is about to debut.

"Bye, Mami," I say, opening the door even though the car isn't even at a full stop.

"You're awfully eager to get to school this year," she says, suspicious. Her eyes follow mine to the spot where my friends are standing. She squints, lingering for a moment on Wilson. "Ah," she says.

I shrug, annoyed. This is not a conversation I'm having with Mami, not today or maybe ever. She'll feel obligated to tell Papi, and then it will be a *thing*. "I just want to hang out with my friends before the torture starts, that's all."

She smiles slyly. "Tuck your blouse in, then," she says.

I dash across the grass. No one sees me sneaking up on them, though. They're crowded around Wilson, who's showing them something on his phone. I creep closer and closer and then I jump out at them like a ghoul. "Bah!"

Hannah lets out a yelp and whips around. As soon as she gets a good look at me, her eyes get big. "Merci? You look . . . so different!"

My stomach clutches as she regards me. Different good or different bad? I don't have to ask, though, because Edna is already assessing.

"Not bad, Merci," she says, skipping right over *hello*. "If you like curls."

"And who doesn't?" Lena pulls down her red sunglasses and grins. "You look fantabulous!" She loves "stretching language." She's currently reading up on linguistics and how words like *chillax* and *truthiness* were born.

"Thanks." My cheeks flame, and it's not just because the August morning is already suffocating. It's also because Wilson is now staring at my head, too.

"And nothing about *my* new cut?" he says. "People, that's cold." He slides the palm of his hand along his new buzz, grinning. I kind of liked his hair the old way, longer and natural, but maybe Wilson is trying to be someone new this year, too. Maybe eighth-graders are like Banana, the yellow boa constrictor that lives in our science wing. She sheds her skin a few times a year because her old skin just can't stretch and fit as she grows. Strangely, she goes blind while she's shedding. Her eyes get cloudy in what's called her blue phase. That's when she gets crabby and tries to hide because she can't see. I wonder if we sort of go temporarily blind and scared, too, without realizing it.

"Check out the albino gator Wilson saw over the summer," Hannah says.

Wilson turns his phone screen to show me the picture they've all been looking at.

"Cool," I say, nodding. It's the shot he already sent me, but neither one of us says so.

More and more kids gather near building 8 to wait for the bell. We're talking loud and fast, as if we've all thrown back Red Bulls for breakfast or something. It's a gazillion conversations all at once.

"Martha's Vineyard—"

"Our boat—"

"Spain was—"

"Who's got gym fifth?"

"It has pink eyes 'cause no pigment—"

I'm not really sure how to jump into any of it, so I work on wiggling some blood back into my numb toes. It's not like I have anything interesting to add. I stayed home this summer. I babysat my cousins and tried to spend time with my grandfather when he remembered me. I did chores and watched my brother brood and tried not to worry that Lolo would die. Who wants to hear that?

So, I just stand there, listening so I don't miss out on anything important.

After a while, the first chimes finally sound for homeroom. I take a deep breath, trying not to let the thought of walking into homeroom alone terrify me. There's nothing to do about it anyway, so when the crowd starts jostling me along, I get swept up in the sea of backpacks and uniforms heading toward the doors of the building. It's like being one of those jellyfish that's pushed along on the tide. I look around and realize that I've already lost Hannah and Lena somewhere behind me.

Inside, a whole new crop of teachers waits for us by their doors and helps direct traffic. It's chilly in here.

There's a new carpet smell, too, and all the lockers have been repainted.

Room 810 is around the first corner, but the crowd is thick and slow-moving. By the time I get there, seats are already filling up fast. The furniture is brand-new, from the looks of it. The chairs even remind me of Jake Rodrigo's captain's chair at the helm of the *Nova Warrior*. They have fancy armrests and wheels that let you swivel—as everyone quickly tests out. I look around for an empty seat, trying not to seem too obvious. Avery and Mackenzie are already in the back row. Even from here, you can see they're still pretty tight, especially since soccer camp.

There's an open spot in front of them.

I start to make my way over people's backpacks blocking the aisle. I'm halfway to the back row when someone sticks out their foot to block me.

"What's the password, woadie?"

Wilson grins up at me.

"You're in 810, too?" I clear my throat. My voice goes up when I'm excited.

"Looks that way." He takes a spin in the new chair. I know what he's thinking as he wiggles his eyebrows at me, grateful that he keeps it to himself. *Command Central, this is Captain Rodrigo. Do you read me? Over.* He doesn't mind being an Iguanador Nation nerd like me, but we try to keep it under control at school.

I glance at the seat next right to him, wanting suddenly to sit there. Ha! We'd be like cocaptains of our private ship. I weigh my options. Somebody might give us grief about being nerds. If I sit with Avery and Mackenzie instead, no one would tease me. What's better?

I pick my inner nerd.

But just as I'm about to take my seat, a boy I don't know slides into it.

"Snooze ya lose," he says, and turns to his friend on the other side of him.

Just then, the lights flicker. "Good morning, everyone!" Ms. Jenkins is at the front of the room trying to quiet us down. She's youngish and looking a little strict, too. Never good. "Take your seats quickly, please."

I have to act fast, just like in soccer sometimes. "Scan the field for opportunity," Coach Cameron always says. The spot near Avery and Mackenzie is still open but it won't be for long. It's not my first choice, but it might not be a bad thing to have some of that A-list shine rub off on me right now.

"Catch you later," I say and then I practically dive for the back of the room.

"Hi." I sort of stumble into my seat next to Avery.

"Hey, Merci," she says, but then she keeps talking to the girls to her right. It's like we never saw each other at the mall. So, I tuck my backpack into the saucer-shaped holder under the seat and face front, trying to pretend I imagined the whole thing.

For the entire ten minutes of homeroom, I listen to Ms. Jenkins's boring welcome speech, basically a list of rules that we've heard on the first day of school every single year we've been here. She assigns us our laptops and has us power them on to make sure everything works. During the pledge, I look over at Wilson, who catches my eye and stares at the ceiling, mouth slack, to tell me he's bored senseless, too. It would have been more fun to sit next to him for sure. I mean, Avery and Mackenzie are polite enough, but now that I'm here, neither one of them is exactly begging to talk to me. We're teammates, period, as per usual.

When the bell rings, I gather my things as fast as I can, hoping to catch Wilson on the way out. But the aisle fills up fast, and he's already out the door before I can reach him. I just get a glimpse of his shirt as he disappears into the crowded hall.

Hello, eighth grade.

CHAPTER 10

A FEW CHRISTMASES AGO, when Iguanador Nation was first starting to get popular, I asked for an action figure of Jake Rodrigo. I'd seen one on TV, and I knew I had to have him. But I guess it cost more than Mami and Papi could spend because what I got under the tree was a knockoff toy from the Dollar Store that looked like a Tyrannosaurus rex with a man's arms jutting out of its stomach. Don't get me wrong. It was definitely more fun than the new underwear I got that year, too, so I played with it at home just fine. But I didn't take it to school, where a few kids had the real thing, the one with the retractable helmet and glowing eyes. Those guys would know the difference and spot the fake. There's nothing worse than being called cheap or, worse, a poser.

Anyway, a few months ago, I found that action figure again in a box at the back of my closet. I gave it to the twins to play with, but they didn't even pretend to be grateful. Instead, they talked Simón into helping them melt it with Papi's torch as an "experiment."

"We wanted to see if he could shape-shift," Tomás told me as he showed me the result. What remained of the human arms reached out to me from a hardened blob. "He can. Sort of. But only once."

"'Cause he's a cheap fake," Axel said. "You want him back?"

I'm thinking about that mess again because it turns out it's hard to shape-shift in movies and in real life, too. Cool new hair doesn't do it, as I find out. The school universe can still decide to ignore your shift and leave you in the same middle-of-nowhere social spot where you've always been.

Like, for instance, what happened when the teacher's aide assignments got announced today. Back in the sixth grade, I always thought being a TA would be a really big deal. Only ten kids out of the whole eighth grade would someday get picked for the slots, so those people *had* to be special. You had to apply and everything, like for a job, and then your old teachers would have to recommend you. You got to wear a brass TA pin on your lapel, too, which kept teachers from asking you for a pass if they saw you in the hall. And best of all, for Sunshine Scholars like me, TA hours fulfill the community service requirement that we always have to do in exchange for the tuition help.

Glorious, right?

But when the TA announcements start dropping in our in-boxes during homeroom this morning, I find out that becoming a TA isn't such a big deal after all. I pick up that particular piece of intel from Mackenzie loud and clear. She was not chosen for one of the slots. She looks at the list and says, "They're just teacher's pets." And just like that, a once-upon-a-time cool thing becomes a loser badge. Not even cool new hair or sharing a soccer team can change it.

Lolo would say it's the green-eyed monster called la envidia. I know that as soon as Mackenzie says it. But suddenly, I feel embarrassed to see my name on that list, like I'm a suck-up the way she says.

To make matters even worse, I've been assigned to the most boring TA post in the whole school. Lena got assigned to the library, a place where she'd like to spend her eternal life when the time comes. Edna's in the nurse's office, where she'll get ice packs for klutzy kids and pick up people's school assignments if they get sick and have to go home. But me? I'm in the guidance office. That's the place with Ivy League college posters on the walls for the overachievers, not to mention boxes of tissues for weepy kids whose friends didn't like their last post. You can't even walk by there without sensing all those stressed feelings oozing out into the hall.

When the bell rings, I waste no time in going to register my complaint.

"Merci Suárez," Miss McDaniels says from behind the counter when I step into the main office. "I almost didn't recognize you. Your new haircut is very becoming."

Becoming what? I want to snap, salty as I am. But I dig deep and make my opening move instead: a return compliment. It's a harder task than you'd think since Miss McDaniels looks exactly the same every year. Pointy high heels, a suit, button-down blouse, glasses perched on her nose, two frown lines between her sharp blue eyes. In desperation, I point at the only thing that I notice is different at all.

"New pencil cup on your desk? Very classy touch to the office decor."

She smiles primly and folds her hands. "Thank you."

"I'm here to discuss an important matter, miss."

"Is it about your summer reading again? I thought I made it clear in my reply to your email that we were within our rights to assign the work. I checked with the legal office to be sure."

I don't let her blow me off course. "No, miss. I'm here about my teacher's aide assignment."

"Oh, good." She brightens. "Then our conversation will be brief. The decisions are final. Have a good day."

"But—"

"You have just two minutes left to reach first period," she says, tapping her watch face. "Hurry."

What's the point with this woman?

I'm still brooding about things at lunchtime. When I get to the dining hall, I stand at the entrance trying to see where Hannah, Lena, and Edna have set down their stuff. Each grade sticks to its own area, no exceptions, so they obviously won't be where seventh-graders sit, like last year. And it's certainly not near the sixth-graders, whose turf is here by the door. I watch the younger ones figuring this all out as they come out of the lunch line, looking around nervously as they search for a seat. It won't be long before some of them give up altogether and head to the library for shelter. I remember how tough it is to be a lowly sixth-grader in this cold, cruel world. Back then, we used to worry that eighth-graders would jam us into a locker when our teachers weren't looking, the way the rumors said. I've never known anybody who actually got stuffed into one, though. Seems kind of stupid to believe it now.

Anyway, the eighth-grade domain is nearest the doors that lead to the courtyard, all window seats, of course. Wilson has already found a spot there with Darius Ulmer and a couple of other boys. Avery and Mackenzie are a couple of tables over with their friends, boys and girls together, all of whom practically look like high schoolers. They look relaxed together, like they're already having a blast this year. Geez. Maybe some people just have more-fun lives than mine. Avery catches me looking and waves, but she doesn't invite me to their table—surprise, surprise. That's fine, though, because Lena's already spotted me from the food line, too.

"Merci! Over there!" She waves her arm and then points at the table next to Wilson's. Hannah's backpack hangs over the back of one of the chairs, too, so I head in that direction.

Call me strange, but I hate to chew alone in public, especially at an empty table all by myself. I'd reach for my phone to check it, but they're supposed to stay put away.

So, I sit down in the seat opposite Wilson at his table.

"Do you mind if I sit here for a second? I'm trying not to look friendless."

102

He's already digging into one of his mom's extra-stacked ham sandwiches, heavy on the mayo and pickle, just the way I like it. Last year, he shared one with me every day at the Ram Depot. Sadly, I already know what's inside my lunch sack without even looking. Dry turkey breast, a container of unsweetened applesauce, and Veggie Stix. Same as always.

He wipes his chin with his sleeve and grins. "Suit yourself, but I won't be here long. I'm supposed to report to Miss McDaniels when I'm done eating." He pushes an office pass in my direction. "The thought is already giving me indigestion."

"It's day one. What could you have done wrong already?"

He swallows a swig of water. "Can't think of it," he says. "But it can't be good."

I look away from his yummy sandwich and take a deep whiff. God, it smells good in here. Chef is serving one of her specialties, chicken in mango-pineapple sauce, according to the neon menu board, so the whole room smells fruity and sweet, like a little slice of heaven.

He takes another bite and talks with his mouth full. "I got a whole other sandwich in my bag."

A bubble of hope rises inside me. "Yeah?"

"My mom says I'm growing." He shrugs. "Want it?"

"Well," I say, brightening, "if it's extra . . ."

"I won't have time to finish anyway." He tosses a second Saran-wrapped ham roll in my direction. Then he wolfs down the rest of his food and starts packing up, just as Hannah, Edna, and Lena come back with their lunches.

"Good luck," I tell him as he hurries off, and then I scoot back to our spot.

Hannah slides her tray across from me and sits down in a huff. "Where's he off to?"

"An appointment with Miss McDaniels."

"Ominous," Lena says.

Hannah looks over her tray and sighs irritably. "Great. Now I forgot my drink, too. And the stupid line is too long to get one now. This day stinks."

Hannah's usually a pretty sunny person, but she looks super stressed. "What's the matter?" I ask.

She doesn't say anything.

"FOMO," Edna offers.

Lena digs out her refillable water bottle and hands it to Hannah. "Here," she says. Then she turns to me. "She didn't get a teacher's aide job like the rest of us."

"Which is dumb," Hannah snaps, her cheeks getting blotchy. "Why wasn't I picked? I had all Bs. And I did a good job helping in the makerspace last year, didn't I?"

"Well, there's only ten spots," Edna says. "Somebody's got to be out. No offense."

Logical but harsh.

Hannah gives her a look. "But it didn't have to be me."

I have to admit, I feel like maybe now she knows how it feels not to get what you want. I wonder if she'll activate her mom on this, like Edna always does. Still, I try to make her feel better.

"Look on the bright side," I say. "You get to take an elective instead. Is it a good one, at least?"

"Coding," she says, rolling her eyes.

"Oh! They design games in there," Lena says. "Very fun."

I unwrap Wilson's sandwich and lay it out on the table in all its glory. "Plus, nobody is going to call you a teacher's pet," I say, mostly to myself.

They all stare at me.

"What's that supposed to mean?" Edna asks.

My eyes flit to Avery's table. "Nothing. It's just that, you know, some people don't think being a TA is cool."

Edna spears a chunk of grilled pineapple on her fork and looks at it, thinking. "Some people, meaning them?" She points at Avery's group with her fork and snorts.

"Stop pointing," I say.

"They know we're alive?" Lena asks. "I'm shocked."

Hannah tears open her silverware pack. "Still, I'd rather be a teacher's pet than a computer dork."

"Coding is not dorky," Lena says. "It's empowering."

"Forget it," I say. "The point is, you'll be OK, Hannah. Probably better than me in the snoozeland desert known as guidance, anyway."

"Merci's right," Lena says.

My heart sinks. "I am?"

"Not about snoozeland," she says. "I mean about being OK in coding. Besides, we don't all have to do the same thing all the time, do we?"

Edna chews on her pineapple like cud, her eyes still on Avery's glittering group of friends. "They called us teacher's pets?"

"Seriously," Lena says, sighing, "who really cares?"

The answer is supposed to be nobody, but looking around, I know the truth. We all sort of do, even though we know better. It's like your head thinks the right thing, but your feelings refuse to match up.

The rest of lunchtime is OK, I guess. Lena lets me have the chicken from her lunch since she's going vegetarian after bonding with bison. Hannah shares the confetti Twinkies she always brings from home for dessert. Then I pretend to listen as Edna goes on about her la-di-da summer cottage at the beach. I don't even complain about the dead flower stench of her Winter Garden body spray from Lush, which she makes us sniff on her wrist.

The whole time, though, I'm watching everyone at Avery's table from the corner of my eye. Those kids are magnets, even though I don't want them to be. What is it, I wonder, that makes them seem so cool? And more important, *are* they?

CHAPTER 11

THE WHOLE WALK DOWN to my post at sixth period, I'm still trying to decide if being a TA is social sabotage or a good thing. Maybe I can stage a protest in Miss McDaniels's office? Tie myself to her desk or something.

I'm standing outside the guidance suite, considering the pros and cons of hiding in the bathroom instead, when Mrs. Wilkinson, one of the counselors, steps out of her inner office and smiles at me through the glass. I remember her from fifth grade, of course. Who can forget all that eerie cheer and enthusiasm? She's still the shortest woman I have ever known—fun-size, like tiny Halloween candies, as she says—even in platform shoes. She hasn't changed any more than Miss McDaniels has in the three years since she tried to help me "adjust in my transition to Seaward Pines."

"Oh, hello, hello, hello!" she sings out when I step inside the reception area. Her hair is gathered in a messy bun, and her glasses are a little crooked. She clops over in her heels, all smiles.

"I'm your new TA," I say, holding out my assignment sheet from Miss McDaniels.

"Of course you are! I'm so happy it's you, dear Merci! When I heard the news, I was thrilled with a capital *T*." Her eyes slide up to meet mine, twinkling. "Look at how grown you are!"

I glance away uncomfortably and peer inside her office since she left the door open. Her desk is piled with papers, almost worse than Roli's at home. She still has the same beanbag chairs on the floor and the same dish of candies on the shelf, which I hope are fresh since those sweets are one of the only perks of this place that I can think of.

"Right this way, assistant," she says grandly.

The guidance suite is small, but she insists on giving me a thorough tour anyway. Where the copier is and how to work it. ("Do not attempt to solve a jam on your own.") How the shelves are arranged with slips for hall passes, student handbooks, test-prep books, and all that. ("All alphabetical and labeled, see?") She shows me how to press the right button on the phone system to put someone on hold while I ring a counselor's office. ("We prefer the phrase 'One moment while I find you a counselor.'") Then we walk over to the couches where kids are supposed to wait when they have appointments.

"And that's most of it," she says, looking around. "Do you have any questions?"

"No," I say. "I think I've got it."

"Then we should discuss one last thing. The most important thing. It's about our privacy policy." She sits down on the couch and motions me to join her by patting the cushion. "Do you know what privacy is?"

This sounds horrifyingly similar to one of Mami's personal hygiene talks. I brace myself.

"Yes," I say carefully. "I mean, in theory." I don't have much of it at home. Everybody is always in my business. *Where are you going, Merci? Who were you talking to, Merci? Did you remember to use deodorant, Merci? Did you wash your face, Merci?*

"Well, just to be sure, it means that we expect you not to share any information about our guidance patrons with others."

Patrons? Not victims? "What kind of information, miss?"

She takes off her glasses and smiles primly. "Well, most

things, really. We work with students and their families on a range of issues, Merci, and some of them are sensitive. Do you understand?"

I nod slowly, finally understanding that she means I'm under a gag order. You'd think they were keeping state secrets here with all this fuss. Still, I remember the day I cried in here when I failed my first test at Seaward. I was sure I was going to be expelled. I wouldn't have wanted a lot of people to know about that.

"We do not want you to discuss who comes to visit us, whose parents were here, that sort of thing. You were selected because the committee believed you could be discreet with any private information you might inadvertently encounter. Do you think you're up to the task?"

She pretends to zipper her lips and holds my gaze.

I think back to third Iguanador Nation movie, where Jake Rodrigo is tortured by his enemies but never reveals the location of the star key. If Jake Rodrigo can keep a secret while someone is trying to rip off his well-manicured talons, I can certainly handle *this*.

"Sure," I say, and because I'm not sure she's convinced, I pretend to zipper my lips, too.

"Very good!" She stands up—which makes minimal difference, I gotta say. "Put your things in this cabinet, and let's get you started."

She walks over to a metal storage unit near her door and pulls open the bottom drawer.

When I finish putting my stuff inside, she finds a brass TA pin in her desk drawer and hands it to me. I fasten it right next to the one I wear for soccer, the one with enamel winged cleats and a ball.

"It's official, then," she says, beaming at me. "Go Team Guidance!" She holds up her hand for a high(ish) five.

Oh boy.

"Here's your first assignment." She rifles through her papers and grabs a sheet from one of her piles. "Please walk this to the front office for Dr. Newman's signature. It needs his approval before we can make copies to send home with the students next week."

With just a quick glance, I can see it's the master copy of the permission slip for the eighth-grade trip to Saint Augustine.

Guau, guau, guau, as Abuela likes to say.

I try to play it cool, pretending not to care about the juicy details right here in my hands. But I've got the exact date, the bus company that's handling transportation, the hotel where we'll stay, the whole itinerary and cost—which looks a little steep—right at my fingertips. At this very moment, I know everything before anybody else does—and it doesn't feel too shabby.

Maybe this guidance thing will have some perks after all.

I close the door behind me and head toward the office.

It's easy to play Where's Waldo? with Roli's face inside the display cases here in the administrative building, which has no classrooms. The main office is here, along with the headmaster's suite, teacher workrooms, guidance, the nurse's office, and the library. I walk along, playing my private game. He's in almost every case, except the athletic ones, of course, and the one with pictures of deep-pocket donors, who also get benches, rooms, and special bricks with their names on them around here. Some of Roli's pictures go back to when he was in the ninth grade and got to meet the governor when he won the state science fair award. Dark eyes, olive skin, bad acne. (He hadn't started seeing his dermatologist yet.) In every photo, he looks too serious. I've tried to coach him over the years, pero nada. The only way he ever looks natural, the way I know him, is if I sneak up on him and catch him off guard. That's how I got the one of him laughing and holding Axel upside down by the ankles. It's in Lolo's memory book, which has pictures of all of us, to help him when he gets confused.

I pause at one shot of Roli two years ago, when he was

a senior here and leading the science lab team. That's uber corny, but he went so far toward nerd that he wound up at cool again somehow. He just stares at the lens, unsmiling at the camera. My guess is that he was probably working out algorithms as they were taking the shot, but if you didn't know better, you might think Roli was sad. And I mean even sadder than he is now that he's home for the semester.

If you want to play a really challenging game of Where's Waldo?, though, you should try to find me instead. I'm only here twice. One is in the soccer team picture from last year, where I am in the first row, right next to Avery, who, even last year, looked a lot older than me. We didn't win any titles last season—not even close—so it's just a plain team shot in the corner of the athletics department's case.

The second place to see me is harder to find because I'm more or less disguised. It's in the main office's display case and was taken at the One World celebration last year, when Tía's students from her new dance studio got invited to perform. Boy, was that scary, even though you can't tell from our expressions in the picture. Abuela's bright costumes catch your eye, so you barely even notice that it's me in that frilly skirt and head wrap. I was dancing with Wilson, too. Sometimes, if I close my eyes, I can still hear the song in my head that went to the merengue we danced. It was a really old song called "Oriza Eh," I think. Sometimes I can still remember how it felt to hold his hand in front of the whole school, too. Exciting. A little bold. A little embarrassing.

"Where y'at?"

I nearly jump out of my skin.

As if stepping out of my thoughts, Wilson walks toward me. Did he see me gawking at us? My face burns.

"You're alive," I whisper. The bell rang a long while ago, and no one else is in the hall. "What did she want with you?"

"A schedule change," he says, grinning. "Where are you headed?"

"On an errand to the main office." I glance down at the sheet and turn it down so he can't see the words. "Top secret, though. For Mrs. W in guidance. I'm her new TA." I have so much I want to say, such as *Guess what? You can have three roommates in Saint Augustine, and it will take us four hours to get there, and we have one free day where we can go see an attraction of our choice.* But no. The power of the pin keeps me discreet.

He falls in stride with me. "Guidance, huh?"

"It might have its perks," I say vaguely.

We round the corner and walk past the library, where Lena works this hour, in what is probably her version of heaven. Her favorite thing in the world is reading. Right now, she's shelving books from a rolling cart. Unfortunately, our librarian, Mr. Engle, is at the front desk processing new books, so we can't stop in to talk to her or even make faces at her from the hall.

It feels a little weird walking along with Wilson, just the two of us. The halls in the administrative building are so quiet that our steps echo as we walk along. You can hear that Wilson's gait has a tiny pause in it on account of his foot. He's got a new brace, I notice. Not black like last year's. This one is navy blue.

He stops at the glass doors that lead out to the quad and the gym beyond it.

"Where are you going?" I ask.

He grins and flashes me his TA pin. "Turns out, I've got TA this period, too," he says. "That was the schedule change Miss McDaniels wanted to talk to me about."

"No way!" I say as we fist-bump. This could be fun if we plan to run errands at the same time. "Where are you assigned? Let me guess. The math lab." Last year, he took algebra with freshmen in the upper school. He was the best in the class.

He opens the door and a whoosh of air gets sucked toward us. It's like a portal to some sort of magic wind tunnel designed to make your skirt blow up or, if you're

Mr. Tetra from shop, your toupee lift off your scalp. Somewhere down the hall, the gust makes a door slam.

"Not math, though that would have been sweet," he says. "It's in PE."

For a second, I don't say anything. There's the sound of a lawn mower in the distance. An electric pencil sharpener is grinding in one of the offices.

The gym position is the plum assignment, if you ask me. Last year, Mr. Patchett's aide just had to set up drill stations and make sure our equipment was in good shape when we returned it. With a cushy gig like that, at least I'd get to brush up on my free throws or goal shots all I wanted when I wasn't busy. I'd get free tickets to all the varsity games, too.

"*You're* Mr. Patchett's aide this year? I thought it was Michael." It makes no sense at all. Gym class is usually a trial for Wilson, especially when the games get fast and heated. He never gets picked first for teams.

"It was *supposed* to be him," he says, shrugging, "but he got a D in Spanish last year, so he's out and yours truly is in."

I just can't believe it. I would have made a much better PE aide than Michael Clark or Wilson. I'm mad at Miss McDaniels all over again.

"Don't start hating on me," Wilson says, reading my

face. "I was assigned, same as you, remember? It's not like we get a choice."

"You wouldn't want to trade, would you? There's candy involved in guidance. We could go to Miss McDaniels right now."

He snorts. "Yeah, but I'll stick to setting up gym equipment, thanks."

A teacher opens the door to the workroom down the hall and starts toward us. I adjust my lapel to make sure my TA pin is visible.

"I better go," he says.

The latch clicks loudly as the glass doors close behind Wilson. I don't move off right away, though. I watch him walk past the next building toward the gym, his hip shifting slightly so his foot can clear the ground.

Be happy for him, I tell myself. *He's your friend.* But inside, at the jealous part that I have, too, I'm still mad.

CHAPTER 12

I'M RESTING OUTSIDE next to Lolo, my stomach rumbling loudly. Simón and I have been kicking a soccer ball around with the twins while Abuela finishes up the arroz con pollo for dinner. I can tell that's what we're having because the whole yard smells of saffron and because the cazuela she uses to cook it isn't hanging on the hook inside the shed. I take a deep, satisfying breath. Chicken and yellow rice is one of my favorite things to eat except for the "decorative" peas, which I pick out one by one when no one is looking.

I look over at Lolo again. I've been trying to make conversation about school, but it's hard. He used to be my go-to guy for good advice around here. But today, Lolo mostly just listens. I even had to remind him again that I was Merci, which makes me wonder if this haircut was worth it at all.

"So, do you think they're right about being teacher's pets?"

The sun shines against his glasses as he looks past me toward the street. I'm pretty sure he hears me. Why can't he just answer?

"Then again, I think it's la envidia," I say. "What's that dicho you always tell us about being jealous, Lolo?" I continue. "Something about it being hunger and nagging?"

Nothing.

Lolo always had good sayings when he wanted to teach us something important, which he used to say was the gift of growing old. His favorite was *más sabe el diablo por viejo que por diablo*. The devil knows more because he's old than because he's a devil.

I look at him hopefully since he turns my way. But then he says, "The bus is late again."

Frustrating. I know it's not his fault, but it's so annoying. Lolo talks about the bus more and more, no matter what anybody is saying. Like now. He's stuck there, and it makes me mad to be stuck there with him. Weren't the medicines supposed to help him? What's the point of all those pills if they don't work?

I try to find patience, but my voice comes out sharp anyway. "Forget about the stupid bus, Lolo."

A quick whistle from nearby makes me turn. It's Papi, who has apparently overhead us, and he doesn't look pleased. Maybe using the word *stupid* was a step too far. He's been hauling dirty brushes and rollers to the outdoor sink to get them clean. Mineral spirits reek from his clothes. His fingertips are pale white.

"The saying is 'Envy is thin because it bites but never eats,'" Papi says. "Why don't you help Simón with the twins for a while? They're giving him a workout." He gives me a long, steady look, so I know it's not just a suggestion.

"Fine," I say, but I'm relieved in a way.

I take off across the yard to get in the soccer game.

Hannah says identical twins, like Tomás and Axel, are telepathic, which means they can read each other's minds. It sounds far-fetched, but it might explain why my cousins are such good accomplices in everything they do. Lena, who reads everything, says that telepathy is "unlikely," and Roli, who is a stickler for facts, says she's right about "vicarious transmissions." *His* theory is that twins' brains are a lot alike, so they react in lots of the same ways. Mami says no one knows for sure. The brain is still a mystery.

Which is true, I guess, because otherwise someone would have already figured out how to help Lolo.

But all I know as I watch them play is that the twins' brain connection is going to come in handy on the soccer field one day. They're only in second grade, but together, they're already one hundred pounds of fast feet and impeccable timing. It's kind of amazing to see. Just last year, they were clumsy first-graders, chasing the ball together in a glob and fighting over who got to make an attempt on the goal. Now, they've got spindly legs, speed, and killer strategy that looks, well, telepathic. Maybe it's those new sneakers that Tía bought them last week. That, and the benefit of excellent scrimmaging with Simón and me.

Axel dribbles the ball past me, looking like a knobby-kneed foal. I chase him down without much trouble and then try to box him in. You'd think I'd have to go easy on him, but there's no need. He picks up his head quickly and spots his ally.

"Chump," he says under his breath, and then he cross-passes at the last second to Tomás, who's been itching to make an attempt on the PVC pipes we set up as the goal. Simón traps the ball midway, though, and does his ace footwork, even in his paint-splattered work boots. But

Tomás is having none of it. He races alongside Simón on the left and slide tackles it away, a perfect bent right knee and left-foot kick. He braces himself with his left hand against the ground, almost without thinking. In a flash, he pushes himself back on his feet and heads toward the goal with the ball.

I slow down to catch my breath as Tomás takes aim at the grapefruit tree. I know they're usually a pain, but right now, I feel kind of proud of the twins. There's no denying that these two got the sports gene, like me. It's why they learned to pop wheelies on their bikes before their friends did this summer. Why they've never had to bat with a T. Why they play better soccer than half the kids on my school team.

"Goooooooooooooool!" Tomás shouts, arms in the air, as the ball sails between the posts and ricochets off the trunk and back at us.

"Goooooooooooool!" Lolo shouts, too. I turn around to look at him, still in the glider, and feel my heart lift a little. He's the one who taught us how to hold a goal chant really long to really show the player some love. At least he knows it's a soccer game, which is a lot better than waiting for a pretend bus.

"Bueno, ya," Simón says, laughing. Sweat is dripping

along his temples. "Your abuela will have dinner ready soon, and I've still got to help your dad clean up before I go home."

"Cutting out, huh?" I say. "Coward."

"I'm not stupid," he says, grinning. "Those two are fuego. Wait until they're old enough to play on our team!"

He means the one he plays on with Papi and guys from different crews. I can tell by Simón's grin that he's proud of them, too. He grabs the last paint buckets by Papi's van and walks around to the side of the house to join Papi. I wonder if "home" for Simón is ever going to be here at Las Casitas with Tía, the twins, and the rest of us. Not that I'm in a hurry to have more people around. It's just that he comes over almost every day anyway, and on the weekends, he stays at Tía's house until late at night, long after the twins are asleep. He doesn't seem to mind carting them places or playing with them. Their tormenting ways don't ever seem to get under his skin.

Axel asked Tía about Simón a few weeks ago.

"Is he your man?" he asked out of the blue, like something out of one of those creepy dating shows Tía sometimes watches.

She looked at him, shocked. "My *man*? Ay, cielito, I am happy with my two little men right now. And besides, Simón has Vicente to think about. That's plenty."

Vicente is Simón's younger brother. He came to the US last year, and now they live together in a house they share with other guys. He works the grill at a bowling alley since Papi doesn't always have enough work to hire them both.

But I wonder if they'll ever live together or get married. Maybe Tía just likes that Simón has his own place and she has hers, here with us. Juntos pero no revueltos, as Abuela likes to say.

Orange and pink clouds have formed in the early evening sky. I like this time of day best. The air feels cooler, for one thing. Sunset isn't for a couple more hours yet, either, so we can have dinner out on the porch the way I like, crowded around the patio table with a few tea lights to brighten things up. Maybe Roli will be home by then, too.

I'm just about to head inside to get washed up when the sound of a loud engine makes me turn. It's not the bus Lolo has been waiting for, but a shiny red convertible that has stopped at the corner and is practically making the ground shake. It growls down the street, loud enough that Tomás and Axel stop their new chasing game and stare in awe at the flashy two-seater. Then, to my surprise, the car pauses and turns into our driveway.

I try to get a better look at the driver as he cuts off the engine and steps out. He's tall and muscular, in a

T-shirt and jeans, though not the work kind of jeans that Papi wears. These are the fancy kind that men wear with leather shoes. A lady wearing short shorts and a tank top gets out, too. She's tanned to leather and has a tattoo of a rose on her shoulder, I notice, and another one of a vine on her ankle.

"Hello." The man pockets his sunglasses and takes a few steps toward Tomás and Axel. I suck my breath in without meaning to. The twins are between me and the car, but they're rooted and staring. Why isn't Stranger Danger screaming in their heads like it's supposed to?

"Look how big you are," the man says.

"Guys. Come here now," I say. Then I call out to Papi.

The driver turns to me. "Oh, hello, Merci," he says. "You don't remember me, I guess."

I don't answer, even though I know it's rude to ignore people. Who is he?

I squint and try my best to place him. Is he one of Tía's customers from the bakery? A player on one of the soccer teams we challenge? Maybe he works at the botánica? His voice is familiar, but from where?

He glances uncomfortably at Lolo. "And you, señor. How are you? It's been a long time."

Lolo stares at him blankly, but then his eyebrows knit together as he frowns.

Simón and Papi come back around the corner, too. Papi stops short.

"Oh," he says. That's it.

Simón looks on, just as confused as I am.

Just then, Tía steps out into the yard to see who it is, too. She stops in her tracks as if she's found a couple of cottonmouth snakes in the driveway instead of visitors.

"Hello, Inés," the man says. "We were nearby. I thought . . ."

Tía regards them both with a frosty expression in her eyes.

"Hello, Marco," she says, crossing her arms.

My stomach drops at the name, and I turn to him to see if it's true. In a flash, it all comes together. I remember his big shoes by Tía's door, the ones I liked to slip into like clown shoes. I remember the feeling of his big hands around mine as I walked between him and Tía so they could swing me high.

Tía turns to the twins before I can say anything at all.

"Boys," she says, "say hello to your father."

CHAPTER 13

A BOMB COULD HAVE landed softer than Marco has.

Let's just say he isn't really a favorite at Las Casitas. He's the twins' dad, all right, but that's a fact that most everybody around here has tried to forget since the day he ghosted with a new girlfriend back when the twins still shared a crib.

"How long are they going to be over there?" Abuela checks the cazuela of arroz con pollo one more time and clicks her tongue in irritation. We've set the table inside since it's gotten dark by now. Abuela still won't let us eat without Tía. "The rice has turned to paste, thanks to that descarado."

Oh boy. She's already aiming her cannons. *That descarado* is how Abuela has always referred to him. I'm surprised Tía doesn't list him that way in the twins' official school papers when they ask FATHER'S NAME on the forms.

"I can't imagine what this is doing to the boys," Abuela mutters. "A susto can really do a number on a person. Back in Cuba I knew a lady who went bald from one day to the next when the husband she thought was dead appeared on her doorstep. Te lo juro."

Papi takes a swig of his beer and exchanges a dark look with Mami, who's arranging plantain chips in front of Lolo so he doesn't swoon from hunger like the rest of us. I stuff a few more chips in my mouth to quiet my rumbling stomach. Marco and his "friend" went inside Tía's house over an hour ago. What could he possibly want, and why is it taking so long?

I go to the window again and crane my neck to see if I can watch any of the action at Tía's house from here. Marco's car is still there. Not Simón's, though. He left as soon as this little visit got started. Tía whispered something to him, but Simón didn't look too thrilled.

"Get away from the window, please, Merci," Mami says. "You're prying."

"But why is he here?" I ask.

"I'm sure your aunt is finding out," she says.

I sit back down, wondering suddenly how my cousins are feeling about this big surprise. *Hello, I'm your long-lost papi.* It's not like we've hidden Marco from the twins, exactly. It's more like he's never been part of things, which is all on him. He's never remembered their birthday or any holidays. He doesn't visit or go to their school events. He's just sort of not there. They've never asked for their dad as far as I know. It's Papi and Lolo they've always made Father's Day cards for. It was Roli who showed them how to build sturdy LEGO cars. And lately, it's Simón who wrestles with them on the floor and helps them pick flowers for Tía from the yard.

I sit down and grab another fistful of plantain chips to help me think.

"Don't fill up on junk," Mami tells me.

"But I'm starved."

"Join the club," Papi says. "I say we start. We could be here all—"

He stops at the sound of the car's engine roaring to life again outside. Headlights flood the kitchen a second later as the car pulls out.

Abuela holds open her blinds with a wooden spoon and glares as it zooms away. "Finally," she says. She crosses herself and mutters her emergency prayer. "Todo lo malo, echa pa'allá."

A few minutes later, the back door bangs open, and the twins come barreling in from the backyard.

They're not bald, at least. I guess the shock factor was in check.

In fact, they look excited. They're wearing the head-lamps Papi bought them for their birthday last year, the ones they use when they play cave under the bed.

Tomás runs right for the bowl on the table to grab some chips, blinding me with the beams.

"Geez! My retinas," I say, shielding my eyes.

"Un momento!" Mami says, lifting the snacks over her head. She clicks off the lamps on both their heads. "To the bathroom to wash your hands, please."

Tía steps into the kitchen just as Axel and Tomás disappear down the hall. We all stare at her, silent. Is anybody going to be brave enough to pry, or are we just going to sit here?

She crosses to the sink and leans against it, facing us. "Sorry we're so late. I wish you'd started without us."

Abuela holds her tongue for all of two seconds. "And *I* wish that man hadn't shown up." She grabs angrily for her serving ladle out of the drawer that sticks. "Much less with that woman."

"She's his wife," Tía says quietly. "Her name is Veronica."

Abuela looks at her, murderous. She's gripping her ladle so tight, I'm pretty sure it's going to snap in two.

Papi leans back in his chair. "So, what brings him here out of the blue?"

Tía shrugs. "The visit isn't *exactly* out of the blue."

Mami and Papi exchange a look.

Tía sighs. "I reached out a few months back and told him I needed more help with the boys."

Abuela gasps. "Help from *him*? That's a laugh. With what?"

"With money, Mamá. It's not easy trying to pay for everything the boys need now, not to mention keeping the dance studio running, too, and . . ." She gives Papi a careful look and adds, "Other expenses."

Abuela's lips tighten to a line. Without a word, I can tell we are officially in the no-fly zone. Lolo's medicines are super expensive, and Mami, Papi, and Tía all have to chip in every month to pay for them. They've been talking about hiring the aide, too. That would be a new person on Papi's payroll. Where's he going to get that money?

"Look, Mamá, Marco stepped up and sent some money last week to buy the boys sneakers, which they needed for school. That's not a bad thing."

I try not to let my mouth drop open as I think back to that envelope without a return address. My hand goes self-consciously to my curls, too. My new haircut was bought with money from el descarado? Geez. I'm tainted.

"I would have lent you the money," Papi says. "You know that."

Tía gives him a long look. "Yes, but you *always* lend me money, and you have your own obligations to think about. Just think about this month. There's Merci's school trip coming up. And don't think I don't see how Roli is killing himself to pay for tuition. My nephew should be up in North Carolina studying important things like all his fancy amigotes, not here pinching pennies with us."

Papi's ears flame red. "Who says that hard work kills anybody?" he says. "Roli's fine. He's doing what he has to do. That's what makes a man, Inés."

Tía sucks her teeth, like that's the silliest idea. "Being broke doesn't make a man. It just makes you tired. You know that as well as I do." She lowers her voice to make sure the twins can't hear. "Besides, isn't it time Marco did *something* to help his sons? Even if it's just financial?"

"What about love?" Abuela says, outraged. "He forgot all about them for seven years, Inés. What makes you think he'll be dependable now?" She shakes her head. "And look at the silly car he drives! Where is he planning to put the two sons he's just remembered? In the trunk?"

Tía stares at the floor, miserable. "I understand all that. But now he's come, and the boys are excited."

My mind races as I listen.

"Excited about what?" As soon as I blurt out the question, I brace for a pile-on. Nobody around here likes me to interrupt when they're talking about so-called adult things. It's strictly a spectator sport for me, as far as they're concerned.

But this time, I stand my ground and stare back at them. I toss back my shoulders. I'm in my size 8 shoe, sporting my new haircut. I am a teacher's aide who can be trusted with people's private information. Isn't it time for my own family to include me in discussions?

Tía turns to me. "That they have a Papi of their own, Merci." Her eyes rest on Lolo, who's busying himself with the chips. "Having a father to love matters."

CHAPTER 14

I'M STANDING AT THE freezer the next afternoon, ready to get some ice cream for me and the twins, who walked over. Luckily, Mami brought my favorite flavor home from Presidente this morning when she took Abuela for groceries. I'm surprised it didn't melt in the car since it's nearly 100 degrees again today.

I rummage inside—even behind the frozen chickens that have hardened into boulders—but nothing. I'm positive that I saw Mami put the ice cream container in here.

"Hey. Where's the Chocolate Chip Royale?"

The twins turn to me. They're already waiting with empty bowls and tablespoons. Things could get ugly.

Roli doesn't turn from the sink, where he's washing some dishes. He spent the morning bathing Lolo and then arranging his computer setup for the start of classes at community college. He hooked up speakers, an extra screen, and an old printer Mami borrowed from the rehab center. He even posted a schedule of the days and times I am not allowed in our room because he'll be studying for class.

His silence is telling. And so is that bowl he's trying to rinse free of evidence.

"Roli," I say slowly. "Where's the ice cream?"

He turns off the water at last and faces me. "Sorry," he says. "I guess I worked up an appetite and got carried away."

"Noooo . . ." Axel groans.

I slam the freezer door and glare at Roli. It's not even three hours later, and already, an entire half gallon of ice cream has completely disappeared? That's a new record, even for him.

"It's boiling outside," I whine, "and it's not like we can go to Abuela's to see if she's got any in her fridge! She's still spitting nails about you-know-who."

Roli gives me a knowing look. We had a long talk last night when he got home, and I filled him in on the daddy drama.

He checks his watch. "I have an idea. How about if I take you guys to Ivan's? I have some time before work."

Tomás and Axel perk up right away. Ivan's is a new paletería down the road, where they've got a flavor called cola de tigre. It's chocolate, mango, and vanilla ice cream swirled together so it looks like a real tiger's tail.

"Let me get my chancletas," I say. And then, for good measure, "You're treating."

The twins let out a whoop and run out the door toward Roli's car.

Papi surprised Roli at the start of the summer with new wheels of his own, which was supposed to be a huge deal and maybe a way to take the sting out of having to stay home this semester.

"For you, hijo," he said proudly, dangling the keys, "so you can get to work and drive to school like your friends."

Like his friends? I beg to differ, especially since the car is literally older than Roli and his pals. It's a Kia from 2000, to be exact, the year a guy named William Jefferson Clinton was still president. Papi snagged it for cheap from one of Gustavo's condo residents who was moving into assisted living. He calls it a "cream puff" because it has low miles and a working engine. But a cream puff is something you want to eat because it's delicious—and there is nothing desirable about this heap. Here's what I know. The Kia is going to do absolutely nothing for my brother's social life. The engine sounds like Abuela's sewing machine. The paint on the hood has faded to gray in spots. It has crank windows and a CD player in the dash, both fatal flaws. Face it, I've seen ladies at Palm Villa with cooler whips.

Still, I'm not complaining. It's an extra set of wheels in a pinch, like now, and at least the air-conditioning works in this thing. Roli's driving skills have improved, too. He gets up to the speed limit on a regular basis now, and I'm hardly ever choked by my seatbelt when he stops at a light.

Anyway, in no time at all, we're at Ivan's, scoping out all the paletas in the freezer case and making our selections through the fog of our breath on the glass. The two indoor tables are taken, so we head out back to the picnic tables chained to the ground. I stretch my legs out and let the sun bake the itch off them a little. I shaved my legs for the first time the night before school started. Who knew that hair could grow back in a week? And that it would be so prickly? When I rub my palm against my kneecaps, it feels like I'm touching little porcupine heads.

I dig in and let the heavenly coolness slide down my throat. "Thanks, Roli," I say.

He nods, licking the drips before they hit his hand.

"Freeze head!" Tomás cries out. He and Axel still like

to give themselves blinding ice cream headaches on purpose to see who's tougher. That's why they're taking big bites of their strawberry paletas, aptly called vampirito. The name appeals to their bloodlust, I guess.

"If you take big chomps like that, your paletas will be gone really fast," Roli warns. He licks another drip of his dulce de leche. "I have no more cash for another one."

Normally, they'd keep it up, just to be obnoxious, but to my surprise, they cut it out and start to eat slower.

We're quiet for a while until a loud car goes racing down Lake Worth Road. I look over at it, thinking back to yesterday.

"So, what did Marco say when he visited?" I ask the twins casually. "You haven't told us anything."

Roli gives me a look and shakes his head. But what's wrong with a little info straight from the source?

The twins keep eating.

"Your dad," I say, taking another lick of ice cream. "Roli and I knew him a long time ago. Did you know that? When we were all really little. I don't remember him too well, though."

At first, I think they're going to keep ignoring me, but then Tomás says, "He's going to give me a ride in his car."

"It's going to go fast," Axel says, nodding. "Maybe five hundred miles an hour."

"That's how fast planes go," Roli says. "But not cars."

"How do you know?" Tomás asks.

"Because even race cars only travel between two and three hundred miles per hour, tops."

"Why?" Axel asks.

"There's the friction issue, mostly."

"What's friction?" Tomás says.

"Well, during acceleration, the car must exert an average of two thousand six hundred pounds of horizontal force against—"

My withering look stops him midsentence. Then I turn back to the twins.

"So, he's coming back soon?" I ask. "Did he say that?"

Axel shakes his head. "No. We're going to his house."

"To visit," Tomás adds.

"When?" I ask.

"One day," Axel says.

I look at Roli and roll my eyes. *One day* sounds shady. Like "*One day*, I'm going to Paris." Tía.

"*One day*, you'll understand why." Mami.

"*One day*, your eyes are going to stay crossed." Abuela.

Everybody knows that *one day* is maybe never. Plus, I'm remembering what Abuela said about Marco's car. How there's no room for them anyway.

Still, my stomach lurches a bit. Some of my friends

at school have divorced parents. Look at Wilson. He's got two separate houses, not just one, which means he has double everything.

I rake my teeth along the wooden stick for the last bits of chocolate, annoyed. I mean, technically, the twins already have three houses at Las Casitas: theirs, Abuela and Lolo's, and ours. Why do they need another? And where do Marco and Veronica live, anyway? Is it far? And what if they make brand-new bedrooms for the twins at their house and fill them with new toys and stuff that the twins won't be able to resist?

I don't think I like sharing the twins. They're pains, but they're *our* pains.

"Why do you even want to go there?" I ask.

Tomás shrugs. "Because."

"*Because* is a dumb reason," I say.

"*You're* dumb," he says.

Axel lets out a laugh that almost makes him spit out his vampire ice cream.

Roli wipes his mouth and crumples his napkin to a tight ball as he stands up.

"It's OK if you want to go there," he tells Tomás pointedly. Then he holds up his hand to stop me from saying anything else. "He's their dad."

———— ☀ ————

Do you like your dad's house more or your mom's?

Kinda random question, woadie.

But then there are ellipses.

I lie back in bed and wait. Roli is across the room, plugged into his headphones and taking notes. I'm allowed to be in here if I don't say a word.

Wilson's parents don't live together. But I don't know what his life is like in New Orleans, if he feels like it's his house over there, too, or if he's a visitor, sort of like summer camp. The only thing I know is that Wilson goes every summer and that his dad works in a place that builds parts for NASA's rockets.

Just depends. They're both OK. My friends are here. Most of my family is there. So, it can be weird.

He sends a shrugging emoji, then more ellipses.

Why?

I stare at the ceiling, thinking of the twins and how they might choose. How it might feel for them to have an uncle and an abuelo and a cousin, but not a dad of their own.

I was just wondering.

CHAPTER 15

AVERY POKES ME IN the ribs. She's my table partner in language arts because of our two *S* last names, Sanders and Suárez. It's fun sitting here on most days, since so many kids stop by before class to say hi and stuff. *Wassup, Avery. I think I saw you at the mall, Avery. I like your earrings, Avery. I'll hit you up later, Avery.*

"Merci," she whispers. "She's talking to you."

I startle and find our teacher Ms. Tibbetts looking right at me, waiting for my answer.

"I'm sorry." My eyelid starts to flutter a little. "Can you repeat that?"

"Can you tell us if statement number six is true or false?" Ms. Tibbetts says.

At least Ms. Tibbetts isn't one to embarrass you for daydreaming. That isn't always the case. I remember Mrs. Krightman—aka Mrs. *Fright*man, my fourth-grade teacher at my old school. She was the school meanie, plain and simple. You'd lose recess for not paying attention in *her* class. We had to walk in the halls with our fingers to our lips like babies, too. She even gave me a "red light" on my daily report home a few times, even though I tried to explain that all I was doing was telling Herman Espinoza to stop copying from my paper, which he did every single day. She was unmoved. "I have no patience for nonsense," she said, like it was my fault that she sat me next to a kid so I could rehab him.

The funny thing is that it was also Mrs. Krightman who wrote my recommendation letter for Seaward Pines Academy. She said I was "a girl with a curious mind and enormous potential," which made me think that maybe she liked me after all. You just can't tell with people sometimes.

I look down at my screen to reread the question. It's true or false, so I've got a fifty-fifty shot. We're going over the books we read this summer, but number six is a stumper. It's about *The Birchbark House*.

Old Tallow is kind.

I think back to the stories I listened to. Which one was Old Tallow?

Geez. Couldn't Ms. Tibbetts have picked somebody else? Somebody like Elton Bonneville, who waves his hand like a drowning man for almost every question in class?

I take a deep breath and try to be logical, the way Roli always recommends. He says fast thinking isn't always the best, but it doesn't feel that way when people are staring and waiting on me.

Old Tallow. I think she's the woman who hunts. She's kind of a mystery and a loner for most of the novel. She even kills her own dog. But then there's the baby we find out she rescued. And then that big surprise of who the baby really is.

Which things count as kind?

My heart pounds as Ms. Tibbetts waits for my answer. *Say something,* I tell myself. But my mind is just whirling like a boat stuck on a sandbar. The more I rev my mental motor, the deeper I dig into the silt.

"You've read the book?" Ms. Tibbetts asks.

I blink. "Yes, miss."

"Then make an attempt. It's safe here."

My eye pulls even harder. Please. Sometimes it's not even safe to say what TV show you like or what your favorite food is without someone calling you weird.

My mouth feels dry, and my eyelid finally droops.

Why can't I be more like Lena, who reads everything and retains it like a walking encyclopedia? She's super quiet, but she can always explain herself in a way I never really can in class.

I sit up straighter, but my voice still sounds small. "True."

"You don't sound sure," Ms. Tibetts says.

My knee starts to bounce, but Avery looks over at me and smiles in a way that gives me just enough courage.

"True," I say again, louder.

Ms. Tibbetts looks around the room. "Thoughts about Merci's answer? I feel like there are some ideas floating around."

There's a long quiet. Kids are either checked out or else we're scared of an answer that isn't clean and easy. What if people aren't on your side?

Except for Elton. He's shaking his hand so hard that Ms. Tibbetts has no choice but to call on him for the fifth time this class period.

"OK, Elton," she says. "Shoot."

"I think it's debatable," he says. "She shot her dog, didn't she? Who does that?"

"Gross," someone says.

A few kids around me nod, and now I'm sure I'm

messed up. I'm almost tempted to raise my hand to change my answer.

But then Avery raises her hand. "I'm with Merci. It's still true. She did a very kind thing for the baby. And she had no choice about the dog."

The feeling in the room changes. It's as if Avery has cast a spell. She gives me a sidelong look and smiles, which makes me want to burst with gratitude. Avery Sanders has come to my rescue! I want to pinch myself.

The room is buzzing now, and the conversation continues as more kids agree with me. Elton and a few others argue back and forth, but it's clear that most people have decided to come to my side. I sit back, trying to breathe easier as other people take over. At least the attention isn't on me anymore.

"All right, all right. We're off track." Ms. Tibbetts has to hold her hand up and use an outside voice to get our attention again after a few minutes of sparring. Then she perches herself on the edge of her desk and glances at the clock.

"We're almost at the bell. You have only a few minutes, so please be diligent as you work independently on the last section. Drag and drop the completed assignment into the classwork folder when you're done."

I'm just finishing up the rest of questions when I feel a pencil poking in my side again.

Avery has her eyes on my work, just like Herman Espinoza in fourth grade.

"Scroll up a little," she whispers.

I glance nervously toward the front of the room. Ms. Tibbetts is busy checking something on her desktop.

"Why?" I whisper.

"I didn't read the rest."

For a second, I'm frozen.

Avery took my side in the discussion. Don't I owe her? And also, how important is this, anyway? Probably not very. And if I say no, won't she say I'm a suck-up, a teacher's pet, a brownnoser, like Mackenzie claimed?

So, I press the arrow key and let her copy the answers that come into view. But even as I drag my document to the folder, I feel weird.

When the bell rings, I pack up, but Avery doesn't wait for me. She's spotted one of her friends in the hall and goes rushing to meet them. They hug as if they haven't seen each other in years.

I should not have let Avery copy: true or false, I wonder.

CHAPTER 16

SAINT AUGUSTINE'S CLAIM to fame is that it's the oldest city in our country. It's no Disney World or Busch Gardens, but as educational school trips go, I suppose we could do a lot worse. For two whole nights, we'll be at a hotel four hours away from our parents and can stay up as late as we want with our friends.

At first, I was worried I might not be able to go because of the silly no-sleepover decree at our house. There's just no shaking it, even with my closest friends. I've asked why a million times, but Papi gets all tight-lipped, and Mami says, "It's not what we do."

"Why not?" I always say. "Everyone else in the whole world does it." Pero nada. The answer is always no.

The other problem is that the trip costs $450, which I know is a lot for Mami and Papi.

Luckily, it turns out that our trip doesn't count as a sleepover for my parents since there are school chaperones involved. And the money isn't a big problem either because Miss McDaniels sent us a notice about a special fund to help Sunshine Scholars who want to go. We got a lower price and can pay a little at a time.

Anyway, everyone's pretty excited since the first weekend in October is only about a month away. In fact, it's the main topic at lunch today. Not even the "fun facts" one-page reports about Saint Augustine that we were assigned are souring us. Thankfully, Lena, as library aide, is helping us find material. I'm researching a guy named Ponce de León. He was a Spanish conquistador—you know, those guys with the metal helmets and the puffy shorts. Anyway, he came looking for the Fountain of Youth, but had to settle for a spring in Saint Augustine instead. I'm pretty sure the water doesn't work since he is dead himself. But whatever.

Hannah is doing her report on the Timucua Indians. Darius wants to find out about pirates and shipwrecks back in the 1500s. Lena is studying boat-building techniques of the sixteenth century. Wilson says he's reporting on the French, who had a colony there before the Spanish ever did. And Edna is apparently researching one of her relatives, or so she claims. Pedro Menéndez de Avilés, the founder of Saint Augustine, might be related to her, she says, since her mom's maiden name is Menéndez, too.

"Are you sure, Edna?" I say, searching Google. "There's one hundred and ninety-six Menéndezes just in the West Palm Beach phone directory."

"We could easily be distant kin," she says, wiping the corners of her mouth with a napkin at lunch. "He was the first governor of Florida. Leadership qualities run in families, you know."

Wilson and Lena exchange looks. He munches on some Doritos that Edna shared with him. We've pulled our table together with his and Darius's, since they were sitting right next to us anyway.

"Menéndez?" he says. "Why does that sound so familiar?"

"He massacred the French Huguenots for not being Catholic, remember?" Lena says grimly. "It was in the book we found for your research."

"Right! The guy who hung the bodies from the trees," he says.

Edna snatches back her chips and gives Wilson a deadly stare.

Hannah shudders and covers her ears. "Let's talk about something more pleasant. Like our free night!"

"Good idea!" I say.

Our teachers have lined up a few boring stops on our trip, such as tours of two forts and Flagler College. But we can also choose where we want to eat with our friends on Saturday night. And Sunday morning is wide open for us to choose the attraction we want to see on our own, too. "I'm feeling the pirate ship," I say.

"Me too," Darius says.

"We're supposed to do a museum visit, aren't we?" Lena asks.

"No problem. I already checked," I say. "There's a pirate museum nearby—and a gift shop." I pull out a map of Saint Augustine that was in the guidance office. "See? We can go there after. Who's in?"

Hannah raises her hand and looks around at our two tables.

Wilson squints as he reads the map. "There's a medieval torture museum, though," he says.

"Gross," Edna says. "Now who's bloodthirsty?"

"Maybe one of your relatives designed some of the devices," he says.

Hannah covers her ears again as Edna throws a chip at him.

"Funny," she says. "Anyway, Merci, more important: When do we find out about roommates? I don't want to get stuck with anybody I don't like." She turns to Hannah. "I put the three of you down, like we said."

Hannah and Lena will be great roommates, but two and a half days in close quarters with Edna is going be tough, even though I agreed to it. She's just a lot, even though she's not as mean as she used to be. I don't argue, though, because there are four to a room at the Country Inn and Suites, not three. If you don't fill the spot, Mrs. Wilkinson assigns it to someone herself. And besides, it's not like you can ice out somebody you eat lunch with every day.

"After the holiday weekend," I say, "as soon as people bring in their deposits."

"Well, people better pay up, then," she says.

Wilson glances at me and then looks away. He brought his form back to the guidance office for the special trip price, just like I did. Not that Edna—or anyone else— needs to know.

CHAPTER 17

TÍA INÉS FINALLY had the bullet holes in the front window of the Suárez School of Latin Dance fixed. For a while she drew daisy petals around the damage to make them look like flowers in a mural. No one knows how the damage happened since it was already there before she leased the place. Tía, who's squeamish about guns, says maybe it's best we don't know.

"Sometimes it's better to leave unpleasant things in the past," she says.

I guess she doesn't have a choice about Marco, though. He stepped right back out of her past and now there's no getting rid of him, at least not from the twins' minds. Axel and Tomás even found his number in Tía's phone and took turns dialing it so they could ask him when they could come over.

"I don't get why they're so obsessed," I told her yesterday. I was helping hang the laundry. "Do they think he lives at the Taj Mahal or something?"

"I don't think that's what matters to them," she says.

"Then what's the big deal?"

"They just like knowing he exists, I guess. That he's theirs."

But is he? I wondered. I handed her another clothespin from the basket. "And what about Papi, Roli, and Simón, who've been their pinch-hitter pops? Are they out, just like that? That's cold, Tía. I'd put my foot down."

She looked at me through the sheets she was hanging on the line.

"They like the idea of having a dad to love, Merci. I can't blame them. I like having one, even at this age and with all the changes."

The breeze fluttered the sheets like ghosts between us. I guess she's been thinking of Lolo getting worse, too.

"It's good for them to get to know him," she said, "so they can have a relationship with their father. It's not their fault we didn't work out. We'll have to be patient."

Anyway, that's how I found out that today is the "one day" when the twins are going to visit Marco. I have been forced into working surveillance on a perfectly good Saturday. Abuela made me promise that I'd check the place out when we dropped them off and report back in full detail.

Roli pulls into the parking lot at the dance studio on his way to work. He's been listening to a recorded lecture on brain cells that go berserk and make cancer. Abuela put him up to do some reconnaissance, too. She made him drive over to make sure the address Marco gave was real. According to the names on the mailboxes that he stalked for her early this morning, yes, it is.

He lowers the volume as I slip on my sunglasses.

"You want me to wait for you to get in?" he asks. Tía keeps the glass doors of the studio locked when classes are in session, but parents are already gathering outside. It's the last class before Tía closes up for Labor Day Monday.

"Nah." I shake my head. "Aurelia will buzz me in."

I wave as he pulls away and then head to the locked door. I can hear squeals and yelling going on inside, but I can barely see through the glass to see inside. The air-conditioning inside has created enough condensation to make it look like a rain forest terrarium in there. I'm pretty sure the bright pink blob behind the desk is Aurelia, though. That's Tía's so-called office manager. ¡Qué desastre! She was the receptionist at the after-school center where Tía used to teach classes last year, before it closed and they both got booted. Forever the softy, Tía offered Aurelia a job, even though everyone knows that her main skill has always been gabbing on the phone.

"¡Me dio pena!" Tía always says in her own defense, as if feeling sorry for somebody is enough reason to employ them.

I knock on the glass door, waiting to be buzzed in.

"Aurelia!" I shout. "Over here!" I wave my hands, but it's like I'm invisible. Aurelia doesn't even look my way.

Suddenly a bang on the other side of the glass startles me. Two noses are flattened into pig snouts. It takes a second to recognize the distorted flesh, but I'm in luck. It's Tomás and Axel.

"Open up," I shout.

Aurelia is still on the phone, unaware that there's been a serious security breech, as they unlock the door for me and I step inside. Kids are running all over the place, shoving each other, playing hand slaps and having thumb wars instead of getting their things and heading out to their parents. None of this seems to interrupt her phone conversation.

I fish in my pocket for my phone and dial the main number for the dance studio. The light on Aurelia's desk phone blinks. It rings six times before she clicks over.

"Oigo. Suárez School of Latin Dance." She's multitasking, paging through a magazine while her friend is on hold. It's kind of impressive. I walk close to her desk.

"Hello, Aurelia, it's Merci. I'm here to steal some kids when you're not looking."

"Excuse me?"

I clear my throat and pocket my phone as she looks up, startled.

"The twins let me in," I say.

"Why didn't you ring the bell?" she asks. "All visitors have to be buzzed in."

"I banged on the glass," I say darkly. "Hard."

She frowns at me. "¡Ay, muchachita! I just cleaned fingerprints off the window this afternoon! I can't do extra work for nothing."

Tía Inés appears from the back studio before I can answer. Her hair is in a long braid down her back, and she's flushed and sweaty from the class she just dismissed. She waves at me and then stops a kid who's about to swan dive off the waiting bench.

She claps loudly and raises her voice. "Order, please. Everyone please gather your things and sit on the bench so Aurelia can sign you out."

Reluctantly, Aurelia puts away her magazine and pulls out a clipboard.

"Perfect timing, Merci," Tía says when she kisses me hello. "This won't take long. Pickups should be done in twenty minutes or so. Then we'll drop off the boys. Do you mind helping Lolo into the car while we close up? It takes him a while."

I glance inside the studio. Lolo is sitting in his favorite folding chair, an audience of one near the mirrors. Tía likes to bring him with her some days, especially if Abuela needs a rest. She says he likes the music.

Tía signals to Tomás, too. "Get your backpacks—anda," she tells him. "It's almost time to go."

The twins barrel past us to get their things.

Half an hour later, we're heading down South Congress Avenue. I'm shotgun with Tía, sweating to death, naturally. But Lolo is looking out the window happily, the breeze blowing his hair into curls. JFK Medical Center is the sand-colored building on the left. That's where Lolo went when he fainted. I turn around, wondering if he's going to recognize it, but he doesn't seem to—or if he does, he doesn't say so. He just watches the tall flag flapping in the wind as we drive by. A few seconds later, he hums "My Country 'Tis of Thee," which I didn't even realize he knew.

"And remember to say please and thank you, you

understand me?" Tía is talking fast and glancing at the twins in the mirror as she speeds along. "I don't want anybody thinking you were raised wild," she says.

The whole ride here she's been going through a long list of dos and don'ts. I can't see why she cares what Marco would think, anyway. But maybe it's the same reason I can get worked up at school, worrying what people think about my hair or eye or really anything. It's all that judgy stuff and the feeling of people whispering about you.

"Prince Drive." I pinch open the street map to get a better look. "I think it's coming up here."

Tía takes the corner at the last minute, the twins yelling "Whoa!" as they lean into the hairpin turn. Then we creep up the block, looking for the house number. Marco's shiny sports car is parked in one of the driveways on the left, next to a white Honda I don't recognize. Tía looks at it and sighs. She drums her fingers against the steering wheel, looking a little queasy, like that time she ate the bad clams from the supermarket and threw up for three days.

"You don't have to visit if you've changed your minds," she says quietly. But the twins are already unbuckling their seatbelts and wrestling with the door handle. I step out slowly and open the back door for Lolo so he can get some air.

Tía stops the twins before they tear up the walkway. She tucks in their shirts, fixes Axel's hair, and wipes the sweat off Tomás's neck with the back of her hand. Then she lowers her voice again.

"If you want to come home, you tell him that you want to call me. I will come right back to get you. I can be here in five minutes flat, OK?"

They tear off toward the front door and start ringing the bell, worse than how they ring people's doors on Halloween.

It takes a few minutes for anyone to come to the door. For a second, I think we've been spared. But then the front door finally opens, and Marco appears, shirtless and looking surprised to see us. The same goes for Veronica, who appears in a bikini top and shorts. It looks like we've interrupted their sunbathing. Veronica doesn't look too pleased about it, either.

"Hello," Tía says. "Did you forget we were coming?"

"Nah. It's fine," Marco says, as if we're the ones who got the wrong day or something.

I look through the open door behind them into their living room. Even from here, I can see it's a grown-up place. The glass tables are the giveaway. If Abuela saw them, she'd worry that the twins would decide to hang from the edge and get sliced up when it shattered. And uy, those white couches. Tía has to keep sheets on her furniture to protect from the sneaker prints and jelly sandwiches.

"We can come back another time," Tía says.

But Tomás pulls on her hand rudely. "No," he says.

"We want to see the planes and stuff," Axel adds.

Marco grins at them. "No. It's fine. Leave them. I promised we'd go to the airport."

Tía looks unsure. "I'll be back before six o'clock," she tells him. "We're having company for dinner, so this visit has to be brief."

Which is not true.

"You have my number if you need anything." Tía glances at Marco's car. "And you probably won't be driving anywhere, right?"

It's not really a question. More like an "or else" statement.

"We're going to walk to the park, Inés, and then to see the planes," he says, a little testy. "We'll take Veronica's car if they get tired."

"I'm thirsty," Tomás says suddenly.

"Me too," adds Axel.

"Boys," Tía says.

"Get them some sodas," Marco tells Veronica. "We have a couple left in the cooler." He doesn't know Tía's rules about sugary drinks. Ha. He'll find out why soon enough.

The twins race inside ahead of Veronica, like they already own the place. She chases after them in bare feet.

"Six o'clock, then," Tía says, trying to sound happy.

Marco nods and steps back inside his house. I buckle Lolo's seatbelt and then climb in beside him. "I'll keep him company back here," I say.

But really, it's got nothing to do with Lolo. He doesn't even seem to know I'm here. He's too busy picking at pieces of fluff coming through the armrest.

It's that Tía's eyes look watery, and her hands are shaking as she puts us in reverse. We pull out slowly and turn back onto the main road for home.

I take Lolo's hand in mine, and he lets me hold it.

I know Marco is their dad. I know they are excited to visit him. I know she thinks it's important that they spend time with their father.

But I'm pretty sure Tía is finding out that she's not any better at sharing the twins than I am.

CHAPTER 18

FOR MOST PEOPLE, Labor Day is sort of an anti-workday. Its name is what Ms. Tibbetts might call ironic, especially at Seaward, where kids kick back for a day of video games, mini vacays, or shopping trips to air-conditioned malls.

Not for me.

Around Las Casitas we keep the "labor" part of the holiday intact since it's a workday like any other. Today, Papi and Simón are painting the party rooms at Greenacres Bowling Alley, where Simón's brother, Vicente, works. There is a silver lining, though. Part of the deal Papi worked out is that he gets a coupon for a complimentary lane along with his pay. Six people will be able to bowl— with shoe rental included—for free. Papi offered the coupon to Simón this morning before they took off.

"You can take Inés and the boys if you want to use it," he said. "They like bowling."

"And take Merci, too," I butted in, since maybe he forgot that I am clocking time as a babysitter today and deserve something in return.

"Of course!" Simón said as he climbed into the truck.

Anyway, watching them drive off this morning, I wondered if Papi has noticed that Simón has been making himself a little scarce. He claims he's been extra busy with Papi's jobs plus a few side ones he's picked up with another friend. But he can't fool me. The stench of Marco is all over this. Maybe he's jealous, although it's not like Tía is going to get back together with Marco. I think the trouble is because Simón doesn't know how to fit in right now. One minute he was part of the family and sort of becoming like the twins' dad, and now, *pfft*! There's this other dad, the so-called "real one," and Simón is out. It's like he got replaced.

I asked Roli what he thought of my theory. He looked up from the textbook he was outlining. "A strong hypothesis, Merci," he said finally, which is heaping praise from him. "But it's a complicated situation, so do yourself a favor and stay out of it."

Anyway, Tía and Abuela are getting Lolo dressed this morning to give Roli a break, so I'm teaching the twins the ins and outs of cleaning up Abuela's sewing room. It's only fair that they labor on Labor Day, too. In fact, I'm grooming them to take my place on this chore as soon as possible. It's not like we adhere to child labor regulations around here anyway.

"Didn't you hear what I said? Don't stick each other with pins," I tell Axel, just as he's creeping closer to Tomás's bottom. "Just put them in the tomato." I point at the cloth pincushion near the machine. "And organize them by color. Abuela's picky."

I look over at Tomás. He's been on his stomach coloring for a while.

"Aren't you finished yet? We have work to do."

"I'm making something for my papi."

He rolls over on his back to show me his picture. It's him and Axel (wearing the same striped shirts), plus a very big man with a rectangle body and circle hands. Cigar-shaped planes are in the sky above them. The bottom says *DAD*. No sign of Veronica. But no sign of any of us here at Las Casitas, either.

It stabs harder at me than any of Axel's straight pins. "Oh," I say.

"What's this?" Axel asks. He's peering under the otto-man and pulls out a big plastic bag from underneath.

"Let me see it." I sit down and open the bag, smiling

when I see what's inside. A warm memory floods over me. It's part of my favorite game from a long time ago. "Pirate booty."

"Liar," he says.

"Really," I say.

When I was little, Abuela always let me play with the extra scraps of fabric from her sewing room so I could become a pirate. It was fun pretending to be lawless, plus I could dress up without those silly wings and fairy wands some of my friends liked. I'd wrap a piece of cloth on my head like a bandana, one end dangling down my back, and then I'd go in search of this bag. It's where she kept a collection of fake jewelry. When she still sewed for people, she'd use the baubles to help customers see the finished look as they admired their new outfits in her mirror.

Abuela never got mad if I played with these necklaces and earrings.

"Here," I say. "Rubies and diamonds from the bottom of the sea, mateys."

I drape long plastic beads over Axel's head, and I push a few brass bangles on Tomás's wrist. "The king's gold," I say.

Then I fasten a silver parrot pin with a worn-off eye to my own shoulder, a single gold hoop through one of my lobes.

167

"It's not real," Tomás says.

But Axel is willing to play. "Argh!" he says. "Walk the plank!"

Tomás climbs up on the ottoman next to me and does as he's told.

Maybe I'll buy the twins eye patches at the pirate museum in Saint Augustine. Maybe even a hook to wear over their hands. It's not watching planes at the airport, I guess, but I'll make it fun—*more* fun, even.

I dig inside the bag and pull up a fistful of earrings. Most of them are singles, their matches lost a long time ago in someone's shirt, under a bed, in a couch along with spare change and dropped raisins. I asked Abuela about the missing ones once. Something about the unnatural singleness made me sad. They were meant to be pairs, mates, like Tía and Marco. I remember that Marco suddenly stopped coming home to us in a way that I didn't understand.

"If one is lost, they're no good anymore," I told her. "They have to be a pair to be good."

I still remember how she cut the thread with her teeth and turned to me, surprised.

"Nonsense. They're still beautiful and useful. You just have to think of them in a new way."

CHAPTER 19

HANNAH IS MEETING with a group from coding to work on a project, so she won't be at lunch today. Lena volunteered to help a few kids with their research for the Saint Augustine reports. And Wilson is absent, too. That means it's going to me and Edna for lunch.

But when I get to the cafeteria, I don't see her, not in the line and not at our table. I start to get that jumpy feeling of being by myself. Edna's not my super favorite person, but I like her better than I like eating alone. I glance outside to see if maybe I can escape to the courtyard, where the loners around here like to eat in peace. But it rained hard this morning, and the chairs are too puddled to find refuge there.

That's when I see an empty chair at Avery's table. She's with Mackenzie, of course, and Lindsey Poletti, another girl from our team. I walk over, my hands sort of sweaty, even as I tell myself that on the field we have each other's backs.

"Hey, can I sit here today?"

The conversation doesn't stop, but Mackenzie slides the seat toward me with her foot and then turns back to listen. Avery is telling them all about a party that happened over the Labor Day weekend, and everyone is hanging on her words. She sneaked out of her window after her parents fell asleep. She met a few kids on the Sandhill-something golf course so they could go as a group.

I unpack my sandwich as I listen, feeling as babyish as one of the sixth-graders at the tables across the room. My bed is right next to my window, but I'd be too scared to sneak out to a party. It's not that I'm afraid of the dark, zombies and other night lurkers notwithstanding. I mean, even Tuerto looks a little bewitched and fierce when he spends the night roaming. It's more that I'd be terrified of what Mami and Papi would do to me if they ever found out I lied to them and went roaming with high school kids. I'm sure it would be el fin.

Avery dips the last of her french fries into ketchup as she finishes her story and finally looks over at me. She licks her fingertips daintily. "Hey, Merci." Her voice sounds friendly, like that day at the mall. She looks at the other girls at the table. "Should I ask her?" she says.

Lindsey and Mackenzie shrug. I manage a smile, but I am right here, so why is she talking about me like I can't hear them?

"Ask me what?"

"Well, we were talking about you . . ." Avery begins.

I sit very still now. Being "talked about" usually means being made fun of. For instance, Rachel Peterson and Michael Clark are always the topic of gossip since they argue and break up at least once a week. Everybody calls their squabbles "doing the Micha-Racha."

Avery scoots her chair close enough to mine that I can smell her coconut shampoo. When she's not on the field, she wears her long hair loose, which makes her look pretty in that *Teen Vogue*-ish sort of way. It's easy to see why lots of people have crushes on her, even kids in the upper school who normally don't give any of us in the middle school a second look.

"Do you want to be our fourth roommate for the Saint Augustine trip?"

I blink.

"It'll be a soccer-team room," Mackenzie says sweetly, as if she never said a thing about teacher's pets. "Plus, we don't want to get stuck with someone random."

Well. Wow. I am not someone random. That's something.

People don't usually seek me out, so this feels pretty good. Still, I can't kid myself that it's anything special. They're telling me, plain as day, that I'm just a filler against having to room with someone they don't know. I'm just better than the risk of Mrs. Wilkinson choosing for them; that's it. And I guess it makes sense. Mrs. Wilkinson doesn't know who's arguing, who became enemies over the summer, who's made new friends. What's going to happen to all the randoms, though? The ones who don't have three friends, but maybe just one or two? Mami claims that's all you really need in this life, one or two true friends, but it makes stuff like a school trip murder. Are they going to want to go to Saint Augustine if they have to be forced into rooming with somebody they don't know or like? You'd have to get in your pj's in front of strangers. And brush your teeth. And what if you got gassy at night or if you snored? It could happen! People might talk about that, and you'd never live it down. Uy. It's not as if our teachers think about any of this stuff, not even Mrs. Wilkinson.

What would it be like to have a soccer-team room, though? Maybe it would be fun.

I guess I'm taking too long to answer because Avery

looks at me, disappointed. "Oh, you probably have roommates already." She glances toward my usual lunch table, empty today. "Can't you tell them you changed your mind?"

I blink hard so my eye doesn't stray. I've already agreed to room with Hannah, Lena, and—God help me—Edna. I should just tell her I can't, but turning Avery down feels like I'm walking away from something lots of girls would kill for. But how would I ever feel comfortable? I think about all the times Lena and Hannah have slept over at my house, when I couldn't go to theirs. How Lena sometimes sucks her knuckles when she's tired. How Hannah can't sleep after scary movies. That we are all three early risers and big fans of banana pancakes with a lot of syrup.

"I . . ." The words are a paste in my mouth.

She leans back and flashes a grin. "You'll be sorry if you miss rooming with us," she says. "It's going to be so fun!"

Just then, Edna appears at the entrance to the dining hall. She scans the room, looking for one of us, I guess, but I don't think she spots me at Avery's table. In fact, she doesn't even glance this way, thank goodness. What would I say? Would I get up and join Edna at our old spot? There was a time Edna was one of the queen bees around here, too, and a mean one at that. Now, she's down in the trenches with the rest of us mere mortals.

I lower my eyes and concentrate on Mami's dry sandwich, trying to blend into the crowd. Edna turns on her heels and leaves.

CHAPTER 20

MISS MCDANIELS IS NEAR my desk in the guidance office, checking her watch as she waits for Mrs. Wilkinson. Waiting is not her best skill, though, since she's used to keeping our school on a schedule down to the last nano-second. Her toe-tapping is breaking my concentration as I work making parent information packets. They're for the clubs Mrs. Wilkinson runs here in guidance, all designed to "support children through a variety of challenges that arise in the middle school environment." I guess it makes sense, but geez, you'd have to have a lot of clubs around here to keep up with our challenges. If it were up to me, I'd have the Stressed About Grades Club, the Bad Fights with Friends Group, the People Who Broke Up and Now Claim the Other Person Is Ugly and Has

Bad Breath Club (that is today's Micha-Racha situation, according to the lunchroom buzz), and now, the Who You Should Room with Club.

Anyway, I'm supposed to put a welcome letter inside each one and then label the envelopes with the addresses.

Tap-tap-tap.

"This could take a while, miss," I tell Miss McDaniels. "She's in a parent meeting." I lower my voice. "With Mrs. Kim."

Did Miss McDaniels just flinch?

She sighs and pulls back her shoulders, probably wondering if she should go in and save Mrs. Wilkinson. She's had to meet with Hannah's mom about all sorts of stuff, mostly safety related—everything from Internet safety to proper art room ventilation. The list is pretty impressive.

I happen to know why Mrs. Kim is here this time since Hannah texted me last night in a full-blown freak-out. Surprisingly, it is not about getting out of coding, which Hannah has started to like after all.

> Don't let my mom in the guidance office tomorrow. She wants to chaperone the trip. Lock the door if you have to!

I can't do that, of course, mostly because I don't have keys. (Mrs. Wilkinson wears them on a spiral wrist coil.) Not that there isn't good reason to try. Hannah is sure that if her mom gets her way, she'll have us walking down the street tethered to a rope like preschoolers.

Luckily for all of us, Mrs. Wilkinson is as tough as she is chipper. She believes 100 percent that the trip is supposed to teach us "how to engage in responsible independent behavior" without our parents, a skill she says we'll need in high school next year. Her rules clearly state that no adult who comes along can have a kid in our grade. Mrs. Kim is an attorney, though, so we shall see.

"Are we getting new merchandise for the school store, miss?" I say, mostly to see if she'll stop toe-tapping. It's driving me nuts.

Miss McDaniels looks up at me. "Excuse me?"

"The T-shirt." I motion to what she's holding. It's red and has our school crest on the pocket. Based on last year's sales figures, when Wilson and I were managers, I'd say she could sell those for twenty dollars and turn a profit. I'll have to meet with the new seventh-grade managers and get them up to speed. This is one drawback to making the school store a seventh-grade work assignment: no chance to build institutional knowledge.

"Oh," she says. "These are for the eighth-grade field trip. I thought Mrs. Wilkinson might like to see them before I put in the full order." She unfolds it and holds the shirt against her chest to show me. "What do you think?"

It's boxy and Papi-sized, and the shade is so bright it could probably blind you if you stared too long. Normally, I don't care about these things, but I can already hear Edna complaining about not being able to show off her new shirt or shorts or whatever else she's planning to pack in her matched luggage set. If I can shut that down before it happens, all the better.

"But miss, I thought we were allowed to wear our regular clothes on the trip," I say. "It said so on our permission slip. It's one of the perks." I grab a copy of the permission form and hand it to her. "See point six."

"We have to think about safety when we take students off campus, Merci."

I take a closer look. "You're saying these T-shirts are bulletproof, then?" I say. "Mrs. Kim might want to know."

She raises her eyebrow. I'm right on the edge of snark, always a little dangerous around Miss McDaniels.

"Of course not," she says. "It's just a way to have all our students easily recognizable at a glance. They're roomy enough so you can wear these over your clothes."

An extra layer of clothing in the Florida heat? Never mind that it will be nearly impossible for me to keep mustard and ketchup off my shirt for a whole weekend, especially since I plan to eat as many cheeseburgers and hot dogs as I can without Mami around.

I think fast.

"I'd reconsider that plan, miss," I say. "Three days in the same shirt could be hot . . . and that means smelly." For good measure, I lower my voice and add, "You know how it is with puberty and all." It's awkward, but it's also my Hail Mary play. I happen to know that Miss McDaniels is particularly sensitive to "malodorous environments." I saw it in a memo she circulated to the teachers reminding them to open windows in our classrooms every once in a while. Apparently, we are walking stink bombs.

Miss McDaniels purses her lips, thinking. "That is a good point," she says. "We'll be sure to pack spares in case they're needed."

Touché.

Mrs. Wilkinson's door swings open, and Mrs. Kim steps through to the reception area. I wiggle my fingers at her as a greeting, but she looks grumpy, so I lower my eyes and then pretend I'm working on the folders again.

Mrs. Wilkinson leads her to the door. "Thank you for stopping in, Mrs. Kim. We're always so grateful to hear from our parents."

After she's gone, she turns to Miss McDaniels and heaves a big sigh. "That took some work."

"As always." Miss McDaniels holds up the shirt. "Samples. What do you think?"

"Fabulous!" Mrs. Wilkinson says. "And I'm glad you stopped by, because I wanted to go over roommate requests as they start coming in, just to make sure we don't have any problems with the arrangements."

I lean in, trying to listen. It's always interesting how adults define *problem*. It's usually what's a problem to them, not to us.

Mrs. Wilkinson turns to me. "I won't be available for walk-in student visits this hour. Please have them make an appointment if they need me, unless, of course, it's an emergency."

Oh boy. I really hope nobody shows up with a so-called emergency. The guidance office isn't like the nurse's office, where blood and broken bones are the giveaway that you've got a situation. Here it usually comes attached to lots of crying and mucus. I try not to shudder at the thought.

"OK," I say.

And with that, the door closes again.

I work for most of the hour quietly, only taking two messages for the counselors. (One is from Mrs. Kim again.) But just as I'm finishing up with the last folders, someone comes to my desk.

"Well, this is a cushy setup."

It's Edna.

"You need something?" I ask.

She takes a strawberry hard candy from the bowl on my desk. I brought them from the stash Abuela keeps in her purse since I ate all the other ones Mrs. Wilkinson had in there.

"Do you know if she's finished the room assignments for the trip?" she asks.

I feel my face flush. It's been more than a week since Avery asked, but I haven't turned down her invitation. Every time I decide to tell her I'm rooming with my friends, I imagine someone cooler than I am taking my place, and I can't bring myself to do it. If only I could be in two rooms at the same time.

"She doesn't have all the permission slips in, so I don't think they're that far yet," I say.

She doesn't move.

"So, is that it?" I ask.

She gives me one of her imperious looks. "No. I need to talk to Mrs. Wilkinson," she says. "Please buzz her to tell her I'm here."

"No can do. She's in a meeting with Miss McDaniels, and she said she wasn't taking student appointments this hour."

Edna sucks her teeth. "Oh, give me a break, Merci. It's not an appointment. I just need her for a second."

"Is this an emergency?"

"Will that get me an audience?" she asks.

I can see I'm going to have to take a bare-knuckle approach. I take a closer look at Edna's eyes, trying to decide if I see suffering in them. Nope, her eyes are Visine clear, and I don't see any mucus leaking from her nose, either. She's just being pushy. What a surprise.

"What are you staring at?" she asks. "Is it my bangs? I told Auden he was cutting them crooked."

"It's not your hair," I say, trying not to roll my eyes. "Just come back later, will you please?"

"But I have to give her something."

"The only thing she'd want is aspirin from the nurse. Someone was here to discuss safety concerns about the trip."

"Mrs. Kim trying to horn in as a chaperone?"

"You didn't hear it from me."

Edna looks at me and then we both crack up.

That's when I notice she's holding an envelope a lot like the ones I'm working on.

"Drop off what you have for her. You can put it in her in-box right there." I point at the plastic file holder that's nailed to Mrs. Wilkinson's door. "She checks it a few times a day."

I keep my eyes glued to her in case she tries to bust through the door. Mrs. Kim's got nothing on Edna when she wants her way.

She slides the envelope where I tell her and then stops at my desk, watching me as I finish my work.

"Yes?" I put aside the folder I'm working on and fold my hands.

"I hear Avery Sanders asked you to room with her."

My heart almost stops as I stare at her. How does information get around this place? "Who told you that?"

"I have my sources," she says. "So, is it true?"

"Yes."

She blinks hard a couple of times. "So, what? Are you going to ditch us? You looked kind of cozy at lunch."

Edna's words feel like little knife points. So she *did* see me. What if she's told Hannah and Lena? They'll be mad if they think I'd dump them.

Thankfully, the bell rings just in time to save me. "I can't talk now," I say. "But I never said I would room with her." It's true, isn't it?

I hurry to gather the folders and lock them in the file cabinet where they belong. When I turn back around, Edna is gone.

CHAPTER 21

MAMI HAS A LATE patient today, so I'm supposed to start on my homework while I wait for her to show up.

I'm sitting outside, leaning against one of the pillars as I tackle pre-algebra, when Wilson comes out. He's wearing Beats, red camo ones, which are definitely a step up from last year, when we were both sporting earbuds from the checkout line at Marshalls. He pulls one side off when he sees me.

"Where y'at?" He tosses his backpack and slides down next to me. Then he glances over my work. My class is doing linear equations, which I'm pretty sure *he's* been able to do in his head since third grade. "Number two is messed up. You gotta get all the *x*'s on one side."

I look down and start erasing. "Knew that," I mumble. "Thanks."

I start working the problem again, but now I'm self-conscious. Also, I'm noticing his nice smell, which I remember exactly from dancing together in Tía's show last year. What is it? Body wash? Detergent? Whatever it is, it's distracting.

"Wilson, do you mind?"

He sighs and leans back and picks aimlessly at the Velcro on his foot brace. It must make his leg sweat in this heat. "Sorry." But then he can't help himself. "It's just that the x in the denominator means you gotta multiply—"

I slam my book closed and decide to work on this at home later. I don't like feeling dumb around him.

"I need advice," I say. "On the down low."

His eyebrows shoot up and he scoots closer. "Listening."

"My soccer friends asked me to room with them in Saint Augustine. Avery and them."

"Avery?" he says.

I give him a sharp look. Clearly, he understands her charms, even though he's not as bad as Darius, who has to run away every time he sees Avery walking toward him in the hall.

"Focus. I already told Lena, Hannah, and Edna that I'd room with *them*."

"So, what's the rub?"

I sigh. For a smart person, he can be thick about people. "Never mind."

"Oh wait. I get you." He leans back, shaking his head. "You might want to."

My face flushes. "Too bad I can't be in two places at once, right?" I say.

"Yep. Like Double Take." That's one of the lieutenants from Iguanador Nation. He can clone himself in emergency situations, making him essentially immortal.

Off in the distance we can hear the football team doing their warm-up cadence. Mr. Patchett claps a rhythm and calls out the words. Then the players echo it, like they're in a chorus or something. Really their voices aren't bad.

You can't break my body down
You can't break my body down
Work your body-body. Ooh
Work your body-body. Ooh

"You like being Patchett's TA?" I ask.

He shrugs. "It's all right. He's a little intense. But check this out." He unzips the front pocket of his backpack and pulls out two red tickets. They say COMPLIMENTARY PASS. "I'm going to use them for the first football game," he says.

186

"The Pox matchup is coming up, and Patchett thinks we're gonna crush them."

"Sweet!" I say. The Poxel School is our archrival. Everyone wants to see them eat dirt.

"I have an extra ticket," Wilson says. "You want it?"

My stomach dips.

Is Wilson just giving me an extra ticket, or is he asking me to go to the game? Like, *with* him? My heart starts to race at the thought.

"Full disclosure," he says. "The upper-school kids take the good bleacher spots at the fifty-yard line. Middle school sits at the twenty, near the marching band." He shrugs. "The trumpets blast your eardrums, but at least it's a faster walk to the concession stand at halftime."

What a salesman.

But still, my mind is swirling. I've never been to a night game, mostly because Roli never primed the pump for me with Mami and Papi. He wasn't much into sports events here at Seaward unless you count chess, which he loved to analyze from the sidelines in the library after school.

Just then, Wilson's mom's SUV pulls into the lot. He gets to his feet and pulls on his backpack. Mrs. Bellevue rolls down the passenger-side window and waves at me as Wilson makes his way over.

"Later, woadie," Wilson calls out to me when he gets in. "Remember, you have to get rid of that denominator in number three. Hint: multiply!"

"Oh my God, Wilson," I say.

And then, he drives away, leaving me here, wondering.

CHAPTER 22

COACH CAMERON HAS CALLED a preseason meeting of the girls' soccer team after school today. When I get to the gym, there are still stragglers milling around, and Mr. Patchett is trying to boot them out so he can get to football practice with the upper school. With the big game this weekend, he's in full military mode and barking orders in code that we barely understand.

"Make a hole, people! Make a hole!" he says to get them out. Then he sees Wilson still hauling a net filled with orange cones, field hockey equipment, and pinnies back from sixth-grade PE last hour. "BELLEVUE!" he roars. "Water cooler outside! ASAP!"

Wilson gives me a despondent wave as he hurries into the office to do as he's told. He's learned to "embrace the suck" like a soldier. I won't lie: watching him work with Mr. Patchett makes me a lot less jealous of his teacher's assistant spot in PE.

Anyway, our eighth-grade crew is already here, waiting on Coach. We're not supposed to have food in the gym, but we're all starving, so Avery was nice enough to share her extra packs of fruit snacks. I was hoping I could talk to her alone about the roommate situation, maybe ask her if she told Edna, and then explain why I didn't say anything. But she's near the exit talking to Clayton Browne, the ninth-grader who currently likes her. Clayton is holding his lacrosse stick across his muscled shoulders, his helmet hanging off one end.

I look over at them, trying not to be too obvious, just like everybody else is doing. They're just talking, but the way Clayton is shaking his hair out of his eyes makes him look a little nervous. Weird. What is *he* worried about? He's the ninth-grader, isn't he? I wonder if Avery is actually allowed to go places with Clayton, or if she only sees him when she sneaks out. I know it's more than holding hands in the hall in between classes if Miss McDaniels isn't around.

Not that I care.

The rule at our house is that I can't date until I'm fifteen, which is in two years. It's probably even more unbreakable than the sleepover rule.

I fish inside my packet of fruit snacks for a red one and take an informal assessment of the talent pool that's gathered among the team hopefuls. Some seventh-graders who are interested in trying out this year are sitting a few rows down below us. And of course, there's a huge group of sixth-graders squirming nervously on the bottom bleacher and being silly. They're stealing cautious glances at us eighth-graders.

"Between us, I don't suspect we've got much raw talent down there. Do you?" Mackenzie says, popping a fruit snack in her mouth. "Sad."

I shake out a few green gummies, disappointed. Who invented that lousy flavor? "You can't tell. That one with the skinny legs might be OK. Sometimes there are surprises." I motion to the little sixth-grader who lugs around the Orlando City Soccer Club backpack. At least she's a fan.

Coach arrives, still wearing teacher clothes, their feet looking swelled in those pumps. Officially, girls' soccer tryouts don't happen until the start of October, but Coach Cameron doesn't like to leave anything until the last minute. That's why we have to attend this meeting of former players and prospects to go over the season schedule and clinic dates. Plus, Coach is big on "commitment," which means they like to warn us about not missing practices or games because of other clubs and whatnot. They don't want us to sign up if we're not all the way in.

"All right, if you're here for information on the upcoming soccer clinics and tryouts, you're in the right place." Coach glances over at Avery, who's still talking to Clay. "Sanders, are you joining us?"

Avery lets the door close and starts jogging back. "Sorry, Coach," she says, blushing.

"The rest of you, come sit down closer," Coach says. "My voice has had it."

Mackenzie tosses Avery her backpack so she won't have to climb all the way up, and then they sit together. I grab my stuff, too, but even when I sit on the same row, I still feel like I'm on the edge, not really part of the club that includes Avery and Mackenzie.

It's mostly welcome blah-blah, but we do get the season overview and parental permission slips. I eyeball the schedule and see it's just like last year. Voluntary weekly clinics starting at the end of the month. A whole week of mandatory practice and tryouts in October, with the first official game against the Pox scheduled for December. Last year, they crushed us, but we have sworn revenge, even more than the football team.

"That's all I've got," Coach says after we've gone through it all. "Questions?"

Orlando City girl raises her hand. I'm expecting her to ask regular newbie questions, like how long practices are and whether we've got to arrange our own rides to the games.

"What qualities are you looking for in recruits?" she asks. "And how do you handle player development?"

I snap to attention. Gutsy. How *does* Coach handle player development? I want to know, so I lean in.

Coach blinks and then looks at her carefully. "What is your name?"

"Robin Farmer," she says.

"On the soccer field, we need each other, Robin. We lean on one another's skill and strategic thinking. I'm looking for hard workers, for players who work as a team, and for players who can think on their feet, literally. We're not here to build stars."

"Ooh. Shut down," Avery whispers to Mackenzie, who fist bumps her. Robin doesn't notice.

"As for player development," Coach continues, "it's highly individualized. Every player will have a starting point and a personal goal, to be determined after I assess you in a few weeks." They look at the rest of us. "Other questions?"

"One last thing," Robin says.

Relentless. I like it.

Coach turns to her, pained, but it could be the shoes. "Yes, Robin."

"Who's the captain?"

Everyone's eyes go to Avery, including mine.

People listen to Avery, on and off the soccer field. They notice her on the pitch. They cheer for her even if they don't know her. She went to that fancy soccer camp and knows good moves.

But Coach doesn't let on. "That's not decided until after I set the roster, though it's always an eighth-grader. The player is selected by me, based on leadership potential and field skills."

Coach looks around. "If that's all, you're dismissed. I'll see you for clinic. Make sure you have your signed physicals by the due date. No exceptions."

I'm gathering up my nerve to tell Avery I can't room with her, but she heads out of the gym before I can talk to her alone.

Maybe I can just text her and be done with it.

I'm trying to decide what to say when I get home after the meeting. I'm in Tía's kitchen, enjoying a pre-dinner smoothie that always helps me think better. I thought maybe I'd ask Tía for advice, but she's been on the phone untangling a problem with the power company. I think to the stack of papers on Aurelia's desk and get a knowing feeling. That power bill is probably still sitting under a magazine somewhere. Why Tía doesn't hire someone with serious organization skills in that position, I'll never know.

I know I should just text Avery. There's no use dragging it out, especially now that Edna has asked.

But when I reach in my back pocket for my phone, it's not there. It's not on the counter, either. Or under any of the dishrags on the table.

Just as I'm starting to panic, I hear the twins talking and giggling out in the living room. They've taken a page from Roli's playbook recently and started to leave me little photographic presents on the home screen.

Sure enough, when I walk out into the living room, I see they've got it in their grubby hands. They must have lifted it while I was making my smoothie.

"Give it back or die."

They're too busy to hear me. They've got it on speakerphone, listening for the long beep of someone's voice mail.

I snatch it away.

"Stop bothering people."

They look at me, annoyed, and then take off for outside.

I scroll through my call log. Geez. They've made twenty calls to the same number in just the last hour. If they've been bothering any of my friends, like last time, I'll be so embarrassed.

I press redial to see if I can figure out who they've been cranking.

Marco's voice comes on and tells me to leave a message.

I hang up fast.

I check the log again. Twenty calls in a row. I wonder how many messages they left for him? But then I think: Not a single call back.

Maybe Marco is just busy right now, but shouldn't a dad pick up? Wouldn't all those messages make him want to talk to them, see if they're OK?

Of all the questions the twins ask about stupid stuff, it's amazing they haven't thought of the obvious one: Does this guy like us? But maybe they want him to like them so bad, they can't even imagine it otherwise.

I head back to the kitchen, thinking about Avery again. But I don't send the text. I pocket my phone instead.

CHAPTER 23

SOMETIMES MAMI IS MORE understanding than Papi, but you never really know. Sitting here in the car, I'm wondering how she's going to feel about me going to night football games.

I wait until we drive past the practice field on the way off campus to feel her out. The team is doing footwork drills, sort of like the ones we do in soccer.

"The first football game is this weekend," I say carefully. "Wilson thinks were going to crush the Pox."

She looks both ways and pulls out of the school's driveway. "Football," she mutters. "We have a kid right now with a spinal-cord injury he got in a game. He just got transferred back home after his treatment in Atlanta."

Great.

She's almost as bad as Abuela with worries, especially about head injuries. Your brain controls everything, she says, so she's always warning me against headers. I'm not allowed to do them, no matter what Coach says, not even for the winning shot.

We stay quiet the rest of the way home. It's only when we pull into the driveway, though, that I find out why.

"Hang on, Merci," she says as I start to unbuckle.

"Why?" I grab my polyester blazer from the floor.

"Come with me first," she says, looking toward Abuela's house. "I'll need moral support."

"Moral support for what?"

"I think I found someone who can come work with Lolo." Mami sighs. "And now I have to discuss it with Abuela. Your Papi and Tía thought she might listen to me best."

I look toward Abuela's house. So. It's going to be an ambush.

I feel bad for Mami, though. She and Lolo have always been close. Sometimes people think she's his daughter, like Tía is. A few times, when she's been helping him do his balance exercises, I've seen her eyes get sad and watery, like she suddenly realizes he's Lolo and not a patient she's helping. I'll bet this is one time she hates being the medical authority around here.

She gets out of the car and waits for me, her human shield, to walk inside with her.

From the looks of the kitchen sink, Abuela has been cooking all day. The smell of lemon and vanilla fills the whole house.

"Hi, Abuela," I say, inspecting the counters. There's a tray of glazed coconut balls on parchment paper. And beyond the coquitos, I notice natilla simmering on the stove, which is the twins' favorite pudding. If I didn't know better, I'd say Abuela was trying to cancel Marco's allure through culinary means.

Mami sits down and makes some small talk while I butter some crackers for my snack. I try to pretend like it's any other afternoon, but honestly, it's like waiting for an explosion you know is coming.

"The milk in the refrigerator is new, Merci," Abuela says. "Pour yourself a glass."

I slide in across the table from Mami and mouth, *I have homework.*

She's quiet for a few minutes and then finally takes a deep breath. "Teresita," she begins, "I have something to talk to you about."

"Pues dime," Abuela says absently. The loose skin under her arm jiggles as she stirs.

"There's someone I'd like you to meet. Her name is Fabiola. She's one of the aides at the rehab center." Mami holds out a piece of paper with a name and phone number. "She's willing to come by this weekend, if you're available."

Abuela looks confused. "Come by to meet me? But why? Does she need something hemmed?"

Mami barely flinches. "No, no hemming. It's that maybe we can hire her to help you with Lolo's routine in the morning."

Silence.

"What do you think?" Mami says after a few seconds.

Abuela turns slowly.

"A stranger touching Lolo?" she says.

"Not a stranger. Fabiola. One of my coworkers. I've seen her work with patients, and she's excellent."

Abuela looks at the slip of paper with Fabiola's name like it's radioactive. "No thank you, Ana. ¡Ni hablar! Lolo isn't a patient. Tell your friend we don't need her services."

I glance at Mami uneasily and take another brittle bite of galleta. Abuela has a point, doesn't she? Patients are sick people in hospitals. Doctors and nurses have to take care of them. Lolo lives here with all of us.

"I mean no disrespect, Teresita," Mami says. "I know this is difficult to talk about. It's been hard for all of us."

Abuela doesn't answer. She sprinkles cinnamon into the pot with a vengeance as the natilla bubbles like pale yellow lava. Then she scoops out a spoonful and brings it over so I can taste it.

"No te quemes," she says. "I once knew a girl who lost her taste buds for life with something hot."

I blow on the spoon to cool it down. *Heaven*, I think as I taste and then nod my approval.

Mami presses on. "It's just that there's so much to do now. Roli is home this semester, but he's working, and it's not fair to him, Teresita. He's barely more than a boy. Besides, we all want him to go back to school after Christmas. That's what's best for him. To finish his studies."

"Claro que sí," Abuela says quietly.

"So, who'll help you then?" Mami asks, softer.

No answer.

"Enrique and I leave too early in the morning to get Lolo dressed," Mami says. "And Inés has the twins and the dance studio."

Abuela shakes her head. "I can manage. I always have."

It's so quiet that you can hear the gurgling pot. I wait for Abuela to say, *Merci can help*, which is what usually happens around here when there's something that no one else wants to do. I think of Roli having to see Lolo's privates. They wouldn't make me do that, would they?

"It makes sense to hire someone who can take the strain off of you, someone who's trained," Mami says.

Abuela bangs the wooden spoon clean and turns to Mami at last. She is suddenly a fortress. "I have been married to my husband for more than half my life, Ana," she says stiffly. "How much more training would I need?"

Tuerto yowls from somewhere in the yard. He always eats as soon as I get home from school, so he's probably hungry and sharpening his claws right now in preparation of an attack on our screen. For once, Mami doesn't complain about it.

She clears her throat. "It's just that we can't run home for small emergencies anymore or attend to all the important things Lolo needs now. Think of the wandering. That's not safe for him." Mami lowers her voice to almost a whisper and gives Abuela a pained look. "And we have to think of what's coming. Even if we want to, we won't be able to do it all ourselves anymore."

I pour my milk and take a sip, but nothing seems to help the dryness in my throat. It almost hurts to push it all down. I stare at Mami, suddenly feeling angry at her, too. What is coming, exactly? Is she hiding something about Lolo from me again?

Abuela is stone-faced.

"No one knows what the future holds for any of us,

Ana," she says. "Only God." She moves the pot off the burner and turns to me. "Merci, go wake up your grandfather, please. He's been napping, and if he goes much longer, he won't sleep well tonight."

I'm only too happy to brush the crumbs off my shirt and slip out of the room.

Lolo is not napping. In fact, he's wide-awake. And he's very busy.

I'm at their bedroom door, but he doesn't look up, not even as I step inside. I walk over to his side of the bed to take a closer look. He's upset, breathing hard, like he's been in a race, and his hair is sticking up in spots. It's his messy hair that unsettles me most somehow. I want to reach up to pat the back of it down neatly, but a prickly feeling inside me makes me change my mind.

"What are you doing, Lolo? I thought you were asleep."

He looks up at me and squints, puzzled, as if he's never seen me before.

"It's me, Lolo. Merci."

He turns back to the socks and underwear that are strewn on the bed. There are more things piled on the floor by his feet. He's gotten one of Abuela's old purses from the back of her closet, too, and grips it by the straps like a robber.

I glance at the door, still open, and wonder if I should close it. Abuela and Mami are dueling in the kitchen, and Abuela won't like this mess, on top of everything else. It might be the match that lights her fuse. She's such a stickler for neatness. Lolo's socks, usually folded and tucked together at the cuff, have been yanked free of each other. Abuela's slips and bras aren't in the drawer underneath, either. They're out here in the open with everything else. Even Abuela's old mint tin—the one where she keeps our baby teeth and locks from our first haircuts—has been opened and spilled on the bedspread. What will she do when she sees her orderly drawers have been ransacked?

No. If Abuela finds things this way, there will be big trouble for sure.

"We have to clean this up," I whisper. "Hurry. I'll help."

I scoop up the baby teeth, the edges still marked with dried blood, and start to close them back in the rusty box. But Lolo suddenly grabs my wrist in a hard grip that surprises me. Where is this strength coming from?

"No," he snaps at me. Clear, hard. "Don't touch."

I drop the tin right away, but he hangs on. I don't cry out, even though I want to. If I tell on him, he'll get in even more trouble.

But his fingers are digging in hard.

"That hurts," I whimper. "Please, Lolo, stop."

He blinks and loosens just enough that I can pull my hand free. I've never wanted distance from Lolo before, but I do now. I hurry to the other side of the bed, safely out of reach with the mattress between us. The sting of his fingers is still on my skin, and my heart is pounding.

He shoves socks, bras, and the empty tin inside the handbag. A second later, he pulls them out again, frustrated, and runs his fingers through his hair.

"Se me va la guagua," he mutters.

I grit my teeth and look out the bedroom window. The stupid bus again, leaving him behind. I hate that he imagines this. Where does he think he's going?

But as I stand there watching him wrestle again with the purse, I think of Roli and have an idea.

"Do you want help packing for your trip, Lolo?" I ask quietly.

I know he's heard me, even though he doesn't lift his eyes. He gets so still.

It's a game of pretend, I tell myself. Like playing with the twins that time we went to Mars in an old box.

Slowly, I reach over for two socks. They're not a match, but I put them together anyway and hold them out to him to see if he'll play. As soon as he puts them in the purse, I make another pair and hold them out, too. He seems to calm down as we work, so we keep at it until the purse is a bloated tick.

"You can sit down and wait for the bus, if you want," I say when we're done. "I'll watch for it through the window."

"Thank you, Inés," he says. He sits on the edge of the bed, still gripping Abuela's purse as he stares ahead. It takes a long while before I have the nerve to walk back to him. His eyes are nearly closing by then, and his breathing is slower. Without a word, I help lift his legs, and he doesn't fight it. Instead, he smiles at me, pats my hand with his old softness. He lies back against his pillows and curls himself around the bag as he sighs. In a few minutes, he's drifted off to sleep.

I let myself out and close the door gently. But as I stand here in the hall, I can't decide what to do next. Out in the kitchen, Mami and Abuela are still talking. More than anything, I want to run, sneak home, but I know I can't. Instead, I take a deep breath and slowly make my way back to them.

Lolo clearly needs our help, but it's harder to convince Abuela that she is going to need it even more.

CHAPTER 24

I WALK INTO Walgreens the following day, looking for Roli. It doesn't take long to find him. He's scanning the labels on bottles of shampoo that he's arranged on the bottom shelf.

"There you are," I say.

"This can't be good," he says, straightening. "What are you doing here?"

I shrug and hold up a box of Milk Duds. "Candy is two for a dollar today, according to your ad. I'm hoarding up for the trip to Saint Augustine."

"You didn't ride your bike all this way in this heat to get Milk Duds. What do you really want?"

I take a deep breath. "I need a ride to the football game tomorrow night."

He opens up a new carton and pulls out a bottle of Alberto VO5 shampoo, the kind Abuela likes because you can get it for a dollar. "So, what does that have to do with me?"

Everything, of course. Hannah is going to the game because she really wants to check out the cheer team. She thinks she might try out next year. (It's the glitter hairspray she can't resist.) Lena doesn't really want to go, but the Earth Club always collects recyclables at the event, so she's willing to take a bullet for the planet. Edna was all for going to the game since "it's the place to see and be seen."

"Sorry. I'm on until seven tomorrow, so you'd be late for kickoff," Roli says. "Ask Mami or Papi."

"I don't mind being a little late."

He crosses his arms and stares at me, waiting.

I can feel my cheeks lighting up. "It's complicated," I say.

Eyebrows.

"Complicated because Wilson is giving me one of his free tickets, and I'm not sure if that means I'm going to the game with him exactly."

He stares at me a second and then he shudders like the AC just got cranked up in here.

"Forget it. Middle school love stories are *not* my thing," he says.

"It's *not* a love story."

"Then why aren't you just asking Mami?"

I stare at my shoes. *Because what if they don't let me go or follow me there and embarrass me by watching me the whole night?* "Please, Roli. I'm just going to see a football game."

"With a boy."

"With a boy and all my other friends around. What can happen?"

He lets out a sigh. "What's his name again?"

"Wilson."

"Right. *Wilson.*"

"He has an extra free ticket for being Mr. Patchett's teacher's assistant, and he offered it to me. Really, when you think about it, *I* should have been the PE aide, so in a way, I'm getting what is due."

"When are you going to let that grudge go?" he says.

"Maybe when I go to the game." I take a step closer. "Mami and Papi are busy worrying about other stuff, Roli. Why make Papi's head explode over nothing?"

A customer walks by and we fall quiet. She's an older lady who asks for a specific formula of Clairol hair coloring. Roli hunts down the right box that he has arranged by shade and number, and hands it to her.

After she rounds the corner, he turns back to me.

"Fine. I'll take you and pick you up again after the game."

"Thanks." I start to feel giddy, like I've already eaten a whole box of Milk Duds even though I haven't even had one. "I owe you."

"You'd better be at the main gates when I get there because I'm not waiting on you. And I want this kid's number, too."

"Is that really necessary?"

He folds his arms. "You wanna go to the game or not, shorty?"

"Fine." I send him Wilson's contact.

"Cashier to front register two!" The manager's voice sounds tinny over the store PA system. Roli squeezes his eyes shut and takes a deep breath. He tosses the scanner into the box and adjusts his shirt. I can tell this job must kill him a little every day.

"Give me those," he says, snatching away the boxes of candy.

I trail him up to the front, where he cashes me out, paying for the whole stash himself. He hands me the plastic bag and receipt.

"Thanks, Roli," I say.

"Next in line," he calls over me.

———— ☀ ————

That night, I'm picking at my food, listening as Mami and Papi talk about Fabiola. Abuela has agreed to a trial run, but she is 100 percent unhappy about it.

"Did I overcook the chicken breast?" Mami asks. "I think the broiler is heating too fast again."

Papi just winks at me when Mami looks away. Honestly, you could crack a tooth on the black parts of this thing, but neither one of us is going to say so. We usually get enough good meals at Abuela's to balance out the fact that Mami is the worst cook in the family. But not tonight. Abuela left an awkward voice mail on Mami's phone saying that she was making soup and sandwiches for herself and Lolo, claiming it was too hot to cook.

"My stomach is just kind of queasy," I say. It's sort of true. I ate an entire jumbo box of Milk Duds after I got back from Walgreens. Mostly it was because I texted Wilson to tell him I could go. Then we had had a betting contest of how many times I could catch a tossed Milk Dud. I made thirty out of thirty-four tries, an 88 percent stat according to Wilson, who figured it out in his head.

"There's Alka-Seltzer in the botiquín," Mami says.

I put my plate on the counter and grab my soccer forms and final permission slips for Saint Augustine that

I left for Mami to sign on the counter. Everything looks in order.

"Thanks for this," I say. Then I fix my face into neutral the way I practiced earlier and say, "The first football game is tomorrow night, remember? My friends and I want to go. Roli said he can give me a ride. He'll pick me up and drop me off at the gate."

Mami's eyebrows shoot up. "Roli offered that?" she says. "That's generous."

"He didn't have anything else to do," I say quickly. "Plus, you've been busy with Lolo and stuff. It seemed easier."

Mami and Papi exchange looks, which I hate. It's like secret communication code, and you're never sure what they're saying.

Papi saws into the last of his chicken breast, thinking. "I don't know," he tells Mami. "Those games go late. They're mostly for the older kids, aren't they, Ana?"

Look calm, I tell myself. "It's over by ten o'clock. And we're all going . . . Hannah and them."

Papi takes a swig of water to wash down the chicken and doesn't answer.

"The eighth grade has a section where we sit together," I say, looking squarely at Mami now. "And Mrs. Kim is going."

That's the ticket.

I feel strange leaving out bits of information. But this isn't like I'm sneaking out in the middle of the night, right? Or is it? Does it make me a liar?

Mami nods and turns back to the sink. "I think it's all right, then. Stay with the group," she says.

CHAPTER 25

THE SUN IS JUST starting to set when Roli pulls up to the gates nearest our football fields. There are lots of stragglers hanging around the parking lot, mostly upper-school kids I don't know. Most people have already gone inside for kickoff, though.

"What are they waiting for?" I ask, looking around. "The game started." In soccer, I like to see the whole game, start to finish. You can tell a lot about who's on fire in the first few plays.

Roli glances around. "Don't worry about them." He slumps in his seat as we idle by the curb, like he doesn't want anybody to see him in his Walgreens shirt or something.

"I don't understand why you're so bothered. The teachers would probably make a big fuss over you, being an academic legend and all."

He looks at me. "I don't want questions about why I'm not at school."

I never thought Roli was one to concern himself with what other people think, since most people think he's just, um, freakishly advanced. But maybe even legends worry about how they look to other people. Maybe nobody is safe from that.

"You don't have to wait," I say.

"I'll be back at ten," Roli says. "Remember to meet me here when it's done. Keep your phone on."

His awkward feelings work in my favor because he doesn't stick around long enough to see who I go in with. He doesn't even wave as he drives off. The tinny sound of his Kia's motor sounds pathetic as he tries to speed away.

Wilson is leaning against the wall near the security guards, checking his phone for my text, like we said. According to his last message, everybody else went inside to save us good seats.

I type a fast message to Wilson.

Look up.

It dings in his phone just as I reach him.

"Hey," I say.

Wilson startles a second and then smiles.

"Hurry up, woadie," he says. "Thought you'd never get here."

We walk to the ticket booth, where he exchanges our passes for two wristbands. Inside the gates, everything feels a little exciting. It's our same old field, but at night, with the stadium lights blazing and all these people gathered, it sparkles and feels electric. There's a smell of hot dogs, popcorn, and bug repellent in the air as we squeeze through the throngs of people toward our seats in the muggy heat. I almost lose sight of Wilson ahead of me a couple of times, but then he looks back and grabs my hand so we can stay together and push through.

I won't lie. It's surprising, but kind of nice.

"Merci! Wilson!"

We drop hands at the same time, a little chill of embarrassment washing over me as I look up and spot Lena, Edna, and Hannah waving at us from the stands. Even from here you can see the blinding white of Edna's new kicks, purchased just for tonight's game. Anyway, they've saved a small space for me next to them. Darius is right behind them on the bleachers, where he signals a spot for Wilson.

I start to charge up the steps to reach them, but then I remember that it takes Wilson a little longer to climb stairs, especially narrow ones like these with no handrail at all. So, I slow down until we make it to our seats.

Wilson's knees are against my back when he sits, and I am still thinking about his fingers around mine. But nestled here with the rest of our friends, I feel a little more settled somehow. Lena has a book with her, as usual, her emergency tool kit for boredom. Hannah is already filming the dance team routine that's happening along the sideline, all glitter and spandex the way she likes. I open my camera phone, too, knowing it probably won't be the best for nighttime photos. Still, maybe I can get one or two good action shots that they'll use in the *Ram Gazette* or even in the yearbook. You never know. So, I look around for some practice shots.

The stands are packed with fans and, of course, the band is right next to us, sweating in uniforms that were clearly designed for people who live in colder states. The red color makes them look like British soldiers of some kind, especially with those fringy epaulets on their shoulders that the band director insists on. When they march, they have to keep a blank, serious expression on their faces, too.

Still, the Pox band across the field looks even sharper with their plumed hats and shiny instruments. Their school colors, navy blue and white, remind me of those cruise line workers you sometimes see down near the port in Fort Lauderdale. They just feel fancy compared to us. I noticed their buses are the luxury kind like the ones big stars use for road tours.

A piece of popcorn lands in my lap. Then another. And another.

When I turn around, I see Avery and Mackenzie a few rows back, along with other girls I don't know.

"Suárez!" Avery says, giggling.

I smile and wave. It feels good that she saw me and said hello in front of everyone, even if it was by throwing food at me. But I turn back around, trying not to look at Edna, who's giving me a quiet side-eye. I hope Avery doesn't come down here and ask me about being roommates on the trip in front of Hannah and Lena. I've been trying to think of some way that I can do something fun with Avery in Saint Augustine, maybe when I'm not with my regular crew. It's like two sets in a Venn diagram. I am the only common member.

Suddenly, there's a roar of the crowd, and everyone gets to their feet.

"What just happened?" I ask.

Lena, who's next to me, marks her page and pushes up her glasses as she stands up. "Touchdown."

"Ram Rummmmm-ble!" the senior on the loudspeaker calls out, all dramatic.

I'm not sure what that means at first, but the fans sure do. Everyone on our side starts stomping the metal bleachers. It's slow at first, and the sound echoes through the air like heavy monster steps. We get faster and faster until we sound like a thunderstorm with our feet pounding against the metal.

"Go, Rams!" everyone screams at the end.

Then the cheerleaders take over.

"Oh, this one is my favorite," Hannah whispers to me, her eyes dreamy on those sparkly kids below. She knows the cheer by heart, mouthing the words as she watches them tumble and clap.

Then the horn section next to us blasts our victory signal. *Brwaaaaaaap!* It's so loud that my eyes tear up.

I feel Wilson's knees again, so I turn around and he grins down at me, pretending to shake his eardrum from the blast. "Told ya," he says.

I turn back around. Every inch of me feels full and happy. I'm so glad I'm here and not home like a little kid with Mami and Papi.

By halftime I probably have about fifty shots on my phone camera. Most are grainy, but I've got a few of the tumblers midair, a couple of our mascot, Ronald Ram, whose identity is top secret, and a bunch of shots of people cheering.

At halftime, we're still up by seven. The band empties from beside us and lines up as they get ready to perform. It turns out, band is a thing for Wilson, more than the game, even. He comes from a long line of New Orleans marching-band people, he says. His cousins have marched in the Mardi Gras parade and everything.

"I'm going to drum in the band next year," Wilson says.

I try to picture him high-stepping with white spats buttoned over his shoes, his hands whirring into a blur as he marks a beat on a big drum attached in front of his body.

"That's barely an instrument, Wilson," Edna says, ever the buzzkiller. "Oh, there's Elise!" She sprints to catch up with our class president.

"What does she know?" Wilson says. "Besides, look at *that* dude on the triangle." He points to a freshman on the sidelines, where the pit dads are rolling out the xylophones. "How hard can it be?"

A soda can clatters down the bleachers near us.

Lena sighs and picks up the can to show Darius. "I guess we better go start with the cleanup. Halftime brings out the slobs in people."

"And I better go check in with my mom before she

sics the security guards on me," Hannah says, rolling her eyes. "I'll be back in a few."

That leaves me and Wilson next to a gigantic swath of empty band seats in the stands. If you put a spotlight on us, it couldn't be more awkward.

He must feel it too because he suddenly says, "You want a Coke?"

We wander down into the crowd near the concessions, where the line is enormous. Darius and Lena are gathering cans from the ground that missed the recycle bins. I notice a few of the middle school teachers hanging around at the end zone, giving side-eyes to a few seventh-graders who are pushing and being loud. It's like they've choreographed their own halftime show designed to have people notice them.

I watch the band show instead, all those strange side-steps that I can't imagine remembering.

But just as Wilson gets to the front of the line, I see Avery again. She's not waiting for food like we are, or even with Mackenzie or any of the other girls on our soccer team. She's standing near the base of the bleachers. I move out of line to get a better look, maybe call out to her, or even pick up one of these pieces of popcorn from the ground and toss one at her to say hi like before. It might be the perfect time to tell her I can't room with her in Saint

Augustine, maybe see if there's something she wants to do while we're there instead.

It's kind of hard to see her, but I manage to find a spot where the speakers and trash cans don't block my view. Then I freeze.

Avery is not by herself. Clayton is with her. They're standing close and his hands are around her waist.

"Here," Wilson says, handing me a cold drink. "They just had a Sprite left so I got the last one to split. Try not to backwash."

I don't answer, so he follows my gaze, and then his eyes get a little buggy.

Avery and Clayton have started kissing, like, *for real.*

Wilson takes a step back like he's just discovered a land mine.

"But, um, you know, maybe we should ask them to check the coolers again for Cokes, just in case they're keeping some aside for their friends. Concession stand workers are shady, woadie. Can't trust them for a second."

"Great idea!" I say, my face flaming as we bolt back to the line.

The booster volunteer who's serving customers is not amused when Wilson demands a thorough recheck and inventory of the soda coolers, but even her ugly look is better than the alternative, I guess.

When we climb back to our spot a few minutes later, Hannah and Edna are already there. Soon enough, everybody fills in around us again, except for Avery, who doesn't come back to her seat for a long time. There's another big roar from the crowd as our team jogs back out on the field for the second half.

By the end of the night, our team scores twice more. Each time we stand up to do the Ram Rumble, I stomp hard and woot at the top of my lungs. But when I sit back down, giddy, I can't help but think of Avery and Clayton.

I keep glancing back at her and then at the space between the slats at my feet. I wonder, what else goes on in all those hidden places? And why have I never noticed before?

CHAPTER 26

SHOULD I KISS Wilson one day? I'm wondering as I let myself into Abuela's mudroom early the next morning. Now that Tía gives Saturday-morning classes at her dance studio, we take turns doing Lolo and Abuela's stuff on the weekends. Guess who the laundry attendant is today? Moi.

I stifle a yawn and wipe the grit from my eyes. I barely slept after the game, not only because I was hyped on sugar, but because my mind kept swirling on this kissing idea, compliments of Avery and Clayton's lip-lock, which I just can't unsee.

I stuff Abuela's laundry inside the tub, hoping the machine starts this time. It's ancient and Papi always has to fix it, but Abuela won't let us get rid of it. She claims that new washers are unnecessarily complicated and break right away by design.

"Who wants all those silly settings?" she says. "I'm not manning a rocket ship."

And forget about the dryer. It works just fine, but Abuela doesn't like us to use it on her stuff, not even for towels. That means I have to drag a basket of wet clothes to the line and pin them. She claims it's healthier, better for the earth, and that it makes the clothes smells nice. But I say everything dries so stiff that it feels like bark on your skin. I don't know how Lolo can even bend his knees in his clean pants.

But whatever. I am not here to make my thoughts known.

Not thoughts about laundry and not thoughts about kissing.

I pour in the detergent and turn the knob to COLOR. Down the hall, I can hear Abuela working with Lolo in the bathroom. I can tell from the tone of her muffled voice that Lolo isn't keen on his shower today. I stay very still and pay attention now, wondering whether I might have to run to get Mami for help. Will he grab her or push her away? Abuela might fall and be hurt. But then their voices quiet and I let out my breath. Miss Fabiola is coming to meet us tomorrow. At least there's that. Maybe the extra help will make things easier.

The washer starts its squeaky motion as the agitator twists back and forth. A faint scent of urine rises from the machine, maybe from Lolo's pajamas or underwear. The odor makes me queasy, and almost angry, too. It's not Lolo's fault that he's forgetting things, like getting to the bathroom in time. I know I shouldn't be mad at him for it.

But sometimes I am.

I'm mad about his bus and about how he forgets who I am. I'm mad that he's not taking care of us anymore.

Which makes me wonder what Abuela thinks about all this.

Lolo used to tend her garden and cut her the prettiest flowers from the yard. They'd have coffee together on their porch, and watch telenovelas on their recliners at night, even though Lolo said those shows were silly. Sometimes, they'd dance. Long ago, they probably kissed, too.

None of those things have been happening lately.

So, what does she love about him now?

Suds start forming, so I close the lid and wait to make sure the clothes don't all end up on one side. Last time it got unbalanced that way, the whole machine shimmied across the floor like it was possessed by a demonio. Abuela thought someone was trying to bang down her door.

I put my cheek against the lid and close my eyes, tired and listening for the sound of balance. Then I start thinking my sleepy thoughts again.

Will Wilson and I kiss? He's my friend, but I like holding his hand. And it's not like I'm a baby anymore.

I grab my phone and stare at the keypad. *Wilson, let's kiss.*

What would he do if I ever sent him such a text? Probably run from the room screaming, I, decide. Or else, he'd laugh, thinking it was a big joke.

So, I decide to think of another text I should send instead, one that is just as scary somehow. It's to Avery because I've put off turning down rooming with her long enough. I try typing a message several times, but I delete each version.

It's embarrassing to think about talking to her in person, especially after I watched her smooch Clayton, not that I did it on purpose or anything. But I know I have to—and soon.

Next week, I decide.

CHAPTER 27

ABUELA COMES IN FROM the living room in a huff. "All these strangers showing up in our family all of a sudden," she mutters. "¿Quién ha visto eso?"

She puts down the tray she used to serve the coffee to Miss Fabiola, but she doesn't go back out to the living room.

Tía keeps her eyes on the coupon magazine from inside the Sunday newspaper and pretends not to hear. I can see her jaw twitch, though. She's gritting her teeth like her dentist told her not to.

Out in the living room, Mami and Papi are still chatting with Miss Fabiola, who came to meet Lolo and Abuela for the first time. She's a short lady with an island accent, and she's sort of dressed up, like she just came from church.

Abuela sucks her teeth, as if she's seeing something shocking. "I should have never agreed to this," she mutters. "Never. Mira pa'esto."

I follow her gaze out toward the living room, where Miss Fabiola is helping Lolo put on his socks and shoes, even though he usually stays in his house slippers on Sundays.

"Shh, Mamá," Tía says. "Give her a chance, will you?"

"A chance to do what exactly? Drive me crazy?"

Tía puts down the paper. "How can she be annoying you already, Mamá? She's just saying hello."

Abuela glares. "She's putting black socks on the man. Those are only for his dress shoes. Where does she think she's going with my husband? Dancing?"

This is looking worse every second. I know Abuela. A sock infraction is strike one. At this rate, Miss Fabiola might be gone before Lolo can grow back his five-o'clock shadow.

"She'll learn the dressing routines," Tía whispers. "It just takes a little time. Besides, he doesn't really care about what socks he wears."

Abuela says, "Well, I care. Or isn't that important around here anymore?"

Tía sighs.

Luckily, the back door opens just then, and our escape

for Sunday appears. Simón is here, and he's got the twins, who were playing outside, trailing him. He's off today, so we're finally going bowling with the free pass Papi gave him.

"Buenos días, Doña Teresita." He always greets Abuela first. "How are you today, señora?"

Abuela manages a smile even though she's still grumpy. "¿Qué tal, Simón?"

"Bien, gracias." Then he turns to Tía and says, "My two tutors here are ready to teach me to play boliche."

"Bolos," Tomás says. "I already told you."

Simón speaks Spanish like we do, but we sometimes have different words for the same thing. Boliche around here is that soft roast Abuela cooks in her pressure cooker.

Tía stands up and grabs her purse, smiling. I've never seen her look so relieved to see him. She kisses Abuela on the way out.

"I'll be back soon to hear all about how it went," she says, "but please give Ana's lady a chance. I beg of you."

Vicente, Simón's brother, is working the grill at the bowling alley today, like he does every weekend, making burgers and serving curly french fries in plastic baskets. Too bad we're not getting any of what he's cooking. Our free coupon is only good for nachos and drinks. Still, Vicente does his best to load up our plastic basket with extra cheese from his dispenser.

"Thanks," I tell him.

"The spicy peppers are on the left," he says, remembering that I hate them. He adjusts his paper hat and hairnet, which, I have to say, is not his best look. Still, it doesn't stop two older girls at the other side of the counter from ogling him as he gathers napkins and straws for us. When he signals that he'll be right there, they practically convulse in giggles.

I eye the hot dogs sizzling on the roller one last time. "Have you ever considered innovation on the menu?" I ask him. "For a small percentage of sales, I'd be willing to share my recipe for Dog Crunchers. It's a proven winner."

He grins. "Maybe one day when I open my own restaurant." Then he takes the coupon from Simón to ring us out.

"I see you're living it up today, hermano," he says.

"A guy can rest every once in a while," Simón tells him. "Do you get a break here or what?"

Vicente glances beyond us to the manager, who's renting out shoes to a big birthday party group. "Not for a while. We've got a party coming in. But don't worry, I'll watch you make a fool of yourself from here."

He points at a rack of bowling balls near the air hockey

table where the twins are playing without the power on since they don't have tokens. "The lighter ones for the little guys are over there," he tells me. "You better grab a couple before the birthday kids swarm."

And then he walks off to help his smitten customers.

Obviously, there wasn't a lot of bowling going on in El Salvador when Simón was a kid.

It doesn't take long to find out that he's a terrible bowler, even worse than Tía, who has an unbreakable habit of releasing balls down the wrong lane—even backward, like she did on her first throw. Had I known he'd be such a wreck, too, I would have insisted on bumpers when we got here.

Simón watches miserably as his ball drops into the gutter yet again. Five frames in and he's still scoreless.

"The problem is my fingers don't fit in the holes right. Maybe I should use my feet?"

"Uh. Not unless you want busted toes."

"I guess I'll try another ball then," he says as the lane clears his pins.

It's the sixth one he's tried so far.

"You're up, Axel," I say.

The twins are barely paying attention to the game. Between turns, they've been running to the arcade alcove to watch the older kids play video games or else, like now, hogging all the nachos at the table, picking around for the red chips like vultures.

Axel gets up, licking his fingers in a way that would horrify Abuela.

"Don't eat them all," he warns Tomás.

He wipes his greasy hands on his shorts and finds his blue sparkle ball in the carousel. It's a six-pounder, which shouldn't have that much power, but in Axel's athletic hand it might as well be a guided missile for the pins.

"Watch him," I whisper to Simón. "He uses the arrows on the floor to aim at the head pin."

Axel holds the ball up to his eyes and then draws his skinny arm back as he approaches. He leans forward and releases, his right leg swinging behind him like a pint-size pro as he finishes. The ball barely makes a sound as it rotates dead center down the lane and crashes into the pins. Only one is left standing. On his next throw, he knocks that one down without any trouble. A group of older ladies bowling next to us starts clapping. They're wearing matching shirts that say STRIKE IT RICH.

"You can play on our team whenever you want, young man," one of them tells him.

Axel shrugs and goes back to his chips.

Tía cracks up as Simón shakes his head, shocked.

"You find my suffering funny?" Simón asks. "And here I was thinking you were a kind woman."

She gives him a sympathetic look and then, making him blush, a kiss on the cheek to match the one she planted on Axel as he went by. I can tell that she's happy today, sitting here with Simón and us, even in rental shoes that, in concept alone, gross her out. Really, I don't think either one of them cares that they stink mucho, mucho, mucho at this game. They mostly just seem to be enjoying the air-conditioning, the fancy lights, and each other. And the truth is, I'm pretty happy, too. It feels good to be away from Abuela and Lolo for a little while, even though I love them. It's a relief not to hear Abuela complain about Fabiola or hear Mami sigh or see Papi rub his temples as they try to help.

"Tomás, you're up," I say.

He saunters over. "We're gonna have our birthday here," Tomás says.

When I turn to look, I see that his eyes are glued on the party room near us, where Vicente is delivering three large pizzas on metal stands. Axel turns around and stares, too. You can see the gigantic birthday cake through the glass doors and hear everyone singing to the girl wearing a cardboard tiara. There must be twenty kids in there, and boxed presents are piled high, not to mention all the gift

234

cards she'll probably get, too. She must have invited her whole class the way I know some kids do.

Dream on, Tomás, I think to myself. Their birthday is in a little over a month, but that's not how our family celebrates birthdays. Usually, it's just our family in the yard or, sometimes, we go to the park shelter where there's a playground and a grill. We get one main present and then gifts the grown-ups think we need, like clothes. Abuela bakes the cake.

"Muchacho," Tía says, "it costs twenty dollars for every kid in there."

"So?"

"So skip count by twenty for each person and you'll see how much that costs."

Axel gets to it. "Four hundred," he says. If Roli were here, he'd be teary with pride.

"See? We can't afford that! We're going to celebrate at home, like we always do. Remember? You can ask Abuela for a chocolate cake this year."

But Tomás looks at her and crosses his arms. "Papi will give us the party, then," he says, stubbornly. "He's got a fat wallet."

Where do they get this stuff? I can't tell if he's being mean or saying what he thinks or else just repeating some dumb line he's picked up somewhere. How can you tell the difference with a second-grader? Really, how can you tell with anyone? I can barely tell the difference when I blurt something out myself. Like the time I was mad at Mami for making me study and I told her that Tía was a more fun mom.

"Atrevido," Tía says. "No one is talking about people's wallets."

"But yours is too skinny," Tomás says.

"And nobody is asking anybody for a bowling party, either," Tía adds.

"I'm going to call him—" Axel starts. He doesn't notice the look on Tía's face, I guess, or how Simón squeezes her hand.

"No one," she says, cold and firm. "We're going to enjoy bowling today and that's it, OK? Now, whose turn is it? These nasty shoes are starting to make my feet itch."

I look at the scoreboard and the glittery lights along the lane, suddenly feeling bad for Tía. She doesn't look like she's having fun anymore. And Simón looks like he's been kicked to the curb. He doesn't have bank, for sure, so what's he going to say?

"Go, Tomás," I say. "You're up."

He's sulking, but he steps forward. He picks up his red swirled ball and zeroes in on the center triangle, releasing it the same way Axel did. I don't even have to watch to know what's going to happen.

Crash! There's an explosion at the end of the throw. A strike.

Tomás raises his fist in victory. You just have to hit the right spot to make everything wobble and collapse, I guess. Sometimes even a little kid can do that.

CHAPTER 28

MISS FABIOLA'S CAR is in Abuela's driveway this morning. Papi says it's a miracle Abuela hasn't fired her—or that Miss Fabiola hasn't quit. Not that it's been easy. It's only been two days, but Abuela keeps calling her That Lady Fabiola. And she keeps adding to a full report of Things That Have to Change to anyone who'll listen.

Exhibit A: Abuela walks over to our house as Mami and I are trying to leave for school. Mami has misplaced her phone again. If she doesn't find it soon, I'm going to need a late pass. She's rummaging under dish towels and the newspaper, getting more frustrated by the second.

"Good. You're still here," Abuela says as she lets herself in the back door.

I look at her in surprise. She's in capris and sneakers, her go-to outfit for being out and about.

"Where are you going so early?" I ask her.

She looks down at herself and primps her shirt a bit.

"Well, since That Lady Fabiola is now in charge of Lolo's morning routine, I've decided I can walk the twins to school again. I'll be getting some exercise, as some people are always recommending." She motions with her eyes to Mami.

"And it's an excellent idea," Mami says absently. She searches in the pockets of her scrubs again.

"Ana, please tell That Lady Fabiola that Lolo uses the kiwi-lime shampoo in the green bottle. She used mine today—the one for extra body. It makes his hair too bulky."

"I'm sure if you mention it, she'd be happy to do as you ask," Mami says. "Merci, go check my nightstand."

"I already did, remember?"

"The bathroom, then."

Abuela seems not to notice we're busy. "And tell That Lady Fabiola that I don't like her putting cologne on him unless we're going to the doctor. She should use the body splash. It's cheaper. We're not made of money."

Mami looks up for a second and then sighs. "Merci, go look on the hall table."

But just then, she spots her phone under her stack of

folders. "Aha! Never mind. There it is. Let's get a move on."

"You won't forget to tell her?" Abuela says as we start heading out the door. "About the cologne? Me da pena decirle."

"Teresita," Mami says, turning. "I truly think it would be better if you told her yourself. Good communication is going to be important, after all. Fabiola is very receptive and wants to help."

She gives Abuela a kiss on the cheek, and then we're gone.

Some days are just upside down, and this is one of them. I made it to homeroom with three seconds to spare, so that was good. But after second period, Hannah rushed over to me at our lockers. "News flash," she said. "The civics homework is going to count as a pop quiz today! I hope you did it."

I can't even find mine.

I look again in my binder to make sure I didn't miss it somehow, but no. It's just not there, and I know for a fact that I worked on those questions, at least the first few. I retrace my steps mentally, the way Mami did for her phone. That's when I remember that I was doing my homework during my TA period in guidance yesterday. I must have left it behind or, worse, maybe it got blown to the floor and thrown away! I hope this doesn't mean I'll have to dumpster dive. But I totally would in this case. A lousy grade right before the start of soccer clinics is a dangerous situation. Mami might not let me go.

"Can I have a pass?" I ask Ms. Tibbetts. "I left something important down in the guidance office."

She checks the clock. There's five minutes to the bell. "It wouldn't be civics homework, would it?" she mutters. Everyone has been panicking.

I nod.

"Have you finished your classwork?"

"It's in your Dropbox."

She hands over the pass. "No need to come back. Just go to your next class when you're done."

I hurry to the administration building, cutting across the grass path. It's muggy outside, and the darkening clouds are low, like the sky wants to squash us. It's a relief when I get back inside the air-conditioned halls.

The reception area in guidance is empty when I arrive, and Mrs. Wilkinson's door is closed. A sign hanging from the knob reads GROUP IN SESSION. DO NOT DISTURB.

So, I tiptoe around quietly and check my work area. Thankfully, I find my homework under the desk, a little crumpled, but basically safe and sound. I only have two more questions left to answer, which I can probably do next hour or at lunch since I don't have civics until the end of the day. Maybe Hannah can help, if I get stuck.

I'm about to leave when something else catches my eye. It's the giant grid of sticky notes on the empty wall near Mrs. Wilkinson's door. It's marked SAINT AUGUSTINE. It's arranged in two rows to look like the hotel floorplan, one row for each floor. There's really no order to it except that the boys are on the third floor and the chaperones' rooms are near every staircase and elevator, like guards.

I knew Mrs. Wilkinson was building the roommate plan as kids turned in their research reports and deposits, but I guess things are getting to the final stages. I brought mine in today, and she's already added the yellow note with my name, along with Lena, Hannah and Edna's names. When I look closely, though, I see a question mark by my name.

Then I see another question mark on the note next to ours. My name appears again, only this time with the soccer girls.

Oh no. Avery must have turned her sheet and roommate requests, too.

Suddenly, Mrs. Wilkinson's door swings open, and a group of kids files out.

"Good sharing today," she tells them. "See you next time."

I press myself against the wall to get out of the way, but then I spot Edna. I couldn't be more shocked to see her in this bunch. *She* is learning to cope with something in a support group? It's hard to believe, since it's usually the rest of the world who needs help coping with Edna.

I stand here with my worksheet, gawking at her as the rest of the kids disperse. I'm dying to ask her what the meeting was about, but the question stays on the tip of my tongue. *Nosy. Buttinsky.* I can practically hear Mami's voice clawing out of my conscience to throttle me.

Besides, Edna stops to stare back at me with an expression that says that she'd like to eat my face off.

"What?" I say.

Her eyes narrow and travel to the grid. "Looks like you're buddies with Avery and them after all."

"Oh, hello, Merci," Mrs. Wilkinson says when she sees me. "What brings you by so early? You're not due to work until later."

All I can do is hold up my worksheet. "I . . . I left this here by mistake yesterday."

"Well, you only have a minute or two to get to class before the bell," she says. "Don't dally."

She walks Edna and me out to the hall. My class-room is in the other direction, but I trail after Edna as she stalks off.

"I know what you're thinking," I say, trying to keep up. "But it's a mistake. I didn't tell Avery I was rooming with her."

"Well, she seems to think different," Edna says. "How did she get that idea, Merci? It wasn't by you saying, *I'm already rooming with my friends.*"

It's Awkward City the whole way. We hurry past the library, moving me farther and farther from my next class. I'll never make it in time.

"I don't know. But I'll fix it. Just please don't say anything to Hannah and Lena."

She stops and stares at me head on. "Why not? They should know if they're about to be left flat."

"But they're not! Come on, Edna. It's just a mix-up."

"Don't try to play it cool, Merci. That's a bunch of bull and you know it," she says.

And with that, she turns on her heels and leaves me standing there.

The bell rings for the change of classes. I jog back in the right direction, trying to decide how to get to Hannah and Lena fast. I can't text out here in the open without the risk of having my phone confiscated. Miss McDaniels has eyes everywhere.

When I reach the glass doors to cut across the grass toward the middle school building, I pause. It's grown very dark outside, almost like night. Thunder rumbles in the distance, and while there's no still no lightning, a steady rain has already started to ping against the fieldstone like gunfire. We're not supposed to be outside when it's storming. That's the rule. We're supposed to go around the long way, inside the buildings to stay safe.

I open the door anyway. It's the fast way. A draft shoots past me like a hurricane. Everything feels a little dangerous outside. The palm fronds are already battered flags in the wind. My plaid skirt flaps wildly and lifts enough to show the shorts I always wear underneath. I grab at it uselessly as I run.

Nature takes its revenge on me. The rain is sharp against my skin as the water douses me. By the time I reach the building, the warning bell has already rung. My blazer is soaked, my loafers are squeaking, and my hair clings in soggy tendrils to my head. People jostle around me, a few staring at the drowned mess in the hall.

I take a detour to the bathroom to dry off and try to text Hannah and Lena before Edna gets to them.

But I'm too late. I'm just reaching for a paper towel to wring my hair when Hannah's group text arrives.

> WTH? Are you rooming with us or not, Merci? Choose.

245

CHAPTER 29

I'VE NEVER UNDERSTOOD kids who completely avoid the lunchroom.

Until today.

I seriously consider eating my sandwich in the library stacks instead of facing the music with Hannah, Lena, and Edna.

Unfortunately, Mr. Engle closed the library for special testing this period, so I have no choice but to go down to the dining hall. I'm shivering, still damp and feeling clammy in the AC. As soon as I step inside the cafeteria, I know there's going to be trouble. They're huddled at our table, whispering—which they stop as soon as I walk up. Hannah's face is a stone. Lena pushes up her glasses worriedly. And Edna's arms are crossed.

"I can explain," I say.

"Uh-huh," Edna says.

I sit down as Lena gives her a pleading look. "It's only fair to hear her out."

"Avery asked me a couple of weeks ago," I say, "and I didn't have the chance to tell her I'd already agreed to room with you. I guess she assumed I'd say yes to her offer and put my name on her list without checking with me."

"You didn't have a chance?" Hannah repeats in surprise. "Don't you have language arts and homeroom with her, like, every single day?"

"I don't know, Hannah. I got tongue-tied."

Edna snorts and rolls her eyes. "Because Avery Sanders is so great?"

"Because all the eighth-grade soccer girls are rooming together, and I felt sort of weird saying no."

The truth of it sits there with us like a heavy weight.

"So, what are you saying, Merci?" Lena says. "Do you mean that you might want to room with them instead of us?"

She picks at the edge of her journal as she waits for me to answer. My eye starts to flutter. "No. It was just . . . nice to be asked."

"Nicer, you mean, than when *we* asked you?" Hannah asks.

Lena pushes up her glasses again. "You could have at least told us."

"Look, I'm sorry this ever happened. I want us to have a fun trip in Saint Augustine like we planned. I promise I'm going to fix it."

Edna leans forward and points at me with a ranch-dipped carrot stick. "Then prove it. Avery's right over there. Go tell her you're rooming with us."

I glance across the lunchroom. Avery is laughing with the other girls at her table, not a care in the world, as usual.

"I'll text her."

But I can see from their faces that they don't really believe me. Not even Lena comes to my rescue.

Edna crosses her arms. "What's so hard about telling her right now, so we can see it?"

Hannah nods slowly. Lena shrugs. It's three on one.

"Fine," I say.

I take a deep breath and walk over to Avery's table in my squeaky shoes. I've never been so glad to be mostly invisible, though. Nobody there seems to notice that I'm approaching. In fact, I have to stand there for a second, waiting.

Finally Avery looks up. "Oh, hey, Merci."

"Hi," I say.

A few of the girls turn my way, too, but nobody asks me to sit.

I shift on my feet and glance back over my shoulder to see Edna, Hannah, and Lena watching my every move. "So, I saw the roommate grid in guidance today."

"Oh yeah! I sent it in this morning."

"It's going to be a blast!" Mackenzie adds.

"The thing is, I can't room with you guys. I already promised Hannah, Lena, and Edna before you asked."

Avery's pretty eyes stay fixed on me.

Crickets.

"Sorry," I stammer. "I should have said something earlier. But . . . maybe we can hang out on the trip? Do you like pirates? You can come with us to the museum on our free day."

Avery's eyes go to Mackenzie, and I don't know, it feels like they're barely holding back a smirk. Maybe they think pirates are dumb. Or maybe that I'm dumb or a jerk or whatever. I wonder if they will talk about me with the others after this.

But she just shrugs. "I'll let you know," she says.

"I'm really sorry."

She shrugs and turns back to her friends.

I try to be logical. She doesn't look upset. Plus, lots of people want to be Avery's friend. She's not going to have any trouble finding someone who wants the chance to take my spot. By the end of lunch, she'll probably already have my replacement. Taking my finger out of a glass of water would probably leave a longer-lasting hole.

Still, I feel sick, like I've lost something, maybe a pass into Avery's circle that lasts beyond soccer season.

I walk back to my table feeling like a loser instead of the faithful friend I'm supposed to be.

"It's settled then," Hannah says, heaving a sigh. "Thanks."

I nod but don't meet her eyes. My stomach is in knots as I gather my things and push in my chair. I hope they don't see how my hands are still shaking.

"Where are you going?" Lena says. "Aren't you going to eat?"

"I've got civics homework to do," I say over my shoulder as I head out. "Later."

Mrs. Wilkinson lets me hang out at my desk in the guidance office since my TA period follows lunch anyway. Even though I'm not hungry anymore, I nibble a little of my sawdust sandwich and spend the time finishing up my answers for civics. Mrs. Wilkinson doesn't chat me up the way she usually does, thank goodness, because she's busy.

She's been sitting on one of the beanbags in her office, organizing huge stacks of T-shirts for the trip by homeroom. I'm supposed to help Mr. Vong deliver them with his hand truck when she's through. I'm not in the mood, though, which is saying something. I usually love to work with maintenance and moving equipment. Not even that feels fun right now.

I run some copies for her that she left in my in-box and then set them inside on her desk. I pause by the grid on the outside wall on my way back to the reception area, my eyes glued to the square with Avery's room. My stomach twists all over again.

"Can I borrow a marker?" I ask. "I see a mistake on my room assignment."

Miss Wilkinson glances up at me as she tosses three more shirts in a box.

"Oh yes, I spotted that discrepancy, too, and made a note to ask you about it."

I take a marker from her pencil cup—a pink one that smells like watermelon—and dash out my name from Avery's Post-it.

"I let Avery know already," I explain. "She forgot that I was rooming with Edna, Lena, and Hannah."

She studies my face, which suddenly feels a little warm

from the white lie. "Well, I'm sure it was a hard choice. Avery will be disappointed. You were teammates from last year, weren't you? I assumed you were friends."

For a second, I don't know what to say. Is *sort of friends* an answer?

"We like each other just fine. But . . . it's just complicated."

"What is?"

I turn to her as she counts out another six shirts for a new box. I can't even begin to explain. "Friends. Choosing groups. This whole board, actually."

"Oh, *that*," she says, chuckling. "You mean the wonderful world of human relationships."

I put back the marker and help myself to a chocolate. "I don't see what's so wonderful," I mutter, flopping down on the beanbag chair opposite hers.

"I see." Mrs. Wilkinson says. "Would you like to discuss anything about that?"

I stare up at the ceiling, suddenly feeling tired, like I could nap right here. Why do adults always want to pry?

"No thanks," I say. "I've got stuff to do. Mr. Vong is going to want to pick up the recycling." The bin near the copier is overflowing with paper. I'm supposed to keep things tidy for him so he can empty it in the large receptacles behind the cafeteria once a week. Unfortunately, with the hall breeze, it's a disaster out here. Papers have scattered everywhere.

"Very true," she says. "Thank you for staying on top of things."

I get up and head to the copier area to organize the mess. For once, I don't mind. At least this chaos is a whole lot easier than dealing with friends.

CHAPTER 30

I LOVE SOCCER CLINIC.

We meet on the pitch after school in our gym shorts and sneakers, which feels like a release from prison after a day in a blazer and loafers. I don't even care that the sun is still blazing at this hour. I've piled my curls into a teeny puff on top of my head and rolled my T-shirt sleeves tight into the shoulders. My shin guards are already making me sweat, and I notice I'll need new laces on my old cleats since these are caked with mud. I can't help but notice Avery's new Nike Mercurial Superfly 8 Elites, which have those knit ankle collars. Mackenzie has the same ones. They bought them for soccer camp, claiming that they're engineered to help you turn better. Everyone at clinic likes them. "I'm obsessed," Lindsey said when she saw them. None of them has said a word about me choosing not to room with them, but I still feel a little prickly around them.

Coach splits us into groups today at clinic. We're arranged in four separate lines to practice our ball control by maneuvering around the cones that Wilson set up earlier.

Coach watches and scores us as we work. If you ask me, you can already tell which of these kids will not make the team. A few are huffing and puffing as they make their way along the zigzag course. Some lose the ball around turns or trip over it and face-plant. And then there are the ones who just give up.

Robin Farmer isn't bad, though, especially for a sixth-grader. She clears the course with no trouble. And when we scrimmage near the end of clinic, you can really see her talent.

Despite her skinny legs, she's lightning fast, streaking along in those bright green cleats, her braids whipping like snakes. She hits the ball cleanly on her laces when she shoots, too. Her only trouble is that she wants to shine a little too much. She's a ball hog and doesn't listen when Avery yells out, "Back and left," to signal that she's open.

Coach marks something on their clipboard and calls for subs. "Suárez, you're up." Then they point at Robin. "You, Farmer, stay in."

Avery jogs over and tosses me her pinny.

"Play extra tough," she tells me, arching her brow. "That little kid needs to be schooled."

I look at her cautiously and glance out at Robin, who's waiting on the field, showing off some fancy foot skills on her own. Usually "schooling" someone means it's going to get crazy physical, mostly for the sake of knocking them down a few pegs.

But why? Robin can definitely play. She's got quick feet and good aim. She's tenacious, too. Besides, I already know I'm bigger and more experienced. My legs are longer, and I'll be able to outrun her almost every time. What do I have to prove?

I don't argue with Avery, though. Instead, I jog out and listen for Coach to blow their whistle.

At first Robin holds her own. But sure enough, Mackenzie and I pull plays from last year. I steal the ball away in two moves and pass it down to her so she can score a nice shot that sinks in on the left. A few minutes later, we do it again like we're on instant replay.

By the time Coach blows the whistle again, Robin looks frustrated enough to cry.

"Same time tomorrow, folks," Coach says. "Eighth-graders, you're on cleanup."

Moans.

I start to gather the pinnies while Avery heads out on the pitch to pick up cones and balls. Before she goes, though, she looks at Robin and makes a little dig.

"Tough out there, huh?"

The words aren't nasty, but something about the way Avery says it feels cold.

"Why don't you help me box these up?" I tell Robin as Avery moves out of earshot.

"You guys manned me like that on purpose in front of Coach," Robin says. "Now she's going to think I can't play."

"First of all, Coach uses they as a pronoun. Second, they're not stupid. They can see you're no joke. And third, why did you keep hogging the ball? You had people to pass to. Use them."

She gives me a scowl.

"You have to work with your team, Robin," I tell her. "Grabbing the spotlight isn't going to help us win. Did you notice that both times I took the ball from you, I passed it to Mackenzie to score? Besides, if you're a sixth-grader who wants to start, you better learn how to take heat. The Pox won't go any easier on you for sure."

"You're lucky I was tired," she says.

"You think so, huh?" But I smile, so she knows it's all OK. I think back to being in sixth grade, how scary eighth-graders seemed. "Look, you didn't do so bad." And since she still seems unconvinced, I add, "*Really*. There aren't many kids from your grade who could have held their own like you did."

Coach's whistle makes us look up. They're signaling for Robin to join them at the gym doors. Robin looks at me, worried for a second.

"You'll be fine, but here's some advice, Robin. Be willing to learn something," I say.

And with that, she takes off.

Just then, Avery calls to me from behind. She's dragging back the bag of balls on her shoulder. Mackenzie is still out in the field gathering cones. I stick the last of the pinnies in the box and jog back to help her drag the heavy net along.

"You think we were too hard on that kid?" I ask her. "I mean, she's new." Robin is far ahead by now, already at the gym doors talking to Coach Cameron.

But Avery is barely listening. She stops walking and scans the far fields for the lacrosse team. "Who cares? She'll get over it."

Will she? When someone hassles me, even with little things sometimes, I always remember.

I look back toward the gym. Maybe Coach Cameron is telling Robin the same thing I did. "Help each other." That was the mantra our first year.

I stay quiet as we walk along. I sneak glances at Avery, wondering if she's mad about Saint Augustine. Maybe not. Maybe she said "Who cares?" about whether I was going to be in her room, too.

Her phone buzzes, so she drops her side of the net to check the message. Her eyes light up as she types a fast response. It has to be Clayton.

"Take this the rest of the way, will you, please? I've gotta go. Lacrosse practice is over."

She doesn't even wait for my answer. She just flashes me one of her big smiles and runs off to catch Clayton.

I stuff the box of pinnies into the ball net so I can drag the whole thing the rest of the way on my own like some sort of hot-weather Santa dragging along his gifts. I manage to get it back to the gym, but it's not easy all on my own.

Coach is still there by the door, sipping on a Gatorade as I arrive. I'm sweating and out of breath. Avery is already almost out of sight, but Coach seems to have her in their sights.

"That Farmer kid is pretty good," I say as I drop the net inside the door.

Coach nods, still watching Avery.

"Thank you, Suárez," they say, holding the door open for me. "Good work today."

CHAPTER 31

CAN A DAD NOT like his own kids? I've never even thought of the possibility, but why not? I've got plenty of friends who don't like their parents, so maybe the dirty secret is that it can happen the other way, too.

It's early Saturday morning, and Marco and Veronica have stopped by on their way out of town. I guess the twins' constant phone calls finally wore them down.

Veronica sits in Tía's part of the yard and plays a game on her phone. Maybe she's not a morning person, or maybe she's checking messages. I don't dare walk over to check. Whatever it is, it's more interesting to her than the twins.

Anyway, they are going to Orlando, Marco explained. Just stopping by for a few minutes.

"Are you going to ride Thunder Mountain?" Tomás asks. Their friends have told them stories.

"Or go to Diagon Alley?" Axel asks, remembering the book Roli's been reading to them.

"No, we're not going to theme parks," he says. "We're going to a resort for some R and R."

"What's that?" Tomás asks.

"Rest and relaxation," Marco says, laughing. "Maybe one day you'll come along."

Veronica glances up, worried.

"One day," Marco repeats.

I wonder if the twins' telepathy is working right now. Tomás has a puss on his face and Axel is not much better. Can they tell when someone likes them and when someone is just sort of pretending? Usually, I can, especially with adults. It's something in the smile, sort of plastic. Something like Marco's face right now.

"Tía," I whisper. She's out here with me on the patio, trying to sort out a paperwork mix-up for the studio. She's pretending not to listen, too. It's hard, though. Voices carry, even though we're trying to stay out of the way. "Do you think he means that?"

She puts a finger to her lips to quiet me.

I look over at them worriedly. Marco is jiggling his keys, eager for his trip.

"I think he's lying," I say.

She leans toward me. "Not everyone will be able to give you what you want from them, Merci," Tía whispers. "I found that out a long time ago."

"Well, what kind of dad is that, then?"

"The kind they have, mi vida. We can't change our parents. Not who they are and not who they become. Axel and Tomás will have to decide what they think about him on their own."

By the afternoon, the yard is finally quiet. Marco and Veronica are gone, and Tía took the boys to the studio with her.

"Merci, niña, ven acá."

Lolo's voice surprises me, and, for a second, I think I've imagined it. It's thinner and sounds far away, but the sound of my name is the same, the way he says it with the hard r in Merci.

When I look up from my phone, I find him standing on the other side of the screened porch with Miss Fabiola. It looks like they're taking a stroll around the path in our backyards. I look at his feet. White socks and his sneakers. Abuela-approved attire. Progress?

"Hi, Lolo," I say, my heart suddenly beating faster. "Hi, Miss Fabiola."

She waves at me. She's in scrubs today, like Mami wears. "Ah, your granddaughter," she says to Lolo, nodding. Then she turns to me. "Your grandpapá wanted to visit you today while your grandmamá showers," she says.

Usually, I hate Alzheimer's. It's what makes Lolo have hard days when he won't take his medicine or shower. Why he can't remember how belts or shoelaces work. Why he gets stuck on his idea of missing his bus.

But sometimes, like now, I can live with it. That's because even though it's a forgetting disease that no one can cure yet, it sometimes forgets itself, too. Without warning, it takes a surprise vacation from Lolo's mind, going away long enough that he can be with me for a few minutes, almost the way he used to be.

Lizards jump off the screen as I unlatch the door and walk outside to join them. I give Lolo a quick hug and peck on the cheek. His knees are always a little bent now, like he's about to spring up at something, but otherwise, he seems pretty steady today. Tuerto slinks out of the house and circles Lolo's legs, meowing loudly, too. Lolo used to scratch his cheeks until Tuerto purred, but he can't reach down that far now. I gather up Tuerto and let Lolo pet him in my arms.

"You're studying?" he says.

"Nope, not this time. I'm planning my packing list for

my trip to Saint Augustine. It's next weekend, Lolo. I'm going on a trip with school."

"Saint Augustine!" Miss Fabiola says. "Such a pretty city on the water." She turns to Lolo. "Have you ever gone to visit it, Mr. Suárez?"

Lolo smiles and looks off. "We took the children once, I think." He turns to me. "Do you remember? We went to the fountain and then to the beach."

It was Tía Inés and Papi who went when they were little. There are old photos that Abuela has in a picture collage in her sewing room. Papi and Tía in front of the Fountain of Youth.

I ignore that. "I'm going to the fountain to bring you back some of the water. Maybe it will work on your wrinkles!"

He pets Tuerto one last time before the cat squirms away. "So I can be young and handsome again."

Miss Fabiola has a gentle laugh. "Let's step into the shade," she says, and guides him to a cooler spot.

"Hey, watch this, Lolo," I say, spotting one of our soccer balls near the bottlebrush tree. "Wait here." I get the ball and dribble it back to the clearing, where he and Miss Fabiola can see me. "We're working on pass accuracy at soccer clinic this week."

I cradle the ball in the pocket of my ankle. Then I toss

it up and square my shoulders at the grapefruit tree across the yard. *¡Fuácata!*—it sails across in a beautiful arc and hits the trunk dead on.

He grips the handles of his walker and squints at the sight. "Goooooooooooool," he says, his voice warbling.

Everything is light and happy. It's as if I've scored a winning point in a World Cup championship. I raise both my arms in the air and run in a big circle and then back to him for the tightest hug I can give him. Tight but gentle, so we don't both go crashing to the ground.

CHAPTER 32

THE TOUR BUSES are already idling in the drop-off loop when we pull into the parking lot on Friday morning. I can barely keep still in the back seat.

"Hurry, Mami," I say. "There's a spot over there."

"Take it easy," Papi tells me. "We made it in time."

I lean back and glower at him. It's already 7:20 a.m. We were supposed to be here twenty minutes ago. Lolo wasn't feeling well this morning, though, and Mami had to go over and take his blood pressure and whatnot. Of all days!

"Can't Miss Fabiola do it when she gets here?" I begged as Mami collected her medical things. "They're going to leave without me!"

But Papi gave me a warning look, so I had to sit back and just stew until they were ready. They both insisted on coming to see me off to Saint Augustine. Really, I think Papi just wants to check out the drivers and make sure none of them looks like a homicidal maniac, his deepest suspicion.

When we arrive, the buses are still here, thank God. It's a sea of red T-shirts all around, but I still manage to detect my friends right away. They're standing in the queue next to bus number three, where we've all been assigned—even Avery and my soccer friends. Miss McDaniels is walking around with a walkie-talkie and a clipboard, checking off names as people arrive. Dr. Newman, who has done nothing for this trip as far as I can tell, is busy pumping hands with all the important parents, which explains why Edna Santos's mom is at his elbow, and also why my parents are not.

As soon as Mami cuts off the engine, I hop out and drag the duffel bag I borrowed from Roli across the back seat. Papi grabs it. "What's in here?" he asks, hoisting it up. "A dead body?"

"Snacks and stuff," I say, pulling out my smaller stash for the bus ride. "Hurry, Papi." I zip the duffel bag closed. "They're starting to board."

I rush ahead.

"There you are!" Lena says as I run up. Her red spikes are almost the exact shade of her shirt.

"Did you oversleep?" Hannah asks me.

I glance at Papi, who's handing my bag to the bus driver so it can be loaded into the storage compartment. He gives the guy a hard look, checking out his name tag carefully. Any minute, he'll start asking how long he's been driving.

"No." I roll my eyes. "It was just my grandparents. They needed us for a second."

Edna walks over. She's in skinny jeans and has the bottom edge of her T-shirt knotted at her hip stylishly. She's even worked in a red headband to pull it all together. She takes one last drain of her iced coffee and puts it in the trash. "I can't wait to get out of here."

From the corner of my eye, I see Avery and my soccer friends in line, too. I give a small wave, but I guess Avery doesn't see me.

"Merci!" Mami and Papi come over. "Aren't you forgetting something?" Mami gives me a hard hug and a quick kiss. If I weren't standing here in front of all these people, I might hug her back. But parental PDAs are weird.

"OK, you guys can go," I say. "I'll be fine. See you Sunday."

"Don't trust any strangers in the hotel," Papi says. "And don't talk to anybody you don't know on the street.

There are sinvergüenzas everywhere. Keep your phone on, with the location thing. And—"

Mami starts to pull Papi away as she waves. "This way, mi vida," she tells him.

"Do you think he's been talking to my mom?" Hannah whispers as we watch them go.

Edna shrugs. "Forget them. Three days with no parents," she says, heading for the bus steps. "Let's go."

Talk about a cushy ride! You can barely feel any bumps on this bus. You sort of float over them, like you're on a boat or something. My seat even has its own air-conditioning control, a footrest, a cup holder, two USB ports, *and* we have overhead TV screens above the aisles, too, where we're watching the very first Iguanador Nation movie. It's the one that explains Jake Rodrigo's sad origin story. His scientist parents accidentally gene-spliced him with dinosaur tissue in an experiment gone terribly wrong.

As far as I'm concerned, this is heaven. I don't even mind the fact that our seats are dangerously close to the bathrooms in the back. Edna staged a small protest over it, holding up the whole line, but Miss McDaniels climbed aboard and backed up the driver who explained that no one is allowed to do "number two" in the facilities, except in emergencies.

But to be sure, every time somebody gets up to pee, Edna puts her foot out in the aisle and gives them a warning look before they can pass.

"Really? A stink eye, Edna?" Wilson asks as he steps over her foot.

"It's better than any other kind of stink," she says loudly. "Remember the rules."

"No anal emissions," Lena mutters, in case it needs repeating.

He rolls his eyes and shuts the accordion door behind him.

About halfway through the ride, Avery starts down the aisle toward the restroom.

To my surprise, she stops at my seat and takes a cheese puff from the bag I have open. "Hey."

"Hey," I say. My heart starts to beat faster.

Lena and Hannah look up, but no one really makes conversation. Edna gives Avery a careful glance, too.

Two different islands.

I decide to try to unite them.

"Did you want to come to the pirate museum with us on Sunday?" I ask.

She takes another puff. "Can't. We're going to Ripley's Believe It or Not! Odditorium. They have a metal Chucky and a vampire-killing kit."

"Oh man," Darius murmurs. He's been listening in, more or less mesmerized by Avery from across the aisle.

I feel Hannah shudder beside me.

Instantly I wish I could go. I've done a little research about Ripley's, and personally, I wouldn't mind seeing Walt Disney painted on a black bean or the dried cockroaches posed like famous musicians. I know Miss McDaniels warned us against spending "good money on foolish things," but who decides what's foolish? Personally, I think it's silly to visit a museum to see a 2,400-year-old rug made of ancient Egyptian cat hair, but we've still got the Villa Zorayda Museum on the agenda, don't we?

"That does sound fun," I say.

"You should come, then," she says, but she doesn't invite anybody else. She's looking only at me. She doesn't say we should *all* come.

I can feel Hannah tighten next to me. She's hearing herself being cut out. Across the aisle, Edna and Lena are watching us, too. My face heats up as I get ready to say no.

But Avery doesn't wait for my answer. As usual, she's in her own bubble of cool and already walking away from me toward the bathroom.

"'Come, then,'" Hannah mimics in a whisper.

The four-hour ride goes by in a breeze. Before we know it, we're all piling out in front of the Country Inn and Suites. We wait in the parking lot while Miss McDaniels and Mrs. Wilkinson check us all in. Blinking into the midday sun, I can see this town is nothing like West Palm Beach, even though it's still in Florida. There are big oak trees with Spanish moss hanging from them like spiderwebs. The buildings look older, the streets narrow.

When Miss McDaniels comes back, she hands out maps of the old town district, trolley passes, and our hotel keys. Then we get the required lectures and warnings. Keys secure. Stay in groups. Blah-blah.

"And most important," Miss McDaniels says, "remember that you are representing our school community. We expect quiet voices and excellent manners, please." She checks her watch. "We are on a tight schedule. Go settle into your assigned rooms, ladies and gentlemen. Lunch will be served poolside in exactly twenty-one minutes, and then we will depart for our first tour immediately following. Tardiness is not accepted."

We scramble.

It's tough lugging my duffel bag up the stairs, but I don't have the patience to wait for the elevator. When we get to our room, sweating and breathing hard, Hannah and Edna shoot rock-paper-scissors to see whose key to use to get in. Edna wins and waves the plastic card by the sensor.

"It's a palace," I say as soon as we step inside.

The room is twice the size of mine at home. It has a desk and a comfy leather chair, plus two perfectly made double beds, the size of Mami and Papi's.

Edna throws open the curtains and peers out. "Ugh. Should I complain about the view?" she asks. "We're not overlooking the pool."

"The soaps in here are shaped like lemons!" Hannah calls from the bathroom.

"And the TV works," I say, clicking on the ginormous screen and scrolling.

"We can check it all out later," Lena says, tossing down her bag. "I'm starved and lunch is in a few minutes."

I put my things next to Lena's and use the restroom since I held it the whole way to spare myself Edna's warnings. Back out in the hall, you can hear loud talk and laughter from all our rooms. (So much for quiet voices.) The door to Avery's room is open next door as we go by. Inside they're already playing trampoline on the beds. A girl named Alicia DeSilva from the field hockey team is rooming with them now.

I linger at the door as Hannah and the others keep walking toward the elevators.

"Are you coming?" Lena asks, looking back.

"One second." I duck inside Avery's room quickly. "Hey. You want me to save you guys a seat outside?"

Avery and Mackenzie stop midbounce, their faces flushed.

"We'll be right there," Avery says, and then she throws the pillow at me before bouncing to her butt, laughing.

"Merci!" Lena calls from down the hall.

"Coming!" I run down the carpeted corridor. Up ahead, Hannah is pretending to be Wonder Woman by holding the doors open wide for me.

Downstairs, a sign that says WELCOME SEAWARD PINES ACADEMY EIGHTH GRADE leads us to a bricked patio area where two banquet tables have been piled with boxed lunches for us. Wilson is already in line. When he sees us, he points at the picnic table that Darius, who sunburns easily, snagged for all of us in the shade.

I pick up a box marked HAM AND CHEESE and then stroll over to the pool to have a look. Little kids are splashing in cheap scuba masks in the shallow end. A cool dip would be the perfect answer to this noon heat. A tiny frog has jumped in, I notice, thinking it found a pond, I guess. The poor thing won't survive the chlorine for long, or else it'll drown when it can't climb out. I put down my box and try to stage a rescue.

"Swimming is this evening," Miss McDaniels says as she walks over, sunglasses perched on her head. "There are other adventures first. Time is ticking, Merci."

"We have an amphibian 911, miss." I motion to the pool. "You don't want to have a frog demise on your conscience, do you?"

She wrinkles her nose and shudders. "Go eat. I'll find a net."

So, I sit next to Darius and the others at the picnic table. The Spanish moss is so long, it practically dangles in our hair.

"Save four seats for Avery and them," I tell him. "They're coming."

Darius looks like he might faint. "Oh my God. Here?"

"I don't know why you bother with her," Edna says to me as she flips open her boxed lunch. She tears the plastic straw open with her teeth. "No offense, but she barely likes you."

I glare at Edna. What does she, of all people, know about being friends?

"That's not true," I say. But my face burns, wondering if it is. Shouldn't Avery have tried to beg me to reconsider when I turned down her offer to room with her? That's what I do when I really want Hannah or Lena to do something they're not crazy about. I mean, it's a little like Marco and the twins, isn't it? He's there, but he's not as enthusiastic as he ought to be if he really cared about them.

"Let's not start," Hannah says.

"Amen," Lena adds.

"I'm just saying . . ." Edna says.

"Well, don't," I snap.

The soccer girls do come down a few minutes later. I try to wave them over, but I guess Avery doesn't see. Instead, they grab their boxed lunches and settle together on a chaise lounge near the deep end.

Edna stabs me with an "I told you so" look and takes her first bite.

We don't say much else to each other for the rest of lunch.

CHAPTER 33

THE PARK RANGERS AT Castillo de San Marcos wear three-corner hats and bright blue jackets over their red vests as they demonstrate how to shoot cannons. Their costumes must be killer in this heat, even worse than our band uniforms at school. The whole time he's talking, our guide keeps wiping the sweat off his forehead. We're all fidgeting as we wait for the big *ka-boom*, but it takes a million little steps to light one of these bad boys.

"¡Fuego!" the commander finally shouts. There's a deep *boom* and a puff of smoke.

We all stand there for a second, completely underwhelmed.

"That's it?" Wilson says, disappointed.

"I know, right?" I whisper, applauding half-heartedly.

A breeze blows up from the bay as we're leaving, thank goodness. We follow Miss McDaniels and Mrs. Wilkinson toward the trolley stop. Our agenda says that we've still got to see the oldest jail, a one-room schoolhouse, and then Flagler College.

Mrs. Wilkinson points out a gnarled oak nearby. "Has anyone noticed anything odd about this tree?" Weirdly, a palm tree is growing right out of it.

"They're love trees," she tells us. "Legend has it that if a couple kisses here, they stay in love forever. There are several of these specimens in the city. Keep your eyes peeled and see if you can locate them!"

Lena pushes up her glasses. "Interspecies trees happen when a seed from one kind of tree nestles in the crevice of another trunk," she says.

But nobody listens. A few kids have started snickering and making smooching sounds. I don't dare look at Wilson, just in case he can read minds.

The trolley pulls up just then and we board. But as we rattle away a few seconds later, I wonder if maybe Lolo and Abuela kissed under one all those years ago when they brought Tía and Papi here. I know there's a logical explanation for love trees, but it's kind of nice to think about magic, too.

I'm still wondering a little while later when we are all walking along Treasury Street, the narrowest street in the country. It's smaller than even our school hallway. It's supposed to only be wide enough for two people carrying a treasure chest between them. Wilson and I try it, using Darius as a stand-in for the chest.

"Try this instead, woadie," Wilson tells me. We just put our backs against the buildings on either side of the street and stretch our arms toward each other to see if we can touch fingers.

We can, which is kind of nice.

Eventually, we make our way to go see Flagler College at the end of the day. It's a super fancy place to learn, for sure, even more deluxe than Seaward Pines is. Inside the rotunda it looks a lot like Hogwarts if that were real. My feet throb and my T-shirt sticks to my skin as we shuffle behind a kid, about Roli's age, who tells us about how Henry Flagler, the so-called father of Florida, first built this place as a fancy hotel.

I look up at the curved ceiling and all the dark wood as the guy is talking, and I wonder about how exactly somebody becomes like a Henry Flagler. I mean, he was a businessman like Papi, but it doesn't feel the same. What makes one person become a really rich guy who can build hotels, railroads, and churches, while another guy has to keep working? Is it luck, brains, breaks, or what? Maybe you have to roll with really rich people like Flagler did. I look around at the kids on this trip. I wonder if they are going to be Flaglers or if I'm going to be one. Who's got a chance?

By the time we finish with the tour—the last one offered for the day—the sun is starting to set. We trudge on blistered feet to the restaurant listed on our agenda, where we sit at long tables and share brick-oven pizzas.

But the best part of the day is actually the very last thing.

Back at the hotel, we're allowed to go for a night swim, just like Miss McDaniels said. All the moms and little kids who were here earlier are gone, and there are only two couples talking in the Jacuzzi, which we're not allowed to use anyway. Our chaperones watch us from the chaise lounges, where they sip iced tea and check their phones.

Most of the boys are across the pool playing Marco Polo. Avery and a bunch of other kids are having a water volleyball match with a beach ball someone found floating in the deep end. Hannah, Lena, Edna, and I take turns doing handstands to see who can hang on the longest. After, we hold hands and float on our backs, pretending we're synchronized swimmers. I've never been to a pool at night, believe it or not. Gustavo doesn't let us swim at the condo pool after dark. I like how it feels so different, how everything feels sort of magic, sparkling with lights strung along posts, even though it's only October.

I'm lying back, listening to the muffled sounds of people's laughter through the water. The clouds move over the moon, and the tree branches look like a witch's fingers against the sky. Suddenly, someone grabs me from underneath and yanks me down.

"Shark!" Wilson says, laughing as we both sputter and splash at the surface.

"Hey!" I say, but not an ounce of me is mad. Wilson looks different in the pool at night, too. Like we're not the plain Merci and Wilson we are every day.

"Ten p.m.," Mrs. Wilkinson calls out. "Time to get out, please. And remember, lights out in your rooms by midnight. It's going to be a big day tomorrow, and you'll need your rest!"

Wilson looks at me and rolls his eyes. "Sure . . ." he says. He and Darius are sticking to the plan of seeing all the movies they brought with them.

I slip out of the water fast and wrap myself in one of the towels stacked on the housekeeping bins. Wilson gets out behind me and shakes his hair free of water like a dog. I wrap the towel tighter, shy about showing my body in a bathing suit, even though everybody is wearing one.

Wilson and I sit shivering in the cooler night air, waiting for everyone else to get out. He straps on his leg brace as I find my flip-flops. Then, when our friends are dried off, we head back to our rooms in a herd.

Late that night, I lie in bed with Lena, eating popcorn as we all play another round of Would You Rather, which Hannah plays all the time when she babysits. Would you rather own a dog or a cat? Would you rather be invisible or be very strong? Would you rather eat burgers or pizza?

"Would you rather be with a group or all alone?" Lena asks.

"A group, of course," Hannah says. "I really hate being by myself,"

"You don't have pesky cousins around, that's why," I say.

"I think it depends," Lena says. "Alone can be really nice."

We're all licking our buttery fingers and thinking about that when a knocking pattern sounds through the wall. I check my watch. One a.m.

"Did you hear that?" I ask.

It sounds again. It's the familiar seven beats that our band teacher calls "shave-and-a-haircut—two bits."

I put my ear against the wall between us and Avery's room and nod. Then we copy it and wait.

They knock back with a more complicated pattern, and we copy, too. Even Edna, who's normally so sour about Avery, gets in on it. I'll admit, I feel kind of relieved. Avery wouldn't start a knocking game if she didn't like us at least a little, right? Maybe this is a sort of peace sign?

Anyway, we knock back and forth until we're finally busted a while later by a chaperone who asks us to stop because we are "disturbing the peace" and it's past curfew.

It's after two o'clock in the morning by the time my eyes finally get heavy. No part of home is here. Not Roli's snores or Tuerto's nighttime fights with the drawstring on the blinds. The sheets don't smell anything like what I'm used to. Everything is soft and good.

I listen to Lena's breath deepen next to me and notice Edna's silly satin sleep mask catching the moonlight. Hannah holds her stuffed bear tight.

It's hard to believe that I was back at home in my boring life just this morning.

Would you rather be here or home? I think as I start to drift off.

Right here, I decide. I want this to last forever.

CHAPTER 34

"YOU SAID YOU were going to put on your alarm!" Edna snaps.

"I forgot to turn the sound back on on my phone," I say. "They told us to silence them at Flagler College, remember?"

We've all just bolted up thanks to Mrs. Wilkinson knocking on our door to check on us. Now we're racing around the room, trying to get ready. We've overslept and have less than ten minutes to wash up, get dressed, and eat breakfast before today's tours.

I dive under the bed, searching for my shoes. I also have to pee—bad.

"Edna, please. I need to gooooo."

"Well, I can't go out there with a rat's nest on my head, Merci," she says, hogging the bathroom mirror.

"Use the one on the closet door," Lena tells her through a mouthful of toothpaste. She's at the bar sink brushing her teeth with Hannah.

I don't know how we manage it, but we make it downstairs in our grubby red T-shirts just as people are lining up to leave. The smell of syrup and bacon at the buffet line makes my mouth water. I don't have time to make myself a waffle today, so I grab a pile of bacon and shovel it all down as fast as I can while the rest of the kids start heading out to the trolley stop. If Mami could see me scarfing food like this, she'd faint.

"Shoot," I mutter, wiping my greasy hands on my shirt. "My phone is still on my nightstand upstairs!"

"There's no time to get it," Lena says, pocketing a banana.

"But I can't take pictures without it." I glance around. Everybody is already climbing onto the trolley. Miss McDaniels is starting to do her head count.

"You can borrow my phone for that," she says. "Come on."

We run to reach the group and climb on. It feels strange not to have my phone and camera. It's like a body part is missing. Like something is all wrong.

———— ☀ ————

The Saint Augustine Lighthouse looks like it could be fun, in a creepy sort of way. On the trolley ride over, everybody was talking about how the lighthouse is haunted by the ghosts of three girls who died on the property a long time ago. They drowned in a cart accident, and now they wander around giggling and playing ghost hide-and-seek.

It doesn't look scary as I gaze up at it, though. All that black-and-white swirl is pretty against the blue sky.

"Who would like to make the ascent?" Miss McDaniels asks. We're allowed to climb to the top since we're all taller than 44 inches. "It's two hundred and nineteen steps, remember."

Lots of hands shoot up, including mine. But when I look around, I see that Hannah, Lena, and Edna don't have their hands raised. Instead, they're hunched over the lighthouse brochure.

"Hey!" I say. "Let's go up!"

"No ghosts for me, thanks," Hannah says.

Lena points at a description in the middle of the brochure. "I want to go see the wooden boat-building demonstration instead," she says. "My dad was thinking of working on one."

"You're not scared of ghosts, too, are you?" I ask Edna.

"Don't be ridiculous. It's just that I've climbed plenty

of lighthouses. Who needs one more? I'm going to do the maritime archaeology walk."

So, do I go alone?

I'm still trying to decide what to do when I notice Avery lining up with the lighthouse group. Maybe I can join her.

"OK, well, I'm going up. I'll meet you guys at that playground after," I say, pointing at the climbing structure in the shape of a pirate ship that little kids are playing on.

I turn back to Hannah and the others, but they're already walking across the grass to find their new groups.

"Come on, woadie," Wilson says, trotting up beside me as I walk toward the line. "Ghosts don't scare me."

I wish Edna had told me that the space inside lighthouses feels small.

There's something strange about this circular staircase, too. It makes me feel like I'm inside a conch, with tighter and tighter coils.

The climb is super easy at first, but after about ninety steps, I start to move a little slower on the metal steps and feel my heart beating faster in my chest as the air gets stuffier. I peek over the edge to see how far I've come, but it's not my best idea. The black-and-white checker-board tiles on the floor far below make my stomach lurch a little, although, really, it could be the bacon or this heat, which is getting worse the higher we go.

Up, up, up, I tell myself.

Avery, who's right in front of me, keeps counting the steps. "One hundred and six, one hundred and seven, one hundred and eight . . ."

Geez, not even halfway there and she doesn't sound the least bit out of breath. Meanwhile, my calves are seriously talking to me.

"Make way," someone calls out. Another group is coming down. Only two people fit comfortably side by side in here, so I press myself against the wall to let them pass, grateful that I can pause for a second and that I'm close to the lighthouse wall instead of the railing with the view of the long drop down.

Then I hear someone groan like a spirit. "Woooooo, I want to play hide-and-seek . . ."

Laughter.

I grip the handrails on either side, wishing they'd stop. Behind me Wilson has slowed down a little, too. I didn't really think about the fact that the climb might be harder for him, and maybe he didn't either.

"Why don't we stop here?" I say, spotting a bench on one of the landings. There's a window, too, that lets in some air.

He doesn't argue.

"Play hide-and-seek with me . . ." the mystery voice calls out again.

"It would be sick if there really *are* dead girls up in here," he says, wiping the sweat from his face with his T-shirt. "You think it's true?"

I think of Roli, who scoffs at anything supernatural. "No," I say, but then add, "Maybe. What do *you* think?"

He shrugs just as we hear the whoop of kids ahead of us who've reached the top. "The dead have to go somewhere. Why not a lighthouse?"

"Let's go," I say.

We climb the rest of the way to reach the outside observation deck, which is right under the lens room. Loads of kids are already leaning over the red railing and pointing at all that you can see for miles.

Avery seems to be in charge, as usual.

"Check it out," she tells the group. "I think that's Flagler College over there." She points in the other direction. "And isn't that our hotel?"

The fresh air feels good on my face, but, *oh man*, we're high up, and it makes my legs feel wobbly. I might blow away. The lighthouse seems to be swaying under my feet. I can't bring myself to look at what she's pointing to.

I keep my eyes trained on Avery, pretending everything

is fine, but my eye starts to turn inward, the way it always does whenever I'm nervous. I try to force myself to take a step toward her, but no matter how hard I try, I can't make my feet move. I know I won't fall—there's a railing! Still, I can't shake the feeling that I'm on unsteady ground.

"What's the matter with you, Merci?" Avery says, turning to me. "You're not scared, are you?" Mackenzie and the other girls who are with her turn to look at me.

"No," I say, even as my knees feel weak enough to buckle. "My stomach . . ."

"Well, don't puke from up here. Ugh!" Avery says, smiling, her long hair whipping in the breeze. "You'd hit people below!"

Mackenzie and the others laugh. A few of the boys who overheard her make puking noises, which makes my stomach squeeze even more. Suddenly, I'm afraid I actually *will* vomit, and then what? How embarrassing!

Wilson, who's been taking pictures of the view, turns to me. "You OK?"

"I'll meet you at the playground," I mumble, my mouth watering uncomfortably.

And then it's me who's the ghost.

The rest of the day is better as we tour different sites. Down on George Street, I eat a cold popsicle that seems to settle my gut. I also buy Mami a Saint Augustine snow globe. Suddenly, I sort of wish I could talk to her, maybe just to tell her I was queasy. But I can't. My phone is back in my room, and I don't want to ask anybody to borrow a phone so I can call my mommy like a baby.

Anyway, when we finally get back to the room late that afternoon, it's time to get ready for our independent dinner. I grab my phone and see right away that I have four missed calls. They're all from Mami. Maybe she has that parent telepathy and knew I was sick. She hasn't left a message, though, so she's probably just checking up on me out of habit.

It's my turn in the shower first, so I don't call her back. And after, while I'm waiting for the others, I get busy downloading all the pictures I sent myself from other people's phones today.

Edna takes the longest to get ready, of course, and when she gets out of the bathroom, the whole room smells like Tropical Delight body spray.

"Where's your red T-shirt?" I ask.

We're all clean but stuck wearing our dirty T-shirts.

She turns sideways and points to a tote bag. It's our red T-shirt upcycled into a shoulder bag. It has a fringed, knotted bottom and the sleeves cut off to make the handles.

"Oh my God, I love it!" Hannah says, coming over to take a look.

"Miss McDaniels is gonna give you grief," I warn.

"Why?" Edna says. "I am wearing it, just not as a shirt."

"Technically, you do have a point," Lena says.

"We totally have to make these in the makerspace!" Hannah says. "Show me how."

So that's how we all end up with matching bags. When we're all done snipping and knotting, we pose ourselves in front of the closet mirror and take a picture that Edna posts on her Insta.

Then we let our chaperone know we're heading out to the burger place we chose.

Everything is perfect at dinner, and not just because the burger is greasy the way I like and the fries are crunchy on the outside and fluffy on the inside. It's that it's just us and nobody tells me I should order something healthier. It's that I figure out the tip for the waitress with the calculator on my phone, making sure not to be cheap. It's that we are just here on our own having fun with no adults bossing us.

We're just finishing up dessert when I get a text. At first, I think it's going to be Mami again, but it's from Avery's number.

Top secret!!! Meet at 10 pm near the pool. Sardines!

I love that hiding game, where you find the person

and get in their hiding spot, too. It's going to be fun in the dark and in a place we don't really know.

I'm half expecting everybody's phone to start pinging, but after a minute or two, I realize that they're not getting the message. No one's phone vibrates or sounds. Not in one minute or in five or even twenty as we're walking back to the hotel.

The whole way, I'm wondering why Avery cuts Lena, Hannah, and Edna out like a surgeon. It's not like they don't know how to play a hiding game like sardines. But they're clearly not being asked.

I don't know what to do.

We get back to our hotel room just after nine o'clock. Edna whips out her nail polish kit and offers to do manicures and pedicures, which Hannah is all for, especially since Edna brought along gold glitter top coat. Lena curls into the leather chair with her book to wait her turn, and I lie back in bed and turn on a movie I've already seen a bunch of times. I'm still thinking and worrying. Why haven't they been invited? It would be so fun with all of us.

When ten o'clock rolls around, I make a decision. I'll go downstairs, just to see who's there, maybe see if Avery made a mistake or didn't have everyone's number.

"Where are you going?" Hannah asks when I slip on my shoes and head for the door.

"I just remembered that I need to tell Avery something. It's about soccer."

Edna looks up from blowing on her fingernails and stares at me.

Liar, I hear in my head.

"I'll be back in a little bit." I silence my phone and close the door behind me.

Out in the hall, I put my ear to Avery's door, but it's completely quiet in there. Nobody is in the hallway, either, so I creep past the chaperone's door and slip down the back stairs. Sure enough, my soccer friends are already waiting near the areca palms, along with about eight other kids I don't know too well. I'm surprised to see that Wilson is here. *He* got invited? The sight of him makes me feel better, but where is Darius? Was he cut out, too?

"Where's everybody else?" he asks me.

I shrug.

Avery's eyes are shining with fun.

"OK, I'll be It first. Close your eyes." We wait five minutes and then we go searching. Whoever finds her will climb into Avery's hiding spot with her until there's only one last person left who's searching.

"Watch out for the chaperones," Lindsey warns. Then we spread out to search.

It takes about ten minutes for us all to be behind the laundry bins, giggling. I won't lie. It is so fun. Wilson is the last one to find us, so he gets to hide now.

We wait, counting the minutes, and then we all go out in search of him. Most people head toward the hotel building, but every Jake Rodrigo fan knows he likes open spaces.

I roam the pool slowly. I check near the hot tub next, and then I notice the tall oak tree. It's pretty dark over there, though, and the branches look like witch hands. I think, all at once, of the love trees.

I creep closer.

"Aha!" I say.

He looks up at me from where he curled up near the base playing dead like a possum.

But then he grins.

"Shh!" He pulls me toward him. "Don't give us away."

We huddle close, curled tight and trying not to giggle.

My heart is beating in my ears from nerves as I sit close. It's nice to be here, hiding in the dark with Wilson. I hope no one finds us. Maybe this is what Avery was thinking with Clayton underneath the stadium stands. Would it be so terrible if Wilson and I kissed and no one could see? And no one could tell?

Suddenly we hear more and more voices on the pool

deck. They're loud, though. Wilson puts his fingers to his lips and inches even closer to me.

"Merci Suárez! If you are hiding, come out at once, please."

Miss McDaniels's voice is cold water on my back.

Wilson and I exchange terrified looks. We're in for a lifetime of detentions for sure.

"Merci Suárez!" Her voice is much louder now. "Come out right now if you are hiding, please."

From the corner of my eye, I see the kids we were playing with making a break for the stairs. Avery sneaks away the fastest.

But Wilson and I would have to cross the whole deck to get to the stairwell.

"Merci Suárez!"

"There's no escape, woadie," he whispers.

I swallow hard and step out into the light shining from the lampposts.

"I'm here, miss," I say.

To my relief, Wilson comes out to stand next to me a second later.

"I'm here, too. We were just playing sardines, Miss McDaniels," he says. "That's all."

Miss McDaniels is on the pool deck wearing silk pajamas and a matching robe. I can't read her face at all as she blinks and takes a deep breath. "We will handle that matter another time," she says. "There are other issues right now."

That's when I notice that Miss McDaniels isn't alone. Lena, Hannah, and Edna are all trailing behind her, looking scared. But there's someone else with them who is even more surprising.

"Mami?"

There's a pause when no one says anything.

"Come along with me, Wilson," Miss McDaniels says. "Girls, go back to your rooms."

Lena, Hannah, and Edna turn slowly, but they all glance back worriedly as they go.

Mami crosses the deck to reach me.

"I tried to call you," Mami says when she reaches me. Her voice is tired, quiet. "When you didn't pick up, I decided it was best to come right away."

There's a prickly feeling rising inside me. She's come all this way to check up on me? Is this what happens just because I don't answer the phone? I stand there, trying to understand that ridiculous idea.

"I'm fine. I left my phone in my room by mistake, that's all. You didn't have to come check on me."

She takes my hands. "I'm not here to check on you," she says. "I'm here to drive you home."

Nothing makes sense as I stare at her. "What are you talking about?" I say. "I'm on a *field trip*."

Mami's lip gets quivery. She leans her forehead against mine.

"It's Lolo," she whispers.

CHAPTER 35

BAD THINGS CAN HAPPEN, even when they are not supposed to.

They happen when you are far away and don't expect them. Or laughing with your friends on the best trip ever. Or playing sardines and wishing for a kiss.

Even then. Something very, very bad can find you. And when it does, it is the worst kind of surprise.

Mami tries her best to get me home in time. She drives with the windows rolled down to stay awake. She plays the radio loud.

The whole way home, I keep my eyes on the headlights and on the stars above as we speed along I-95. My hair blows crazy, and my ears whoosh with the sound of wind that keeps repeating all the medical words she has used tonight to explain what I still cannot understand.

Collapsed. Hospital. Hemorrhagic stroke.

Papi is waiting for us in the dark on our stoop although it is three thirty in the morning. I see his shape in the dim light cast from Abuela's kitchen.

He stands up, but when he sees me, his shoulders seem to collapse, and he heaves in big gulps of air.

In the end, no matter how fast Mami drove, it wasn't enough. The blood that spilled inside Lolo's brain was much faster.

He died before I had the chance to hold his hand and say goodbye.

I had to borrow Tía's shoes for the funeral. They made it hard to stand when people came to give us their pésame. Gustavo and Zenaida. Señor Humberto and Lolo's friends from the bakery, one by one. Señora Magdalena. I saw Lena with her dad, and Hannah and Edna, who came with Mr. and Mrs. Kim. Wilson and his mom were there too. They sat with Miss McDaniels.

There was a stench of carnations. Papi fidgeted in his tight suit. Tía's eyes were swollen and she talked in whispers with Simón, who walked the twins around outside when they couldn't behave for Marco, who came by himself and sat in the back row, jiggling his keys until he could leave. People kept taking Abuela's hand to say lo siento.

But I was trying not to feel anything.

I wedged myself between Mami and Roli and closed my eyes. I wouldn't open them, no matter how many times my parents asked me to in whispers.

When we finally came home, I put away all my pictures of Lolo and me. I found the photograph book I made for him and pushed it to the back of my closet, too.

Then I plugged in my earbuds and played music loud enough so that I wouldn't hear his voice calling "preciosa" or hear the faint rattle of his walker coming along the path.

Even now, a week later, I haven't gone out into the yard where he should be walking or watching us play soccer.

I love Lolo but I have to erase him.

I need to rub my memory clean, leave no trace of him at all.

Because even the tiniest thought of him now plunges into me like broken glass.

CHAPTER 36

MAMI DOESN'T PULL into the car loop this morning.

This has been the longest I've ever been absent from school. Six days. That's even longer than the time when our whole family got a bad stomach flu and we fell ill, one by one. She's going back to work today, too, after helping all week at home. There were papers to fill out and things to pack up. There was Abuela, her whole body so still as she sat, stunned by Lolo's absence. I watched from my bedroom window when church ladies came to pick up bags of his clothes. I wanted to yell at them to leave them alone. Who would be wearing the shirts Mami gave him or his favorite pants that I used to hang on the line? Would I catch a glimpse of these impostors at the grocery store or on the street?

For once Mami is not rushing me out of the car. Instead, she shuts off the engine and turns to me.

"Do you want me to walk you in?" she asks.

I shake my head and keep watching kids hop out of their parents' SUVs, laughing, running for their friends, the same as always. Everything has kept going without me, which somehow seems impossible. It's like I've been existing on another planet while they've kept on laughing and talking, slamming lockers and going to tryouts and practices as if the whole world didn't change.

"Do you have everything?" she asks. "Your lunch?"

I glance at the backpack at my feet. Did I grab my lunch sack? I can't remember. But it doesn't matter, since I won't be hungry. I haven't been for days. But at least she doesn't ask about my homework. It's usually Mami's first question, but maybe she already knows I've done no work at all, even though it was all posted online in our class folders. "Complete it when you can" is what my teachers said in their notes to me. But when will that be? Besides, I didn't know what they'd gone over in class, and I couldn't muster the energy to text or call.

I haven't talked with anyone, either. Not even with Lena, Hannah, Edna, or Wilson, who texted into the void until they got tired. They made me a card in makerspace and mailed it to me the old way instead.

Not with Avery, who didn't text me at all.

Mami waits quietly. The warning bell rings, and she glances over at me, still sitting here.

"Remember that Mrs. Wilkinson asked you to go to her office first thing today. That might be easier than going to homeroom."

I stare straight ahead. If I could, I'd crawl back under the covers at home and sleep.

"Do I have to?" I ask her.

There's a long pause. "No," she says. "But I think it's probably a good idea."

"She didn't even know him," I say bitterly.

"No. But she knows you," Mami says.

We wait together in silence until the late bell rings and the quad empties. Then Mami turns on the ignition. "I'm going to go to work now, Merci."

"Who's home with Abuela?" I ask suddenly, my eyelid growing heavy with tension. I need to stall.

"Zenaida promised to check on her," she says. "Tía will be there this afternoon until her classes start."

She waits again, but when I don't move, she says, "Merci, mi vida, it's time to go. You can call me during the day if you need anything."

I don't answer, but my eyes start to fill. People are

going to ask where I've been. They're going to stare at me. They're going to want me to talk.

A knock on my window makes me turn. It's Miss McDaniels. I'm sure she's going to start in about tardiness.

Mami powers down my window. "Good morning," she says.

I stare straight ahead.

"Good morning, Mrs. Suárez." Then she looks at me and clears her throat. "I saw you here, Merci, and I was thinking that you might like some company walking in today. Would that be all right?"

Her words catch me off guard. Miss McDaniels is never one to be soft, but her voice is missing its usual sharpness.

Mami leans over and gives me a long hug. "Anda," she whispers in my ear. "I'm a phone call away."

I grab my backpack, droopy without books, and head toward the academic building with Miss McDaniels at my side.

Mrs. Wilkinson is drinking a cup of coffee at her desk when we arrive. She's wearing a cream-colored suit today with a matching pair of wedges. I stand at the door to the guidance suite but don't step inside. If she doesn't see me, I can slip away and tell her later that I came.

But Miss McDaniels knocks.

Mrs. Wilkinson looks up and sees me just as I'm starting to back away.

"Ah," she says. "Thank you, Jennifer." Then she motions me to her office chair. "Come in, Merci. I've been expecting you."

I grip my backpack tighter as I stand in her office. The hotel chart for the trip is gone from her wall. It feels like Saint Augustine happened long ago, like maybe it was all a dream. I stare at the bare spot, wondering all at once if my friends ever went to the pirate museum without me. If they kept having fun. Then my thoughts creep to that last night, hiding near the pool with Wilson while Lolo was so very sick and I didn't know.

I have to shudder to shake the idea away.

"Please sit down for a moment." Mrs. Wilkinson leans back in her chairs as I settle in. "Your mom shared with me that your grandfather died last week."

I study my shoes, scuffed already. Abuela will want me to shine them.

"I am here for you, Merci," she says, leaning forward. "It's difficult when someone very close to us dies, especially unexpectedly. The experience is different for everyone, though, and that's OK. I'm here to help you find a way forward that feels right for *you*."

A way forward? I sit still as an iguana, stuck.

"This room is a space for you if you need to be quiet and by yourself for a little while during the school day, or if you'd like to talk to me."

I wait until the tug on my eye goes away. I nod, my mouth still glued.

"Good." Mrs. Wilkinson opens her top drawer and pulls out a green paper that she begins to fill out. I've seen these special passes before. Sometimes kids come here with them. It means I can let them sit on the sofa until she comes back to see them.

"You know how these passes work. Show this to your teachers if you feel that you need to come see me. All right?"

I take the pass and shove it deep inside my backpack so no one can see.

She plucks a chocolate from her candy jar and hands it to me. Then we walk together to the door. A fast breeze rushes at us through the hallway.

Preciosa, it seems to whisper.

"I'm here," she says. "We'll check in when you come back for your TA period. I'd like to know how it's going."

When we were little, Roli and I used to play slo-mo. It was a made-up game where we'd slow down everything we did and pretend we were stuck in slow motion, like on TV.

Today, it feels like a game of slo-mo that I'm playing alone.

I can't remember my locker combination. I lose track of what period I'm in and what class I have next. I forget what page we're on in class. I'm in a daze all morning, feeling bone tired, as if I haven't slept at all, even though I've never napped so much as I did last week. All I want to do is put my head down and close my eyes, which I do, a couple of times.

If they notice, my teachers don't complain. But I do see Wilson glancing back at me from the front of Ms. Tibbetts's class once or twice during our quiz, which I'm sure I will fail. He's not the only one, either. I can feel other people's eyes on me, too. I was one of the big stories on our trip, I suppose. I provided the drama.

When we're done, Ms. Tibbetts asks us to exchange quiz papers so we can check each other's work. Avery takes mine—and then exchanges it back again when Ms. Tibbetts isn't looking.

She leans toward me. "We can fix our answers and she won't ever know," she whispers.

That's all.

Her empty smile turns my skin to gooseflesh. To Avery, I am here for what she needs.

I don't touch my paper at all.

At lunchtime, Lena, Hannah, and Edna have saved me a spot the way they always do. I try to busy myself looking for my lunch, so that I don't have to feel them watching me, too. I grope around inside my backpack long after I realize that I've forgotten my lunch sack after all. It's probably sitting on the kitchen counter. Maybe Tuerto has found it and is feasting while no one is home.

"I'm glad you're back," Lena tells me. "I missed you."

"We all did," Hannah adds.

Nobody mentions that I left them for Avery's game. In fact, nobody really knows what to say after that, especially not me. I'm so afraid of what the next words might be. I can't talk about Lolo. I don't want to cry here in the cafeteria. But these are the Seaward Pines friends who knew him. They're the only ones who have been to my house, the only ones who know my family well enough to call him Lolo and not Mr. Suárez.

I swallow down the hard lump that's widening in my throat.

Edna gets up. "Come on," she says to Hannah and Lena. They follow close behind her to the food line.

A few minutes later, they come back with their trays. Lena hands me half a roast beef sandwich. Hannah has bought an extra carton of milk and a bag of my favorite chips. Edna sets a slice of à la carte key lime pie near my elbow.

"Extra whipped cream," she says. "I had to beg."

I stare at the gifts.

"I'm sorry," Edna says in a softer-than-usual tone as she sits down next to me. "For everything."

"Thank you," I say, and I mean it.

When I check in with Mrs. Wilkinson later that day during TA time, we have more chocolates, and she lets me play a word-search game on my phone instead of making copies. She promises to talk to my teachers about how to make up only the work that really matters. She assures me that Coach Cameron will understand why I missed tryouts with everyone else, that they will make adjustments.

"Is there anything you'd like to share?" she asks.

I tell her about lunch.

She listens, jiggling her shoes off the end of her toes.

"True friends feed us in lots of ways," she says.

CHAPTER 37

THE TWINS FOUND a dead lizard today while they were playing. They're studying it with their new adult-looking magnifying glasses, which have built-in LED lights for nighttime bug safaris. They were an early birthday present from Roli, who thought it would keep them quiet while he clipped the bougainvillea that's gotten overgrown and thorny on the back fence. Papi hasn't been able to do it. There was the funeral that kept him away and now all the work for him and Simón to make up.

This dead anole in the garden gets their attention. They stare at it solemnly, which is a big improvement over their squabbles lately, always ending with them both red in the face and screaming. They've brought Tía to tears a couple of times.

"Look."

Axel shows me the carcass on the end of a stick as I cross the yard. I'm on my way to Abuela's, where I'm supposed to be helping Mami and Tía clean up. The lizard is stiff and dried out by the sun. The eyes are gone from the sockets now, and its feet are curling. The sight chills me. I've been having nightmares. I can't stand to think that Lolo's body is buried in the ground.

"Get it away," I say. Normally, Axel might toss it my way and try to scare me. "Put it in the trash."

Roli looks up to see what's the trouble. "Axel," he warns, "Enough."

But Axel doesn't throw it at me at all. Instead, he crouches down in the garden with Tomás beside him. Heads together, they stare at it through their magnifiers.

"Wake up," Tomás says. He puts his hands above the lizard dramatically, like a magician working a spell.

Roli and I exchange looks. Then he tosses aside the hedge clippers and comes to kneel on the ground with the twins. Roli's hands are filthy. Two long scratches from the bougainvillea thorns run the length of his forearm.

"Dead things are not sleeping," he says. "Their bodies

have stopped working. They can't wake up to play again, even if we wish it very hard."

The twins look at the anole miserably. Tomás pokes at it one more time to make sure.

"Like Lolo," Axel says.

"Yes."

They were at the funeral, of course. But something about his absence must feel impossible to them, too.

There's a long quiet and then Tomás says, "Does it hurt to die?"

Roli thinks for a moment. "Sometimes," he says. "But it didn't hurt Lolo. It's mostly us who are hurting because we miss him."

Was he scared? I want to add as I listen. *Was he angry that I wasn't there?*

But I am too afraid to open my mouth. I still can't say his name. If I do, I might start a cry that won't ever end. I take a long, deep breath the way Mrs. Wilkinson says to do when those prickles start in my chest.

Roli looks up at me. "You OK, Merci?" he asks.

I shrug and hurry away again along the path.

Abuela's kitchen has been abandoned.

Nothing is cooking on the stove. A bag of bread is molding. There are no little garlic peels floating on the floor or dishes in the sink. It doesn't feel like her kitchen at all anymore.

I step inside the back door and watch as Mami and Tía empty the refrigerator of food that has expired. They're talking in low voices about Abuela. Tía thinks she should come to the studio when she's ready, maybe give Aurelia a much-needed hand. She looks up and sees me.

"Merci, please bring me a garbage bag," Tía says, grimacing. "This yogurt is growing mold."

It's been two weeks since Abuela has cooked anything. We haven't had a meal together, either. It's Papi or Simón who picks up food at El Caribe and brings it for us to eat, everyone in their own space. It's as if we can't figure out how to be together. No one has mentioned this change, though. How would we sit together now with a gaping hole beside us?

I walk to the mudroom to find the cleaning supplies on the shelf. Abuela's laundry basket is in the corner. There are only a few pieces of her clothing there, just hers, nothing else. I can't stand the sight of it.

I bring back the trash bag.

"Can I go, please?" I ask Mami. "I still have homework to make up."

She tosses out a watery cucumber and scratches her nose with the back of her gloved hand.

"Maybe you can check in on Abuela first? I'm sure she'd like to have your company, Merci."

My skin prickles again, and I take another deep breath. I've been avoiding Abuela. The thought of being alone with her scares me now. The feelings are too big. Then my eyes flit to the living room. Lolo's recliner is still there, a blanket folded neatly over the back. The indentation of his body is still in the seat cushion.

"For a minute. That's all," Mami says when I don't answer.

Tía stops what she's doing and turns to me, too, with a pleading look. "She's in the sewing room having coffee," she says.

There's no getting out of it.

I walk down the hall that leads to the bedrooms, my heart already racing. It still smells of Lolo's after-bath cologne in here, as if it has seeped into the walls and tiles. Pictures of our family line the hallway, but I won't look at them. I turn away from their bedroom.

A minute, I tell myself. *That's all.*

The door to Abuela's sewing room is open. She sits in a chair near the window that overlooks what's left of her old garden and, beyond, our house. Her cup of coffee is growing cold on the table nearby, the milk making a filmy circle in the middle of the cup. The candle with the image of la Caridad del Cobre is still burning for Lolo on the cutting table. Even from here, I can see that Abuela looks thinner. Mami bought her those special shakes but they're still untouched on the kitchen counter.

She turns to look at me.

"Mami sent me to see if you need help with anything." I shift on my feet, hoping she'll send me away.

Abuela nods slowly and turns her gaze outside again. "What are they doing out there?"

"Cleaning the refrigerator."

She shakes her head. "No, not Inés and Ana. I mean the boys," she says. "Out there in the garden."

I don't know what to tell her. *Talking about dead things,* I want to say, but instead I walk over to stand beside her near the window. This close, I can see the circles under her eyes and catch the scent of her unwashed hair. I look out through the gauzy curtains. The twins are still out there, although now they're wetting the soil into mud with Lolo's old watering can. I think of them only a year or two ago when they'd pretend to be chefs. Lolo was always good at pretending to taste their dirt cupcakes, a pebble as the cherry on top. Anything for his caballeros.

"Making cakes, maybe," I say quietly, even though it's a lie. It's probably a burial. "It's their birthday next week."

She turns to me, surprised. "Verdad que sí. Seven," she

says under her breath. "Dios mío, how time leaves us." Then she stares at the paper napkin she's been twisting into a cigar shape in her lap.

Abuela watches the twins like they're a TV show. She's always been so sure of herself, so busy, sometimes so bossy. She never seemed to have time to play with us. Instead, she was making sure we were clean and looked right, that we got home from school safely, that we weren't devoured by a gator or felled by another horrible villain she conjured in her mind.

It's been easy to overlook her and want to be with Lolo instead.

What happens now with all this space around her that he used to fill? What's the way forward for Abuela, the way Mrs. Wilkinson says we have to find?

I sit down on the ottoman and press the straight pins deep into her tomato-shaped pincushion. I'm thinking of the days she let me pretend in this room with all those dangling single earrings that everyone thought were junk.

"Maybe we should bake them a real cake next week to celebrate."

I don't look at her as I say it, keeping my eyes on the pincushion instead. Will there be a happy family party ever again? It doesn't seem right. My mind fills with all the rest of what I can't say. That the whole world feels too big without Lolo in it with us. That I feel like I will miss him forever. That nothing will ever be the same.

But when she reaches for my hand and squeezes it, I feel like she's heard me anyway. We watch the twins together for a few more minutes.

Then she says, "Let's make a list of what's we'll need."

She unrolls her tattered napkin and reaches for a pen.

And that's how I know that she is trying to find a way forward, too.

CHAPTER 38

SOMETIMES I CAN forget to be sad about Lolo.

It happens when I get busy on a group project in class, like the debate we are planning in civics. Or it happens when something funny goes on, like Darius stuffing two grapes under his top lip to make himself look like a gopher at lunch.

But when I realize I have forgotten even for a little while, I feel afraid. I worry that it might mean that I will forget Lolo. The way he laughed. Or his hands. Or his favorite moves in dominoes. The way we used to ride bikes before he got sick.

Mrs. Wilkinson keeps telling me that moments of happiness are normal and a healthy sign. I don't know whether I believe her.

"I'd like to extend an invitation," she tells me one afternoon.

I'm at the copier watching the counter tick down the copies she asked for. 75, 74, 73.

"There's a group of students who meet with me for H and H Club."

"H and H?"

"It stands for *hope* and *healing*. It's for kids who have experienced the death of someone they were close to. I thought you might like to come."

I keep watching my counter. A club for sad people to be together? I don't want to be part of that.

"It's a private place where we can remember the person aloud, if we want to, or just talk about the things that we might find hard to say to our families and other friends."

32, 31, 30.

"Merci?"

"It sounds depressing, Mrs. Wilkinson," I say.

"Sometimes there are moments of emotion, but there are also moments of relief. We work on projects that are fun. And there are snacks, too."

I glance at her.

"We meet during your PE period," she adds.

"I like PE," I say. "I don't like to miss it."

"This would only meet on Fridays."

"I'm not sure," I say, although we usually do health workbook stuff on Fridays.

She nods. "Give it some good thought. I've already asked your mom if it was OK to invite you."

My head snaps around. It's just like Mami to force me to do things.

"What did she say?"

"She said it was up to you."

The machine finishes belching out the papers into the sorted piles. I gather them up separately and start stapling.

"I'll think about it," I say.

"Of course," Mrs. Wilkinson says. "Remember, you can even try it out once and then decide. No pressure."

But everything about this idea feels like pressure.

Later, I stalk Edna's locker. It's close enough to mine that I can smell the car freshener she keeps in there whenever she opens it. I wait for most people to clear away before I walk over. There are only a few minutes until the bell, so I have to talk fast.

"Question," I say.

"Make it quick," she says, sliding a fat science book into her leather pouch. "There's an open-book quiz."

"What's the group you're part of in guidance?"

She looks at me with suspicion and frowns. "And why do you need to know that?"

Edna and I are alone out here, but I lower my voice anyway. "Because Mrs. Wilkinson wants me to join a group, too, and I don't know if I want to. Hope and Healing or something. It's for kids who've had someone die."

She gives me a careful look and then sighs. "Sounds cheery. Not that ours is any better. It's called Socially Speaking for"—she makes air quotes and rolls her eyes—"improving social skills with others."

I stare at her. She may have to be in that group for life. "So does it help?" I ask.

She shrugs and slams her locker closed. "You tell me."

The warning bell rings, so she turns and walks backward a few steps. "Try it out," she calls to me. "No offense, but you can't feel worse than you do."

Friday afternoon, I find my way into Mrs. Wilkinson's office instead of going to gym. I'm early, but to my surprise, I'm not the first one there. Someone has already claimed the most comfortable beanbag chair.

"Robin?" I say.

"Hi," she says.

I guess this isn't a space where eighth-graders' rules

apply, so I take a smaller cushion near the window and wait for the others to arrive.

When we're all here, Mrs. Wilkinson puts a tray of muffins and crackers in the middle of our circle. There are only four of us. She asks us to say our names and our grades and, if we want, the name of our person who has died.

Brandy is in the fifth grade, and her dad died last spring. She does not say how.

There is a boy from seventh grade named Peyton, whose older sister, Cassie, died in a car accident last year.

"I'm Robin Farmer in the sixth grade, which you know," Robin says, looking at me. She reaches for the mini muffins and peels the waxed paper off, not looking at us. "My mother was sick with addiction. Now I live with my aunt Lucille and uncle Derek."

I look around nervously. "I'm Merci Suárez, eighth grade." I don't want to hear Lolo's name aloud, so I say, "My grandfather died."

Mrs. Wilkinson tells us how glad she is that we're here. She asks us about the word *grief*, which she says is the kind of sadness that stays inside you for a while when you have lost someone very important to you. After we talk for a while, she says we should play a game.

She pulls out a bag of Scrabble tiles and tells us that we are going to make words with them but not using the board and not counting points the way you do in the board game. She'll give us a topic and we'll try to make words that go with that topic. We can connect them, if we want to, but we don't have to. She doesn't care if the word is spelled right, either.

"This is going to be a lot easier than playing Scrabble with my brother, Roli," I say. "He weaponizes the dictionary and challenges you for everything."

"Sounds like a stickler," Mrs. Wilkinson says.

"Uncle Derek lets us use made-up words," Robin says as she gathers letters. "*Hangry* counts."

Mrs. Wilkinson gives us the first topic. "Words that make you think of grief," she says.

We work quietly for a couple of minutes, and I finally settle on *quiet,* using Q, which would normally be ten points. The quiet that is blanketing our house in the afternoons, at mealtimes, in the yard. Robin makes *tears* from my *T.* Brandy and Peyton add *angry* and *lonli.*

"You can be mad about what happened," Brandy says as she places her tiles. And we all agree.

After we talk about those words, Mrs. Wilkinson gives us the next topic. "Words that remind us of the things that make us feel better," she says.

famile, cake (that's mine), *walk, sprts*

We talk about our words again and the other ones we like.

"Words that remind us of positive things that might come as a result of grief," Mrs. Wilkinson says for our last category.

That one takes us a long time. At first, none of us reaches for our stack of letters. Robin lies back on her beanbag chair and stairs at the ceiling. Peyton puts his head down for a while. It takes me almost until the bell, because it is so hard to imagine anything good about Lolo dying.

But in the end, we each spell out what we can today.

```
                P               F
        M   E   M   O   R   I   S
                A           I       T
                C           E       R
                E           N       O
                            D       N
                            Z       G
```

CHAPTER 39

WILSON WALKS BY the guidance office during TA time while I'm cutting out letters for the bulletin board the following week. He's been kind of quiet at lunch, so it's a surprise to see him here, motioning me into the hall.

I check to make sure Mrs. Wilkinson is still on the phone and then step out. We walk a little way down the corridor, so she can't see us through the glass.

"What's up?" I ask.

"You're on," he says.

"On what?"

"You made the soccer team, woadie. Again."

"How do you know that already?" I ask, suspicious. "The roster doesn't get posted until this afternoon."

"You're not the only one with top-secret intel," he whispers. "Coach Cameron just sent down the list. And look who's captain."

He looks over his shoulder to make sure we're alone and hands me a sheet of paper with the names of twenty players who made the cut. My name is right there in the group of eighth-graders, along with Avery and Mackenzie, too. But there's an unmistakable star shape next to my name. That's the captain for the year. Coach picks one eighth-grader to do the coin tosses and rally the team when we're in a slump.

Is this real?

I lean against the lockers in disbelief. Soccer tryouts happened the week I was out. Coach did me a big favor by using my clinic performance to rate me, just like Mrs. Wilkinson said they would. And now *I'm* going to have the captain's jersey, not Avery, the way everyone expected.

My first thought, though, isn't celebration.

Is there going to be a price to pay when Avery finds out it's me and not her?

And then a big well of sadness opens up inside me. I won't have Lolo to ask what to do.

I picture him suddenly, standing there in our yard with Miss Fabiola as I took my shot, his mind clear for just a few moments. I stare at the list and try to shake the image from my head. Confused, happy, and sad have gotten all twisted up into a new feeling that needs a name. I'll have a new Scrabble word for our game with Mrs. Wilkinson. *Conhapsad.*

"I thought you'd be more pumped," he says. "What's wrong?"

"I am. Mostly." I shrug off what I'm thinking.

He nods but doesn't leave. "And there's this. I've been meaning to give it to you."

He holds out a brown paper bag that has seen better days, for sure. Its mouth has been wrung into a long, wrinkled tube, and the body is sagging, so it looks like a gourd. "I've had it in my locker for a while. I was waiting for a good time. Sorry."

"It better not be one of your mom's sandwiches," I say, sniffing the top of the bag to be sure.

He shoves his hands in his pockets, waiting.

When I reach inside, I don't find a festering ham-and-mayonnaise mess. Instead, there are two things that make me gasp. A pirate's hook and a matching eye patch.

I look up at him carefully.

"You didn't get to go to the pirate museum like you wanted," he says.

My heart is beating so hard in my chest, but it's not in

the way that usually makes my eye turn on itself. This is like something that wants to lift me up into the air.

He didn't leave me stranded when he thought we were in trouble with Miss McDaniels for playing sardines. And when I disappeared from the trip, he thought about what I would miss.

He's looking out for me right now by bringing me this team list.

Lolo would have called Wilson a caballero.

There are so many feelings that are confusing. Not just *conhapsad*. Wilson is my friend because we like so many of the same things, and he is also something more because of how I feel when I am with him. I don't understand this all the way through, one of so many things I can't wrap my head around. Not people, not feelings, not the bad things that find you and seem unfair.

So, I make a decision, right there in the hall. I lean into the sliver of happiness that is in my belly and hug Wilson tight. And then I give him a lightning-fast kiss, right on his mouth. It feels like a surprise, soft and cushiony.

"Was that OK?" I ask.

He looks like he's been hit with the Jake Rodrigo stun gun, but he swallows hard and nods fast.

The phone in the guidance office rings. I have to

answer it, so I hurry away. I turn around and hold up the bag of presents right before I duck back into the office.

"Thank you, Wilson. I love these. They're perfect."

Still speechless, he breaks into one of his wide, goofy grins as he leans against the wall to watch me go.

That afternoon, I swing by the athletic office to look at the list with everyone else. I have to pretend I don't know so that Wilson won't get in trouble. A crowd of kids is already there, along with Coach, who's in Mr. Patchett's office talking to a few sad ones who didn't make the team this time around.

Robin and another girl are the only sixth-graders on the roster. They're hopping up and down together as the seventh-graders are high-fiving nearby. Lindsey, Mackenzie, and Avery are already here, too, studying the names, but they don't look nearly as happy. Maybe it's because we're old enough that we don't make spectacles. But I feel my skin prickle anyway because I know this isn't what they expected. I can see that Avery looks a little stunned she's not captain.

"It's mostly symbolic, though," I hear Mackenzie say. "Just like for the coin toss and stuff. It doesn't really matter."

Lindsey puts a hand on her shoulder.

But even Mackenzie must know it's more than that.

Then Avery spots me. I brace myself as she turns and walks over. It's going to be hard to play with a team if people hate each other. And that can happen so fast around here.

But Avery isn't mean. She never has been, not exactly.

"Looks like you're captain this season." She puts her hand out so we can shake. "Congratulations."

"Thanks," I say, grinning. "We're gonna crush it as starters."

She breaks into a big smile. "One hundred percent."

And that's enough. She isn't a friend I can count on; I know that now. But maybe not every friend is a lifeline. Maybe being teammates is enough for both of us.

CHAPTER 40

THE NIGHT BEFORE THE TWINS' birthday, Abuela and I pull out her old mixer and the dented bowls from the cabinets.

"That one, there," she says, pointing to one of Lolo's old Danish cookie tins. This one isn't filled with the cookies Lolo liked to share with me, though. This one is hers, the place where she keeps her recipes. The index cards are old and stained, unorganized, which is strange for Abuela since I've never seen her use them anyway. She's always known how to cook everything by heart, the memory somehow in her hands. Maybe it's the same way with all things that are important, even people. They just become part of everything you know.

I squint to read through the oil stains and sound out the español as she watches.

"Dos tazas de harina, seis cucharadas de mantequilla derretida . . ."

She listens patiently as I stumble through some of the words for the ingredients. It was Lolo who taught me to read in Spanish a few years ago. We used one of the twins' library books with the story in Spanish on one page and English on the other. He showed me the sounds of the vowels that day. He listened and helped when I sounded the new words out. When I'd made my way through the book, he brought me to Abuela to brag about what I could do, and then they looked at me with those big smiles that told me they were proud.

But now it's Abuela alone who is teaching me. She shows me the right settings to work the heavy mixer so that the batter whips up thick and creamy. She helps me melt the chocolate without burning it. She even lets me lick off the paddles later, this one time, even though I'm not supposed to.

"And now we wait," she says.

I set the old kitchen timer, and soon the air fills with the smell of chocolate as we wash and dry the dishes. When we're done, we decide to escape the oven's heat. But when we wander toward the living room, we both hesitate before going in. Lolo's recliner is still in the corner, along with the basket where Abuela always kept his napping pillow, the set of dominoes, and the memory book I made him with pictures of all of us.

Abuela takes my hand as we walk through the doorway, and we slide in beside each other on the sofa. Then I tell her the news that Coach Cameron picked me to be soccer captain this year. I show her the armband that will have to be sewn onto my jersey, the one that will tell everyone that I am the head of our team.

"Will you sew it on for me?" I ask.

"If you like," Abuela says, running her fingers along the letters. "Or I can show you how to do it. You're old enough to take care of important things."

I nod and we stay quiet for a long time. Then I take a deep breath and tell her what I have not had the courage to. "I miss Lolo, Abuela. I wish he could see this."

"Ay, Merci," she says, squeezing me close. "Some days, I don't know how I'll live without him."

And then I put my head down in her lap, where, at last, I let her see me cry.

"Not bad, Merci," Roli says as he licks a taste of frosting from the uncut cake the next day. It is only a little lopsided.

"What do you mean?" Abuela asks him. "It's perfect. And don't put your fingers on it. Wait until it's cut."

Tía and Mami exchange hopeful glances. Abuela's little spark feels good.

The twins have had a happy-enough day, even though we're not at a bowling alley eating pizza like they might have wanted. Tía put streamers in the yard, and Papi cooked hamburgers and hot dogs, American style. Now Simón is hanging the piñata on the grapefruit tree while Mami clears the last of the torn gift wrap from the patio.

Only Marco and Veronica are missing. The twins invited them, but they called to say they couldn't come and promised pizza another night soon. The twins were sad for a while, but they seem to have forgotten about it, at least for now. I think Marco is a sort-of dad, the way Avery is a sort-of friend—nice enough, but not really there for all the important things. Maybe one day he'll be something else. He'd have to figure out how to be there for Tomás and Axel, even in the not-so-fun times, maybe make them their own bedroom at his house and act like they matter. But I don't know. He might just stay the same way forever. Whatever happens, at least the twins will still have lots of dads who have been right here all along.

Anyway, they've had presents and attention all day. Mami bought the twins new shorts and T-shirts. I got them the new Iguanador Nation video game, *Albalacerdus and His Appetites*.

"Just so you know," I tell the twins, eyeing the used bowling balls that Simón and Vicente bought them, "these are not cannonballs. Don't try to shoot them at anything. Or anyone."

Which makes us all laugh, hard.

Then it's time for the piñata.

Tía straightens her shirt and kisses Abuela's head. Abuela is already looking worried about eye safety. She's always liked Cuban piñatas better, the kind with long strings you pull from the bottom to release the treats. It was a long-standing argument with Lolo every year, which he always won. The twins loved baseball, he insisted, and why not let them show off the expert swings he'd taught them?

We look around at one another, unsure. Lolo would have been the one to tie their masks tight so they couldn't peek out through the bottom.

But then Papi stands up and takes out the bandana he keeps tucked in his back pocket.

"Arriba, Tomás. You were born first, so we start with you," he says. He ties on the blindfold, his eyes all watery. Simón hands over a yardstick with one end carefully wrapped in a thick dish towel and rubber band. He gives Tomás a gentle spin in the right direction.

Tomás takes a swing, then another two, and then his last makes contact. There's a gash and we all cheer, but it's not enough. So, Axel steps up for his turn to swing for the fences. On his third hit, the donkey's belly cracks open, and Dollar Store candies spill everywhere.

I give the twins a head start on the ground, but then I'm on my knees, wrestling against Roli, who suddenly wants to be little again, I guess. And before we know it, even the grown-ups are down here with us, all of us gathering as many sweet things as we can.

CHAPTER 41

OUR MATCHUPS AGAINST the Poxel School are always a sellout. There's no marching band like there is at night football games and no cheerleaders, either. But it's a beautiful December afternoon, the weather finally breaking into the mild winter that was always Lolo's favorite season.

Time is made very strange when someone dies. It drags its feet when you don't want it to, but then you realize that weeks have gone by. It has been almost two months since Lolo died. It feels like it just happened and also that it was long ago, both those things at once. Some days, when I stop in at Abuela's, I still expect to see him there in his recliner, waiting for me to come home. Other days, I worry that I can't remember the sound of his voice.

I strap on my shin guards and fish inside my bag for

my hair tie. Luckily, today is a day when it seems like Lolo is right here, that he's not gone at all. Maybe he's not here in his sweatshirt and cap, but I still feel him all around. He is making jokes with Lena, Hannah, Edna, and Wilson, who are sitting in the bleachers, waiting to cheer me on. He is alongside Roli, who will be going back to school soon to become a doctor so he can help people who get sick. He is holding hands with Abuela on the bottom bleacher, right beside Mami. He is with Tía, Simón, and the twins, all armed with vuvuzelas. They're ready to show our team some love by yelling *goooooooooool* when we score. I feel him watching me from the shady trees where Papi, who looks so much like him, likes to stand and whisper the moves he wants me to make on the field.

Coach Cameron pulls us together one last time to remind us to use the plays we've practiced all week, to look out for each other and to be there for one another when we can.

Then they look at me. "Ready, Merci?"

And I think I am.

I lead my team out to the field.

Face-to-face with the Pox's captain, I feel calm. Nothing about this opponent scares me now. Today, I will play the way Lolo would have wanted. I will play my best game, hard and fair.

"What do you call?" the ref asks me.

"Heads," I say, and the quarter sails up in the air. The sun is so bright against the blue sky that, for a split second, I lose sight of it.

Still, I'm not worried. It's a game of chance, after all, and there's no telling whether things will go our way at first. But it doesn't matter. I am here with my team, all of them, the ones on the field and the ones who are watching from everywhere. The one who is inside me forever, too.

The whistle blows to start the game.

ACKNOWLEDGMENTS

In 2016, I began writing a story about a plucky, business-minded eleven-year-old who was the daughter of a Florida paint contractor. "Sol Painting, Inc." was part of the anthology *Flying Lessons & Other Stories* (Crown, 2017). I instantly fell in love with the girl who was learning for the first time about how the world works around immigrants—and dreams.

From that seed, I grew Merci and a whole universe around her into what became the Merci Suárez trilogy that ends with this novel. It's hard to believe that this book will be the last in the adventures of Merci and her complicated and loving family. I will miss them—along with all the friends and foes at Seaward Pines Academy. They have felt real to me, and I hope it has been that way for you, too.

I don't write my books alone; no writer does. We get help, large and small. The biggest support I always receive is from my family every day, so I'll start with a big thanks to Javier, Cristina, Sandra, and Alex, whose love and encouragement make everything seem possible.

I'm especially grateful for having taken this book journey with my editor, Kate Fletcher, who seemed to understand Merci at all points of her growing up, and who has also always understood me as a writer over the many projects we've published together. Her heart and wisdom are all over these pages.

My Candlewick Press family have all ushered my books into the world with passion. Thank you, Karen Lotz, Susan Batcheller, John Mendelson, Jennifer Roberts, Phoebe Kosman, and Anne Irza-Leggat, for leading the charge with innovation and heart. Thank you, Alex Robertson, for your early thoughts on the draft—especially about Avery—and for always checking my Spanish. Thank you, too, to my copyeditors and proofreaders, Maya Myers, Jackie Houton, Sarah Chaffee Paris, and Martha Dwyer, for catching all my inconsistencies and flubs. Thank you Erika Sanchez for helping our Latinx community discover Merci on the shelves. A huge gracias to Joe Cepeda for the cover illustration and Pam Consolazio for creating the beautiful visual design. And finally, an electronic fist bump to the social media team, especially Ally

Russell and Raquel Matos Stecher, for all their efforts to get the word out.

Writers depend on experts to get their facts right. I want to give a shout-out to some folks who provided expertise when I needed it. Adrienne Giles, at James Madison University, helped me understand the obstacles college students face and how someone like Roli might meet them. Steve Peterson was my daughter Sandra's soccer coach many years ago. He has remained a good friend and was very willing to chat with me about players and the many ways they sometimes act out on the field.

As I always do, I want to thank my friends in the writing community—too many to name!—who offered terrific ideas when I needed them and who have been so supportive over the years. Where would we be without each other? Lamar Giles, our morning phone calls got me through many a hard writing day.

But mostly for this book, I want to thank all the readers, teachers, and librarians who have laughed and cried with Merci over the years. You are part of my family now as surely as these books are. Merci navigated so many ups and downs in middle school as she dealt with the harder truths of life: her mistakes, her disagreements with friends and classmates, and ultimately, the unbearable loss of her beloved Lolo. I hope her story gave you lots to think about. I hope it will live inside you and inside the readers who will discover these novels in the coming years as well. I hope Merci's story will help you as you grow up and face hard things, too. The future is yours.

Mil gracias, amigos.

Un abrazote,
Meg Medina